"Give me your bl

Fear pounded in En.... ...., and she licked her dry lips. "You found no blades when you pawed through my clothes. The maid found none on my person. Perhaps that is because I have none."

"I don't trust you."

She smiled. *As well you shouldn't.* However, she said, "How can we have a marriage with no trust?"

"Come with me." He forced her toward the door. "You will not return to this room."

"But my clothes!"

"You will have new clothes. Clothes with no holes for pockets. Clothes that provide no access to the blade at your thigh."

"Nonsense." Unthinking, she struggled and then, to her consternation, he picked her up and tossed her over his shoulder. She cried out in fear and horrified humiliation. "Put me down!" She pounded on his broad back. "Put me down, you monstrous serf!"

He strode silently through the halls. She squeezed her eyes shut, unwilling to see the others witnessing her humiliation. "Put me down. Put me down at once!" she gasped. She bit her lip, trying to stop the weak tears of a woman, not a warrior. She sniffed and finally stopped struggling, and hung down his back. His belt about his jerkin was within reach. If only she could loosen it, she could cinch it around his massive neck! It was only a hopeless fantasy, of course.

"Where are you taking me?" she demanded, voice muffled. Perhaps if she pretended submission he would return her to her feet. And if she found a dagger, she'd gladly plunge it through his heart.

"To my chambers."

"Nay!" she gasped out, and struggled in earnest then. "I have decided you are unacceptable to me. You have none of the finer qualities I require in a husband."

Also by Jennette Green

Romance Novels
Her Reluctant Bodyguard
Ice Baron

Castaways
(a young adult novelette)

Murder by Nightmare
(a novelette)

Toot of Fruit
(a children's story)

The Commander's Desire

Jennette Green

Diamond Press

THE COMMANDER'S DESIRE

A Diamond Press book / published in arrangement with the author

Copyright © 2008, 2010, 2013 by Jennette Green
Cover design by Rae Monet

ISBN: 978-1-62964-004-4

Library of Congress Control Number: 2010936492
Library of Congress Subject Headings:
Man-woman relationships—Fiction
Love stories
Historical—Fiction
Scotland—Fiction
Middle Ages—Fiction
Princesses—Fiction
Revenge—Fiction
Arranged Marriage—Fiction

Diamond Press
3400 Pegasus Drive
P.O. Box 80043
Bakersfield CA 93380-0043
www.diamondpresspublishing.com

Published in the United States of America.

Dedication

To my husband, Dale. Without your love and support, I could never have come this far.

CHAPTER ONE

Castle Cor na Gaeth, Galwyddel, 715 A.D.
October

"PEACE. Are you sure it will work, brother?" Elwytha pushed at the warrior circlet that banded her head. It felt constricting, and not for the first time, she wanted to tear it off.

Apprehension simmered in her as she watched her brother slouch on his carved wooden throne, stroking his thick black beard with his fingers. Four years her elder, he had ascended the family throne when their oldest brother, Thor, had died six months ago. Richard shared her dark hair and startling blue eyes—the color of a loch on a bright summer day, when the water reflected the sky.

Richard smiled, and she wasn't sure if she liked it. He said, "They are eager for peace, since our forces have decimated theirs in the last five battles."

Elwytha wondered if this was true. Their castles had been at bloody war for over a century. Why would either side wish for peace now? More puzzling, however, was why Richard would want it. Especially after their enemy's latest despicable act, which had stolen her brother's life. "If we are winning, why not kill them all?" she asked. "Why strive for peace?"

He shook his head. "Sister, your heart is too true, too pure. Of course I do not want peace. I wish for vengeance, and I want to annihilate them all."

She waited, feeling troubled. Vengeance. King Thor had been her favorite brother. Gentle for a warrior. He'd made her a swing in the castle grounds when she was five, had been her champion all of her life...and she missed him terribly. One horrific day six months ago, he'd been cut down in their woods by the enemy Prince's Commander—stabbed in the back in cold blood. The very cowardice and foulness of that act...the evil of it blazed pain and fury through her heart yet again.

Elwytha burned for vengeance as her brother did, but something disturbed her about Richard's plan. The sneakiness of it. The deceit. It didn't matter if the Prince played those un-scrupulous, unjust games. Did they have to sink to his level, too?

She said, "This is the only way?"

"Yes." Richard gave her a direct stare. "Vengeance for our brother lies in your hands. Are you ready to make the bastard pay?"

"How will I know him?" she consented, fingering the blade strapped to her upper thigh, hidden beneath the flowing blue lines of her gown. A slit in the fabric gave her direct access to the weapon. It was one of many weapons she wielded with a skill matching her brother's. War had been their play since babes.

He laughed. It was an unpleasant one, which revealed his straight white teeth. "You will recognize him because he's as ugly as sin. He looks like the monster he is."

Elwytha had killed in battle before, but never like this. Premeditated murder. And she'd do it in the palace of their bitter enemy, Prince Rex. In truth, he was their last remaining enemy. None of the other petty kings of Galwyddel dared to attack her home any longer, for each had tasted the bite of their blades and wished for no more. Only the huge kingdom of Northumbria, to the far east, remained a threat to Castle Cor na Gaeth. But for now they had peace with King Osred—as long as they paid the tribute he demanded.

So their last enemy—rooted in hatred and watered by the bloody war spawned by their mutual great-great-grandfathers a century earlier—remained the Prince, and his fiendish Commander.

She said, "You are sure he will accept this marriage contract?"

Her brother smiled. "The Prince will not be able to resist when he sees you. And he will grasp at the chance to keep his throne. Never fear, sister mine. All will commence as I have planned. I've written everything in this missive." He tapped it on his leg and extended it to her. "Make no move to kill the Commander until you hear my battle horn, announcing my arrival to witness the nuptials in two weeks."

"I will not truly have to marry the Prince, then?" Her flesh prickled at the very idea. The Prince had a repulsive reputation.

"Never, sister. I will rescue you as soon as you slay their Goliath."

She bowed her head. "Yes, brother. I will leave at first light."

"My guard will escort you to the palace with a white flag of protection. Godspeed."

"Success," Elwytha promised, swallowing another churn of apprehension. Tomorrow she would face the enemy Prince. Would she be able to maintain her charade of peace? She had enjoyed make-believe as a child. But acting a part for two weeks seemed nigh to impossible.

⸶ ⸶ ⸶ ⸶ ⸶

Castle Iolaire, Galwyddel

"Enter." Elwytha's escort had deserted her at the Prince's drawbridge, which had been lowered so she could cross the deep, swift flowing burn that protected the castle entrance. Elwytha had never visited the enemy keep before, and in a glance had taken in the deep moat about it, the high stone walls at the front, and the tall, spiked wooden poles that surrounded the castle at the rear. It looked impenetrable.

Now she walked silently beneath the arched entrance into the courtyard of the ancient fortress. Men in thick leather chest armor, inlaid with linked metal pieces, walked beside her. Enemy men. Their weapons were sheathed because of the white flag she carried in one hand, and the scroll of peace she held in the other. She felt several of them looking at her, perhaps eyeing the warrior circlet upon her head. No doubt they thought it was a crown for the princess she was. Her lips tightened, suppressing a smile at their foolish gullibility. None knew of the two knives she wore beneath her flowing aqua gown, which was made of the finest linen and decorated with strips of intricate beadwork. Or the dagger at her ankle, just above her delicate kid slippers. Fools, all of them.

Of course, she was no better—a liar. An ambassador of peace, while she plotted murder. Discomfort squeezed inside her. How could she carry off this farce?

A helmeted soldier, who smelled like old sweat, took the white flag from her and pushed open the door to the palace. "Enter," he ordered, as if she were a subservient maid, and not the princess of Castle Cor na Gaeth.

With a lift to her chin, Elwytha walked with stately elegance to the double, curved wooden doors ahead. Two guards opened these, and before her lay the main hall of the palace.

A soft gasp escaped her lips as startling white blinded her eyes. The floor was made entirely of inlaid quartz pebbles, and they sparkled in the light streaming through slit windows in the stone walls. Overhead, candles in circular candelabras burned, brightening the room still more. Rich tapestries in elegant dark reds and blues and purples covered the walls. Men in helmets stood in two lines before her, lances crossed overhead, marking her pathway to the Prince, who sat upon his throne at the far end.

The Prince sat erect on a polished, elaborately carved wooden chair, with a plush footstool before him. He wore dark pants and boots, and a fine white tunic embroidered with gold threads. A bulbous crown of gold, encrusted with jewels, sat upon his head. Elwytha had never seen such a splendid crown before.

She moved slowly toward him, mindful of the lances above her. Her neck itched. If only they knew of her treason, surely they would wield them upon her.

The Prince's straight black hair reached his chin, and he was smooth shaven. She saw more as she neared him. He possessed a thin face, aquiline nose, and a self-indulgent set to thin, cruel lips. His eyes were as black as coal, and opaque. An involuntary shiver rippled through Elwytha. She stopped ten paces distant and knelt to the floor.

"My lord," she said, in her best obsequious voice. "Thank you for agreeing to speak with me."

"Your forces surrender?" His voice sounded too smooth, as though falsely polite, and her flesh crept.

"Not surrender. My brother wishes for peace. He writes of it in the parchment I carry."

"Peace." The single word sounded contemptuous. "Rise. Bring it hence."

She was surprised. He would allow her to approach him? Was he a fool? She could easily kill him. Of course, she would forfeit her life, and thankfully her brother had not sent her on a martyr's mission. She arose.

The Prince said, "My Commander will escort you."

Elwytha's breath caught. Alarm pierced her, mixed with hatred—and fear. The Commander. The monster who had murdered King Thor. The man she was ordered to kill.

A man appeared behind the ranks of soldiers that stretched to the Prince. Elwytha's courage faltered as he descended the steps toward her.

He was huge. In a quick, observant warrior's glance, she took in the essentials. Dark stubble prickled up from his shaven head, and his pugilistic face was shaved clean. Half of his nose was pushed to his right, as if broken and never reset. A scar puckered down through his right brow to his eye, which seemed to make him squint. He had a thick neck and bulky, muscular shoulders covered in a short-sleeved, dark leather jerkin. Beneath this was a long-sleeved, brown woolen tunic. Cloth trousers of the same color encased legs the size of tree trunks.

Elwytha involuntarily gulped with fear. She would be lucky to match his shoulder height. And she was to kill him?

He stopped before her and inclined his head. "Princess." His voice was uncommonly deep.

Elwytha snatched back her courage, reminding herself that she was a warrior, trained to kill men. All men. Including this one. She inclined her head. "Commander," she said with fake sweetness.

"Follow me," he rumbled.

"Of course." Perfect. If only she could kill him now! How swiftly she would unsheathe her dagger and plunge it through the monster's back, as he had done to her beloved brother. Hatred shivered through her, and she clenched her fists, willfully controlling herself.

Three steps from the Prince, the Commander stopped, and so did she. He turned and held out a huge hand. "The scroll." He spoke with a courtesy that belied his rough appearance.

Elwytha could not look him in the face, for fear her eyes would betray her fury and hatred. Pretending submissiveness, she bowed her head and relinquished the scroll. The giant moved to the side, so she had a full view of the Prince as he unrolled the document. He read quickly, and the beginnings of a smile twisted his mouth as he reached the end.

"Well," he said. "A fine prize your brother offers me."

Elwytha lifted her chin in an effort to appear regal, and not as merchandise about to be bartered for peace. The Prince's eyes drifted down her form, which made her want to shrink in revulsion. With an amused smile, his eyes returned to her face.

"Unfortunately," he said. "I have no wish for a bride."

Her spirits plummeted. Now what would she do? She should have killed the Goliath when she'd had the chance.

"How disappointed you look." He chuckled. "I am flattered you desire me so intensely."

Elwytha swallowed back repelled words of denial, and said instead, "Shall I tell my brother you do not wish for peace?"

"Nay." He slapped the document into the hand of his Commander. "I will agree to a marriage of peace. What do you think, Commander?"

Confused, she looked from one to the other. "You do not want me for a bride. Therefore, you do not wish for peace," she reminded him.

The Prince watched the Commander, who had finished reading the document. She was faintly surprised the hulking giant could read. The Commander imperceptibly nodded to the Prince.

"Good," the Prince said. "It is agreed."

"What is agreed?" She frowned with wary suspicion, disliking the silence. Disliking the silent communication between her two enemies.

"Your brother's marriage of peace has been accepted. I will agree to peace with him if you, Princess, will agree to marry a man of my choosing in my stead."

Her frown deepened. "How can that be peace between your crown and ours?"

"I will sign your brother's peace agreement at the marriage supper in two weeks. Peace is peace, is it not, Princess?"

Elwytha drew a deep breath, uncomfortable with the Prince's trickery. And then she remembered it was a trick—all of it. The marriage would never happen. Peace agreements would never be signed. What did she care if the Prince chose her future fake husband? The wedding would never happen.

She lifted her chin. "Very well. I accept, in the best interests of both of our peoples."

"Good." The Prince smiled, and stroked his chin with one finger. "You are a fine specimen. And my Commander agrees you will satisfy him as a wife."

Her heart faltered. "What?" she sputtered. A sudden roaring filled her ears. It didn't matter if it was all a lie—she could not countenance even a fake betrothal to that monster! The man who had filthily murdered her brother.

"Never," she breathed. "*Never!*"

"No, Princess?" The Prince's eyes narrowed. "You do not want peace?"

"I wish for peace, but not to that monst..."

"Monster," the Prince finished. "Do you hear that, Commander? She thinks you are a monster."

The bulky shoulders tightened, but he did not answer. He did not look at her.

Elwytha heaved a breath and dropped a brief, disrespectful curtsy to the Prince. "I will tell Richard that peace has been rejected." She spun on her heel and marched back the way she had come.

"Halt," the Prince said. Instantly, lances clicked down, barring her passage to the door.

Reluctantly, she turned. "What have we left to discuss, Prince?"

"You have displeased me. And if you return empty-handed, you will displease your brother. I have heard he can be most cruel to those who disappoint him."

Elwytha had heard those rumors. "I am his sister."

"And a threat to his crown. Perhaps you should take this opportunity before he kills you." The Prince chewed on a nail, the picture of casual relaxation.

Fear fluttered in Elwytha's heart, and she hated it. How dare that man place fear in her mind for her own brother? But a better question might be; why was she listening to him? Was it because she knew, deep in her heart, that the Prince might be right? She had heard many stories of men who had mysteriously been killed because they had displeased or failed Richard in some way. And if she resisted peace—a fake peace at that—wouldn't that anger her brother? His plan would fail. A plan never designed to relinquish her to their enemy at all.

She took a deep breath. "My brother would never harm me. But I...I..."

"You wish to reconsider," the Prince said with a thin smile.

The giant turned to look at her, and she swallowed back a horrified wave of fear and revulsion. The Commander would not harm her. He would not touch her. She would make sure of it. If he tried, she would kill him early—even if that disrupted her brother's plans.

"Very well," she said, in a scratchy voice she barely recognized as her own. "I accept your proposal, Prince."

"You mean you accept the Commander's proposal." The Prince nodded to his first-in-command. "Claim your bride. You have well earned her."

Unsmilingly, the Commander strode toward her. When he reached for her arm, she flinched, and jerked it close to her side. "Pray, do not touch me," she gritted. To the Prince, she said, "I must summon my maid and my trunks."

"No maid," the Prince said. "One of ours will serve you. If you are literate, write a letter now to your brother, agreeing to our peace proposal. Then my guard will deliver it and retrieve your trunks for you." He did not wait for her to agree. "Garroway, lead the Princess to the parchments."

Eyes narrowed in displeasure, and heart filled with a small amount of panic, Elwytha followed the page to a low table. There, she quickly wrote her missive. The Commander lurked at her side, a frightening, hulking presence. He took the note from her when she had finished, and read it. Then he handed it to the Prince. The Prince nodded and then sealed it with wax and the imprint of his signet ring. "Garroway, deliver it to her guard, who is waiting on the edge of the wood."

"Very good, sir." The page bowed, and hastily disappeared with his missive.

"As for you, Princess, I leave you in the Commander's capable care. You are dismissed." With a flick of his hand, he averted his eyes, as if she no longer existed.

"Follow me," the giant said, and with stiff, reluctant steps Elwytha followed. Her fingers itched for the dagger strapped to her thigh. She longed to fell him now, before being forced to go anywhere alone with him. Who knew what unspeakable horrors he would force upon her? She swallowed back fear.

"I require a maid. Now," she informed Goliath's back.

"You shall have one," the quiet voice rumbled, but with no inflection of emotion. A shiver of unease rippled through her, but she forbore to ignore it.

He led her through many halls, but Elwytha kept track of each turn, each staircase; plotting her escape with every step. Finally, he opened a thick wooden door leading to a lavishly decorated room. Animal skin rugs lay scattered over the flagged stone floor, and tapestries hung on the walls. Overhead, heavy wooden beams supported a huge candelabra, unlit now, for light poured in through two slitted windows. But what sort of a room was it? Then she spied a chair and table, and beyond them, in the far corner, a large partition.

"You will wish to refresh yourself after your travels," he told her. "Disrobe and bathe behind the partition. A maid will attend you."

Elwytha possessed neither the desire nor the intention to disrobe and bathe. And a maid would only attest to this mutiny. "I can bathe without a maid," she said, and waited for him to leave.

"I will remain, to ensure you don't try to escape," he said, and folded his arms across his massive chest.

"How little trust you place in your future bride," she said, and then unwisely dared to accuse, "I suspect instead you wish to dishonorably inspect your pound of flesh before our marriage nuptials."

He frowned, which distorted his ugly mug into frightening creases. "I wish to inspect your clothes. If you do not want a maid, disrobe and throw your clothing over the partition."

Matters were going from bad to worse. Elwytha flushed with horrified mortification, and also with unreasoning anger at Richard for placing her in this position. Why couldn't she finish the fiendish brute now and escape out the window? How simple it would be. But no. Anger pushed rash words past her lips. "Perhaps you would like to search me, as well?"

His gaze ran down her form. "All in good time," he said.

Alarm shot through her. With all of her heart, she longed for her own maid; for a friend she could trust in this lair of the enemy. But it was not to be. Elwytha struggled to think logically, like the trained warrior she was. She could not allow one of the Prince's maids to come—at least not yet—or her daggers would quickly become obvious when she took off her clothes. At the same time, she felt vulnerable—not to mention the inappropriateness of the situation—to be alone in a room with a man. And not just any man. A dishonorable, murdering heathen, which likely explained his illiteracy concerning social graces.

"Stay near the door and I will comply," she agreed, but with acute trepidation.

He said nothing, and after she slipped behind the partition, she peeked to make sure he stayed far from her. The dark-clad giant remained near the door, arms crossed, one eye squinting beneath his scar.

Only the kind hand of fate had saved his eye, she realized now. Too bad. If it hadn't, perhaps Thor would be alive today.

Swiftly, she disrobed and flung her long gown and white linen shift over the partition. Afraid he might decide to leer at her after all, she unstrapped her three flat daggers and hid them beneath the edge of a rug, which lay near the wall. No one would notice them there now, or perhaps ever.

A rustling sound came from the other side of the partition, and she quickly slipped into the large, steaming tub. Sweet smelling bubbles floated across her shoulders, covering her entirely from any leering gaze. "Satisfied?" she called out. She smiled to herself. How simple it had been to hide her weapons. And after he returned her clothes, how easy it would be to strap them back on her person.

The warm water lapped about her shoulders, but apprehension slid through Elwytha. She refused to acknowledge the fear swirling through her insides like so many viperous snakes. She felt vulnerable in the tub, and wished she had brought a knife in with her. Foolish of her. Now she would have to live by her wits alone.

Perhaps she should wash. Who knew when she'd next have the opportunity? She did so quickly, anxious to escape and speedily clothe herself from his prying eyes.

Now she heard nothing. "May I have my clothes back now?"

"As you suggested, I must inspect your person," the deep voice rumbled. "Or I can call for a maid to do so." To her alarm, the giant appeared at the edge of the partition.

With a horrified gasp, she crossed her arms to cover herself. "Have you no social graces?" Elwytha endeavored to sound disdainful, as though he were a worm, and beneath contempt. But underneath the concealing warm water her limbs trembled. Thankfully, he couldn't see it. Never would she let him see her fear.

"Bubbles protect you. For now." The frightening face looked harder now, as if covering anger. But anger at what?

"I will accept a maid. Leave me," she commanded.

After a hesitation, he disappeared from view, to her relief.

Soon afterward a maid appeared, clutching a white, fine linen robe and a thick woolen towel. Her hair was plaited in a circle about her head, and she looked to be Elwytha's age. Her shoulders were hunched, and she looked frightened. "These are for you, miss."

Elwytha took the towel, but refused help with drying herself off. At home her maid only accompanied her for propriety's sake, for she conversed with many men. Never did she require help with dressing.

"Hagma," rumbled the giant. "Weapons?"

"None." The maid's voice sounded breathless and squeaky. "Miss, he said you are to wear the white robe and then go sit in the chair."

Elwytha stiffened her spine and tightened the sash on the flimsy robe. Although it belonged to the enemy, she couldn't help but admire the fine golden embroidery and beadwork edging the lapels and sleeves. "Very well."

She moved into the main room and stood beside the chair, which was pushed next to a small, round table.

"Hagma, you may go." Voice mild, the Commander dismissed the maid.

"This is inappropriate," Elwytha flared. "My brother will be most displeased with your treatment of me."

"Sit." The word was quiet, with the force of thunder behind it.

She sat, feeling fear curl in her stomach. Perhaps now she should choose her battles carefully.

He fingered her golden circlet headband, inlaid with jewels. Each acknowledged her skill level with the different weapons of war. Swords, spears...and knives. She felt naked without her knives. Defenseless.

He lay the circlet on the table before her, but she made no move to touch it.

"Take it. It is yours." The voice still sounded mild, and that scared her still more. She decided to look at him to gauge his mood, and therefore her responses. Something told her that now was the time to take care.

Her eyes met his for the first time at close range, and a disconcerted jolt went through her. They were a clear, light gray, and keenly intelligent. Disturbed, she looked away. "Yes," she said shortly. "It is mine."

"Tell me its significance."

She narrowed her eyes and lied. "It is a crown. I am a princess. Remember?"

He grunted and paced away, as if thinking.

"May I dress now?" she inquired. "Savage though you are, surely you know the basics of propriety."

He did not answer, and fear mixed with her burning desire to be rid of his vile, monstrous presence.

She stood. "Leave. I wish to dress." Elwytha snatched the clothes his filthy paws had soiled by his touch, and headed for the partition.

A huge hand clamped on her wrist and she gasped, startled. How had he done that? A second ago he had been six paces distant.

"Sit," he told her again.

"I do not wish to sit. Release me." She wrenched at her arm. His grip tightened, hurting her, but she did not cry out. She stared up at his hulking presence and swallowed, unable to deny a sharp sting of fear. If he knew her true identity...her true capabilities...would he kill her? No one knew of her secret, that she often rode into battle dressed like a page. No one except for her only living sibling.

The Commander said, "Give me your knives."

Elwytha drew a quick breath. "I have no knives," she lied coolly.

"You are a warrior." He lifted the circlet with one finger. "You carry knives."

She wrenched at her arm again. "No."

"I am no fool. But perhaps you think I look stupid. You have decided I am a monster with gruel for brains?"

She was fast beginning to think the opposite, which only made him a more formidable foe. "You said it, not me," she returned, seeking for a cool sounding bravado.

"You think I will kill you if I discover you are a warrior."

She glared up at him, lips sealed. Exactly. That was exactly her fear. How easily he could kill her now, since she was defenseless, with no knives. A twist of his hands around her neck and that would be it. After killing her brother in such a despicable manner, what would stop him from killing her, an unarmed woman, if he believed her to be a threat?

Desperately, she glanced about the room, searching for any potential weapon. A sash. Pottery she could smash for a sharp edge—anything.

"You will find no weapon." The Commander's uncommonly deep voice wrenched her attention back to his face and the keen gray eyes, which disturbed her, because she would rather believe him an unthinking brute beast. "I would prefer to treat you kindly, but first you must surrender your blades."

"I have no knives. No blades. Do you live in paranoia in this palace?"

"You are our enemy."

"Then why take a wife who might cut your throat?"

If she had wanted to jar him, she had succeeded. The grip on her wrist tightened, and a large hand gripped her other wrist, too. He drew her near to him. His jerkin was made of supple brown leather with leather laces, she noticed with some fragmented part of her brain.

"Give me your blades," he growled down at her.

Fear pounded in her chest, and she licked her dry lips. "You found no blades when you pawed through my clothes. The maid found none on my person. Perhaps that is because I have none."

"I don't trust you."

She smiled. *As well you shouldn't.* However, she said, "How can we have a marriage with no trust?"

"Come with me." He forced her toward the door. "You will not return to this room."

"But my clothes!"

"You will have new clothes. Clothes with no holes for pockets. Clothes that provide no access to the blade at your thigh."

"Nonsense." Unthinking, she struggled and then, to her consternation, he picked her up and tossed her over his shoulder. She cried out in fear and horrified humiliation. "Put me down!" She pounded on his broad back. "Put me down, you monstrous serf!"

He strode silently through the halls. She squeezed her eyes shut, unwilling to see the others witnessing her humiliation. "Put me down. Put me down at once!" she gasped. She bit her lip, trying to stop the weak tears of a woman, not a warrior. She sniffed and finally stopped struggling, and hung down his back. His belt about his jerkin was within reach. If only she could loosen it, she could cinch it around his massive neck! It was only a hopeless fantasy, of course.

"Where are you taking me?" she demanded, voice muffled. Perhaps if she pretended submission he would return her to her feet. And if she found a dagger, she'd gladly plunge it through his heart.

"To my chambers."

"Nay!" she gasped out, and struggled in earnest then. "I have decided you are unacceptable to me. You have none of the finer qualities I require in a husband."

"This surprises you?"

"I will not marry you!"

"Yet, you mean," he rumbled, and stopped before a door. She took the opportunity of his distraction while opening it and flung her body off his shoulder. She fell with crash to the floor, on her back. The breath whumped out of her. She saw stars for a moment, and then her vision cleared. She stared up at her captor, who regarded her with some surprise.

She flew to her feet, ignoring twinges of pain, but before she could run one step, his hand gripped her arm. He pushed open the door to his chambers with his foot.

"No," she cried out, and fell to her knees, forcing him to drag her. "I will not be defiled by you. Unhand me, or I'll scream!"

"Scream all you wish. It will fuel my reputation."

He scooped her up in his rock-like arms, slammed the door, and strode across the room. He dumped her into the middle of a massive bed. "You are home. You will stay here, where I can watch you."

She sprang up, utterly horrified. "No! You vile, filthy man! This is inappropriate. I will break the peace agreement."

"It is done."

"It is not done until I am wed to you," she snarled.

"Do you wish for a maid? I will send for Hagma."

"I wish for my own room." Elwytha trembled with stark fear, but struggled to cling to her self-possession. "I will not have my reputation soiled by a beast such as you."

"You will have your own room. There." He pointed, and she twisted her neck to look. A door led off his room to a small chamber beyond.

"Never," she gasped. "I wish to be in a different wing of the palace. I wish for solitude to contemplate marriage to one as despicable as yourself!"

"You wish for much. I will grant you a maid. Do you want one?" he asked again.

On some level, she was surprised he asked. But what good would a maid do her? If he tried to have his way with her, would the maid save her? No. And what if Elwytha retrieved her blades? A maid would go through her clothes, her room, and perhaps find them.

"I want no maid to witness my humiliation at your hands." She glared, trying to suppress the fear struggling for control.

He smiled. "I will wait until our wedding night."

Horror spiraled in her. She quickly turned away. Surely her brother would rescue her in time. Elwytha swallowed, and finally part of her warrior mind clicked into action again. Vulnerable though her position was, his was equally vulnerable. Only one door separated her room from his. Perfect for her opportunity to kill him, when the time came. First, though, and quickly, she would retrieve her knives. This faint bit of hope lightened her spirits, and with a lifted chin, she turned back to her enemy.

"How much does your word mean?" she challenged. "How do I know I can trust you?"

The Commander stared at her with his mutilated, squinting face. Her brother was right. He was as ugly as sin. "The Prince trusts me implicitly. You may, as well."

"Trust is earned," she told him. As if she would ever trust a murdering knave who dishonorably stabbed men in the back! "We will see if I can trust your word. In the meantime," she straightened her shoulders, affecting a brave pose, "I wish for my trunks and my clothes to be delivered here."

"No," he said calmly, arms crossed.

Her temper sparked at his unreasonable response. The Prince himself had promised that she could have her belongings. "I insist."

"You wish?" The monster didn't sound *amused*, did he?

Her temper threatened to boil. "I will not beg, if that is what you want. I need my clothes. Give them to me!"

He continued to watch her, arms crossed, as though she were some unusual form of entertainment.

She heaved a breath. Clearly, demands would get her nowhere. "Yes, I wish." She forced out the next galling words. "*Please* give them to me." If only she had a blade, she would end her torture now!

"Very well. You will receive your clothes."

"And my trunks."

"No," he said implacably.

Elwytha clenched her fists. She had secreted blades in her trunks, and other weapons, too. "Please." She bit out the humiliating word.

"No."

She heaved a great breath and stared at him, struggling to find a way to win the advantage over this man.

᛭ ᛭ ᛭ ᛭ ᛭

The Commander looked at Elwytha with her dark hair and flashing, brilliant blue eyes. A beauty. This fact stabbed into his calloused soul. And she clearly found him abhorrent. That was plain, and held no surprise for him. He knew the thick muscles which served him so well in battle could look repulsive to a fine-boned creature such as herself. Although she was not short, which pleased him.

His mind returned to his well-understood deficits. The scar that twisted his brow, and his broken nose... Few women, and usually only drunk ones, would have him.

His eyes traced her delicate beauty. He was not worthy of her. He knew that. But for peace... He grew weary of battle. No. He was weary of inflicting death and pain on other humans. A dark emptiness grew larger in his soul after each battle. He feared that soon it would swallow him alive.

But now, for peace—a peace he suspected was only a game the Prince played with Elwytha's brother—for as long as peace lasted...for as long as he had Elwytha, he would enjoy her fire. A spirit that vibrant could not be broken, and he had no wish to do so. Here was a battle he might enjoy, although he would not trust her one inch. She hated him viciously. Death flared even now in her eyes, and he grinned.

Mutiny gleamed back, and he tried to squash his smile. Here was a worthy opponent. But he would be certain to protect his vulnerable areas. If she attempted a death blow, the game would end.

But for now, he would choose the victory he sought. His mind spun with possibilities. What methods could he employ to tame one such as herself?

᛭ ᛭ ᛭ ᛭ ᛭

Elwytha didn't like the unreadable thoughts flickering through the giant's clear gray eyes. Who knew what tortures he planned, even now. Look at that smile. He was clearly pleased with some nefarious plot he'd concocted to further humiliate her. Perhaps, once again, she should take care. After all, she knew the wickedness of which he was capable. Hadn't she stood at Thor's graveside funeral only six months ago? Unexpected tears stung, but she managed to swallow them back. Tears had no place in her warrior's mission.

She raised her chin and stated, "I will retire to my room. You may summon me when my clothing has arrived." With a majestic sweep of her robe, she stalked to her tiny bedchamber and shut the door. She was surprised when he didn't follow, or try to stop her. Good. He must never know that right now her courage felt about as substantial as a brittle piece of ice.

Her first order of business was to inspect the door. Any locks, to forestall his unwelcome advances?

None. She turned and surveyed the room, searching for weapons—for any tool to help her succeed in her ultimate quest. A quick glance proved the floor and walls were made of stone, and the ceiling of dark, heavy wooden beams. No candelabra for her; instead, dark, cone-shaped torches flanked the wooden door.

The room possessed only one window. It was high and narrow, with bars. Impossible to climb out. If she wanted to escape, she'd use his—she had noticed a larger window in the other room. Her bed was small, and made of wood. A sheet and blanket with a pillow rested upon it. Elwytha heaved up the mattress and discovered slats of wood beneath. Perhaps she could work one of the slats free and use it as a cudgel. Yes. She smiled with pleasure and continued to survey the room.

A tapestry on the wall. Pretty, but useless. A rug on the floor, white and wooly. Again, useless. A wooden dresser with three drawers. All empty, she discovered. No secret compartments existed. However, she could secrete her blades behind the dresser when she retrieved them.

Elwytha completed her survey of the room. A wooden stand with a porcelain bowl upon it stood in the corner. In a pinch, she could break it for a sharp blade.

Not bad. Crossing her arms, she sat on the bed. That's when she realized her room was like a cell. A prison. What would she do in here? Lose her mind, most likely. But it was far preferable to the Commander's presence.

She lay back on the bed and closed her eyes. A light nap would refresh her, and allow her mind to remain sharp. Who knew what further skullduggery the giant intended to pull tonight.

CHAPTER TWO

ELWYTHA WAS UNABLE TO NAP. Instead, she plotted how to regain her daggers. She needed them for self-protection; not to mention her ultimate goal. But how could she retrieve them? Perhaps at night, while her captor slept, she could sneak out and wander the halls until she found her trusted blades. Provided he didn't lock her in her room, of course. Unfortunately, a likely scenario.

Her mind turned to ways of confounding any lock the door might hold. Of course, it would help if she understood what mechanism this palace used to imprison its captives.

Unable to lie idle a moment longer, she sprang to her feet and stealthily tested the door latch. To her surprise, it moved easily in her hand. With suspicion, she cautiously eased the door open a crack. She pressed her eye to the opening and scanned what little she could see; which was only half of the room, and the giant was nowhere to be seen.

Emboldened, she edged it wider and peered out. No one. She was alone. Her spirits leaped in triumph. Now a far greater opportunity lay before her than inspecting the door latch. She could search the Commander's room for a weapon.

She darted out and commenced a quick, efficient search. A small chest pressed flush against the far wall was locked. She made a note to find the key. The bed contained only old footwear beneath it. Clothes filled a tall wooden wardrobe. One chair, a stand for washing, and a window remained. But little else.

In frustration, she put her hands on her hips and surveyed the room. Where did he keep his knives? His weapons of destruction? Perhaps most were in the armory, but a warrior always kept his sword close at hand. And what of his daggers? Perhaps even now he carried them on his person. Likely.

"Have you found everything you require for comfort?" The deep rumble came from behind her.

With a gasp, Elwytha spun to confront her betrothed. He had not improved in appearance during their brief separation. The great shoulders strained at the leather of his jerkin, and the slash on his brow seemed to give him a permanent squint...or frown. She gathered her courage and gave him a cool, bold stare, even though she felt vulnerable without her blades. No need for him to know that.

"I require my clothes," she stated. "They still haven't arrived. And I require sustenance. Unless, of course, you intend to starve me. Is that your standard treatment for captives?"

His lips twitched. "You may dine with me."

"No." The horrified word spit out. "I have no wish to dine with you. A simple meal in my room will suffice."

"I wish for you to dine with me." His expression didn't change, but Elwytha knew he meant it. He was insisting upon her presence with him.

Her skin crawled at the very idea of partaking of a meal with this murderous brute. Likely he ate with his hands and dribbled juice down his chin!

She could not still a shudder.

He waited patiently, saying nothing; allowing her to make up her own mind to accompany him. Everything within Elwytha boiled in rebellion at the thought. He probably meant to parade her as a trophy on his arm before the tables of men he commanded. She gritted her teeth, unable to countenance the thought.

He said, "You will agree?"

She narrowed her eyes. "Or what?"

"No food will be delivered here."

Elwytha's mind worked quickly then, determined to make the best out of a bad situation. Perhaps at the dining table she would find a knife. She could secrete it upon her person. Yes. That would make the coming humiliation worthwhile. Then she'd be prepared to kill Thor's murderer when her brother came...in two long weeks.

Elwytha frowned. "Very well. If you insist. But first, I need appropriate clothing."

"It is coming." At that moment, a knock came at the door, and when the Commander opened it, two guards entered, carrying a large trunk. Not one of her own trunks, she noted with disappointment. They deposited it in her room and departed. The Commander turned to her. "Dress," he ordered.

"Of course. Right away." Her lip curled, belying the servile words, and she retreated into her room. The door slam made her feel better; at least for a moment. She opened the trunk and discovered that most of her clothes were inside. Of course, they were wrinkled now and stuffed in every which-away.

Further outrage simmered as she selected her ugliest garment to wear; a gray woolen with a severe, high neckline. If necessary, and if given a needle, she would modify all of her garments so her enemy would find no cause to lust after her person.

She thankfully found a brush, and brushed out her hair, then plaited it and coiled it up into unbecoming loops. Elwytha smiled with satisfaction into the small, highly polished bit of metal which served as her mirror. It, too, could be used as a weapon in a pinch, but would wield little damage upon her enemy. Likely it was why it had been allowed to her.

Last of all, she tied a narrow cloth about her shin, ready to hide any knife she might pilfer from the dining table. Pleased, she exited the room.

The Commander stared at her.

"I am ready," she announced. "Lead on."

Without a word, he exited the room. She smiled to herself. Her appearance had taken him aback. Good; a small victory to assuage her coming humiliation.

As they neared the end of a corridor, she spied the great dining hall ahead of them. It was hard to miss, as a din swelled down the hall, pulsing into her ears, and the warm smell of crisped venison and fresh baked bread assailed her nostrils. She sniffed deeply and her stomach gurgled. As they drew closer, she noted the huge candelabras burning overhead, as well as multiple torches burning on the walls. A bright, unfortunately festive atmosphere.

The Commander slowed as they neared the entry. "Place your hand on my arm."

"I will not *touch* you." Revulsion galloped through her.

"You are my bride. The Prince has thrown us a feast."

Elwytha saw now that all eyes had turned to them—most likely all of his men who looked up to him. How shamed he would feel if she would not submit to his command.

"I will walk beside you," she decreed. "Expect nothing more."

He heaved a great breath. Displeased, she knew. She flicked a glance up at his gray eyes. That was a mistake. The stormy gaze promised battle. Perhaps later, when no one would see her, or hear her. Without a word, she lightly placed her fingertips on his forearm.

"You learn well."

"I choose only critical battles. No others matter." His defeat, in other words. She gave him a hard stare, wishing she could imprint that warning upon his thick brain. "Don't expect me to smile," she warned, determined to displease him at every point possible.

When they entered the room, all the men stood and gave a great cheer. Her face burned at the hand clapping and coarse jokes, but she lifted her chin and schooled her features into disapproving lines. Her old nursemaid had perfected it. Luckily, Elwytha had taken delight in copying it. This skill served her well now. Unfortunately, it didn't seem to discourage their uncouth behavior, but she felt better about it.

"Up here, Commander," the Prince called from the far end of the room. He sat in splendor upon another ornately carved chair, plumped with many cushions.

Wonderful. Into the enemy's den with a murderer on one side and a conniving Prince on the other. How could her brother have subjected her to such an untenable situation?

Revenge, she reminded herself, and settled onto a bench indicated by her hulking betrothed. He settled to her right. Now only to endure the meal. And to find a knife.

Her swift glance scanned the long wooden table. It was dotted with candles and heaped with hunks of bread, cheese, grapes, bowls of boiled vegetables, and slabs of roasted deer. Plenty of spoons, but no knives were in sight. A warrior on her left scooted a mite closer, but before she shrank back, she noted the bejeweled dagger glinting at his belt. She smiled, pretending cordiality. He grinned back, showing crooked, stained teeth. A waft of putrid air sailed her way, and she hastily pressed a hand to her mouth to stop a gag.

"A fine wench, Commander," the man slurred.

Good. He was drunk. Elwytha smiled with true pleasure then.

"Be careful, Commander," the Prince drawled from down the table, to her right. "Already her eye wanders."

Elwytha frowned. "In civilized courts a smile is merely polite."

The Prince popped a small tomato into his mouth. "Does she please you, Commander?"

"She will do."

More shouts and coarse jesting peppered the warm air. Elwytha longed sharply for her blades then, and for her fellow warriors to cut down this loathsome bunch. Not that the warriors in her palace behaved any better, she had to admit. But still, she'd never been the butt of their coarse jesting before. Not if they wanted to keep their heads, anyway.

The Commander seemed to ignore the revelry around them. A wicked looking dagger appeared in his hand. It flashed as he cut meat for her wooden trencher, and then scooped vegetables in as well. Elwytha tried to get a clear glimpse of the blade. It was long—perhaps almost a foot—with a pair of sapphires embedded in the hilt. It looked wicked, and was obviously his favorite. No doubt he carried it on his person at all times. Well, it was good to be warned of her obstacles in advance.

The Prince raised his hand, calling for attention. "Time for music to honor the Commander and his beautiful bride-to-be. Mac à Chruiteir, you may begin."

The delicate melody of the clàrsach rippled into the hall. Elwytha quickly spotted the man seated behind his triangular instrument, and watched his fingers feather the gut strings. The beautiful music lightened her spirits a bit. So far, it was the only evidence of civilization in this heathen court.

She ate quickly and properly with the spoon. The Prince did as well, but the lout to her left used his hands and slurped mightily from his trencher when it was nearly empty. The Commander primarily ate with his knife.

Which reminded her. The lout's blade. She waited until more ale was consumed and the men jested, roaring with laughter up and down the table. The knave to her left rested his arms on the table now, softly chuckling like a simpleton. He had lost his reasoning abilities...whatever he had possessed to begin with.

A quick scan proved no one paid her the least mind. Quickly, stealthily, and without looking, she slipped the enemy's dagger from his scabbard. Easy. Simple. She hid it in the folds of her dress beneath the table, heart beating rapidly. Victory! Elwytha smiled to herself and sipped more water.

A wide hand curled around her wrist underneath the table. Alarm jolted her. Ignoring a spike of fear, she turned to the Commander. "Take no liberties with me," she hissed.

His eyes bored into hers. "Return it."

She slid the blade with her other hand to her knees, and, using her shins as a slide, allowed the dagger to slide to her feet. She scooted it under one foot. "Unhand me," she ordered.

The grip tightened. "Return it."

"Have you drunk too much ale?"

"I will search you if you do not return it now." The frowning, squinty gaze looked hard, reminding her of the brute warrior he was.

Now was the time to keep a cool head.

She raised an eyebrow. "I'm not sure what you're imagining, but I have taken nothing. See? My utensil remains on the table. As do my trencher and cup. What more do you wish?"

"Return it." His deep voice remained even. Faintly, she was surprised he didn't thunder at her. Probably it was an attempt to retain his pride. He wanted no one to guess that he wielded no control over his future bride.

She smiled at that pleasing thought.

"Put both your hands on the table," he rumbled.

Elwytha froze for a second, and then willingly complied. She gave him a mocking half-smile.

"Now stand," he ordered, "and take a step back from the table."

What about the blade? Elwytha felt uneasy. What did he intend with these orders? And should she submit?

"Am I dismissed?" she inquired.

He turned his full warrior scowl upon her then, and said in low thunder, "Comply."

More fear fluttered. "But I would like more food. I'm hungry," she denied. She needed that dagger. Surely he had not seen her sleight of hand. He would not thwart her now.

"Very well." He turned and abruptly put one leg over the bench, so he straddled it now, facing her. He made to flip his other leg over, also.

"What are you doing?" she asked, alarmed.

"You wish to be carried out. I will be glad to do so."

"I don't wish to be carted anywhere," she snapped.

"Then comply. Now," he growled.

Frustration tightened her lips. He would deny her this triumph. How had he known? How had he guessed? She was glad the blade wasn't on her person.

"I'll stand," she said, with as much dignity as she could muster. She cleared the bench, but her impulsive attempt to slide the blade back with her foot and hide it with her skirt as she swung off the other side was thwarted by his massive leg barring her way.

"Step over."

She rolled her eyes. "My, aren't you trusting?" Reluctantly, she stepped over his shin.

Unfortunately, thanks to her ill-thought plan to shove the weapon with her foot, the dagger now lay in plain view as soon as her skirt cleared.

One massive paw scooped it up. He held it by the blade. "Explain."

She didn't like the threat in the mild tone.

"Explain what? You found a blade on the floor. Is it yours?"

"A blade. Warrior speak."

She shrugged this off. "My brothers taught me a few things. Even a princess must learn to defend herself."

With one swift movement, the Commander returned the dagger to his now passed out comrade.

"Perhaps he dropped it in his drunken stupor," Elwytha suggested with an innocent smile.

"Trouble in paradise, Commander?" inquired the Prince. "Treachery afoot so soon from your betrothed? Perhaps she has supped too often at her brother's table."

Elwytha stiffened. "My brother practices no treachery."

"Perhaps you mistake brothers."

"You speak in circles, Prince."

His eyes narrowed. "Which brother do you favor, Princess?"

An unexpected lump choked her throat and Elwytha clenched her fists. "I have but one brother now, Prince, thanks to..." She bit her lip, realizing it would be foolish to accuse her host of ordering her brother's cold-blooded murder. Or perhaps that had been solely the evil crime of this monster, beside her.

She shuddered with revulsion and backed away from them both. "I am weary. Thank you for the meal, Prince. I must bid you goodnight."

Spinning in her soft slippers, Elwytha fled from the room. Unwanted tears crowded her eyes as she ran blindly through the fiendish snake's lair. How dare the Prince taunt her with her beloved brother's death? A great, aching knot of misery pulsed in her throat. The bold bravado, which she had clung to ever since entering the palace, shattered, leaving her emotionally naked and vulnerable. And she hated it. Weakness had no place in her warrior's heart.

She had no idea where she was going. She flew down shadowed corridors lit by flickering torches, and then found a large door, flung it open, and found herself in the soft night with grass beneath her feet.

A courtyard. The sweet scents of vanilla and late blooming wild roses enveloped her. Gasping, she found a path through the garden and dashed down it, under the pale light of the moon. A bench appeared and she sank down on it, weeping uncontrollably. She sobbed with grief for her dead brother, and for the fear and loneliness she felt here, captive in this enemy stronghold. She wondered if God was listening, and gulped a prayer for deliverance from this unconscionable situation.

She became aware of another's presence.

Alarmed, she looked up and saw the Commander outlined in moonlight, larger than life.

"Get away from me," she cried out, horrified. "I hate you. *I hate you!*"

He sat beside her and she instantly sprang to her feet. "Don't touch me, or so help me, I'll..."

"You have no dagger," he reminded her. "What will you do?"

"Find another!" She bit her lip in dismay at the impulsive testament to her true desire. Brokenly, she said, "I wish to be alone. Leave me."

"It's not safe for you to be alone."

"And I am safe with *you?*"

"No one will harm you when I am with you."

"And who will protect me from you?"

"You must trust me."

"I will *never* trust you!" Her voice shook. "Not as long as you live."

"Do you think I intend to harm you?"

"Isn't that what you do best?" Her voice rose. "Kill. Destroy. Ruin people's lives!" She burst into more tears of sorrow for her brother. "You are a monster! A dishonorable monster," she screamed, unable to help herself. "I hate you! *I hate you.* I will hate you forever!" She ran, but tripped and collapsed to the ground, overcome with rage and grief.

"Elwytha."

She ignored him, sobbing into her hands.

"Elwytha." To her shock, her hated enemy scooped her up in his arms.

"No!" she cried out. She kicked and fought like a wild animal. "Put me down!" She wrestled harder, with all of her strength. She hated his vile presence. His touch made her skin crawl. Being so close to him...touching him...made her sob even harder in dismay.

Still he held her. He would not release her. Her struggles seemed to affect him no more than a gnat flitting at his jerkin. Gradually, she realized it was useless to fight. He would not release her. More logical thoughts drifted in. They still remained in the garden. Maybe he thought she'd taken leave of her senses. Perhaps if she calmed, he would put her down.

With difficulty, she gulped to a stop.

"Put me down," she said in a watery voice.

Instead, he walked toward the castle.

Elwytha felt spent. No fight remained in her. Unless, of course, he tried to force himself upon her. Better to reserve her strength, then.

She sniffed quietly, wiped her face with her sleeve and endured his presence. He smelled of leather and soap, but she ignored this, and instead tensed herself for the return to his chambers.

He strode in, but instead of dumping her on his bed again, like she had expected, he edged open the door to her room and lowered her onto her own bed. A torch flickered in the room, shadowing the bad half of his face into blackness. The good half looked like a normal man, with a straight dark brow and a well cut mouth, twisted down. Only the dark stubble on his head looked unnatural. Why would a man shave his head like that?

"You are all right?" he asked.

She stared at him, barely able to believe her good fortune. "Yes."

"Then I bid you goodnight." Quietly, he closed the door behind him.

Elwytha stared after him. What was that about? Why hadn't he pressed his advantage? Clearly, he could physically overpower her.

After a moment she washed, changed, blew out the light, and crawled into bed. She felt spent and achingly empty. She cried again, but quietly this time, for her brother. Somehow, she would avenge his death. Her misery here would not be for ought.

⸎ ⸎ ⸎ ⸎ ⸎

The Commander paced his chambers, feeling a disturbed, restless energy—as well as guilt—churn through him. Clearly, he had killed someone Elwytha loved. But who? All the faces blurred together in battle. He put the heel of his hand to his head. She hated him. He acknowledged that this would never likely change. It sickened him, but what had he expected?

Still, she was to be his wife. The desire to keep her for his own appealed now, more strongly than before. What could he do so she would look upon his presence with favor?

An idea came to mind, and he smiled. Perhaps it would soften her heart toward him a little. He hoped so.

CHAPTER THREE

THE NEXT MORNING, A GENTLE TAP on her door awoke Elwytha. Alarmed, she sat bolt upright. Yesterday's distressing events streaked through her mind. She was betrothed to the Commander.

Mayhap that was he, seeking entrance to her virginal chamber?

She clutched the bedclothes to her neck, fervently wishing yet again for the friendly bite of her steel blades. Then she reminded herself that she was a warrior, not a fainting violet. No more displays of weakness. Last night she had succumbed to frayed nerves, but this morning she felt refreshed and clear-headed once more. It was time for courage, and for bold plans.

Elwytha took a fortifying breath. "Announce yourself."

"Hagma, miss," came a small squeak. "I have tea for you. And water to wash."

With relief, she said, "Enter."

The other girl hurried in, carrying her burdens. She scurried about, pouring fresh water in the pottery wash bowl, and setting the tea pot and cup on the small dresser. Finished, she wrung her hands, obviously at a loss for what to do next. "The Commander says if you wish, you may have a bath each day. I need only know when, so I can prepare it."

"In the same room as before?" Elwytha asked slyly, thinking of her weapons, snug beneath the rug.

"Nay, miss. The Commander has another room. You will let me know when you wish to bathe?"

"Perhaps this even, before supper," Elwytha suggested, disappointed about the knives, but pleased about the bath.

"Very good, miss. What do you wish to eat to break your fast this morn?"

This special treatment surprised Elwytha, especially since she had refused the services of a maid twice to the Commander. "You don't need to wait upon me," she told the other girl. "At home I know my way about the kitchens."

"But you are a princess," Hagma said with some horror. "And the Commander...he said I am to take good care of you. And I shall."

Elwytha took a quick breath. Was Hagma a spy for the Commander? Otherwise, what would be his purpose in pretending courtesy to her? Whatever the case, clearly Hagma bore no fault. She merely followed orders. Elwytha smiled, to put the girl at ease. "I would like bread, and perhaps fruit. Thank you, Hagma."

"Very good. And miss...the Commander wishes you to join him in the main hall an hour hence."

"He does?" He did, did he? Elwytha narrowed her eyes.

The maid curtseyed and retreated on her errand.

Elwytha decided she would meet the Commander in the hall as he decreed. Otherwise, he may attempt to employ some unspeakable horror to bend her to his will. All the same, she would make the experience as unpleasant for him as possible— and, if quick enough, would accomplish an errand of her own at the same time.

She swiftly dressed in an old, brown woolen frock that she wore for weapons practice back home. Worn and misshapen, it suited her purposes perfectly. And, since her coils last night had been received so well, this morning she would devise a new, even more unbecoming style for her hair.

Elwytha lifted her hair out in different directions, peering intently into her scrap of a mirror, until she hit upon the very idea. She set to work plaiting as fast as her fingers would allow.

When Hagma arrived with breakfast, she gasped when she saw Elwytha, and very nearly dropped the breakfast tray. Her eyes circled in horror. "Miss," she said hesitantly, "do you require...assistance?" She set the tray on the dresser.

"No, Hagma," Elwytha said gaily. "Thank you."

Hagma pleated her hands, and after a moment curtseyed. "If you are sure, miss?"

"Go, Hagma." The maid scurried out, and Elwytha grinned wickedly to herself. Soon the Commander would cease requesting her company, period. All the better, because she needed to apportion time to hunt for her blades. This morning she would steal a few moments. The sooner she found them, the better, should the Commander behave toward her in an uncouth manner. Brother's plan or no, she would not be mauled by that brute.

Yet again, Elwytha tried to guess why her brother wanted her to wait two weeks to kill the Commander. Perhaps to build up trust, so she could attack the Commander by surprise, in secret, and thence escape quickly, before anyone would notice?

That thought caused an uncomfortable knot to form in her chest. It reeked of murderous treachery, which she had not thought about too deeply of late—not since arriving in the enemy palace. But she reminded herself that the Commander was a murdering, cowardly knave, responsible for stabbing her brother in the back. He deserved the same sentence.

She shoved these uncomfortable nigglings to the back of her mind and finished her hair. Elwytha moved the tiny mirror all around so she could see her masterpiece from every angle. She smiled. Ropes of hair stuck out in all different directions. She looked like Medusa, with snakes for hair.

Magnificent. The Commander would be unable to stomach her countenance. Content, she sampled her breakfast. Delicious.

When finished, she exited from her room. Again, the Commander's chamber was empty. She felt some surprise that he allowed her to freely wander his room and the halls. Did no suspicion darken his brain? She blithely disregarded the intelligence she had sensed on more than one occasion. Regardless, she would take full advantage of her enemy's weakness.

A few minutes remained before he would expect her in the hall. Now she'd use warrior skill and cunning to root out her blades. Head turning quickly left and right, she sidled into the hall. All clear. Now to locate the room where she had bathed and been robbed of her blades.

Elwytha skulked left, sure that that was the way they had come. It just happened to be in the same direction as the great hall. Good. If needed, she could sprint to her assignation to hell if time ran short. Her feet were swift, and the baggy dress afforded ample yardage for running.

Elwytha's steps slowed. Here the hall split three different ways. Which direction should she go? She rued the fact that she'd closed her eyes while draped down the Commander's back. Sadly, humiliation had dulled her thinking abilities. A mistake not to be repeated.

While she hesitated, uncertain which direction to turn, a fresh stab of inspiration struck. After her initial meeting with the Prince in the throne hall, the Commander had led her to the bathing room. She had memorized every turn of the hall during that trip. Now she had only to return to the Prince's hall and she'd be able to retrace her steps to her blades.

But where was the throne room? That hall had been huge. It must be hard to miss. How large could this castle be, anyway? She decided to turn left, since she knew the great hall lay to her right. Fleet of foot, she sprinted down the corridor.

"Elwytha." The Commander's voice rumbled down the hall, catching her. She froze. Toad's nails! Frustration churned inside her. Reluctantly, she turned and faced him. A shot of fear stabbed her.

He wore a fully armored, thick leather jerkin, studded with metal, making him appear more massive and intimidating than usual. No helmet, however. Why would he dress thusly to meet with her? The question flew out of her head when she spied his expression.

Shock and disbelief flitted across his misshapen features. Her hair, in all of its glory, had accomplished her goal. She smiled then, with true pleasure.

Then...was that a smile? Did amusement lurk in those light, heathen eyes? No. Surely not!

* * * * *

The Commander looked at Elwytha with her flashing eyes and wide, challenging grin. Clearly, she had found her ugliest dress for their meeting this morn. He had wondered if one could top last night's. And she had fashioned her hair in a way sure to turn a man's stomach.

Creative, the different ways she thought up to displease him. It amused him. He had never met such a spunky, entertaining female before. No doubt it would dismay her to learn that her rebellious attempts to annoy only intrigued him more. He found himself anticipating their morning together even more.

He grinned, and a frown wrenched her brows together.

"Does your hair pain you?" he asked.

She frowned harder. "Why would it? It's the latest fashion. No doubt a brute such as yourself is ignorant of such matters."

He did not reply to this nonsense. "I will ride the perimeter this morn. You will come with me."

Rebellion flared in her eyes. "I wish to go nowhere with you. Leave me at my leisure."

"Your horse requires exercise."

She drew a quick breath. "My horse...is here? I believed he was sent home with the guard."

He did not answer. Instead, he placed a hand upon her small waist, urging her toward the doors. Elwytha stiffened and moved speedily ahead, clearly revolted by the contact. It didn't surprise him, although his choice to touch her had been deliberate. He wanted to accustom her to his touch, so when their marriage night came, it would not terrify her.

However, if her response now was any indication, much work would be required to accomplish the goal of gentling her to his touch.

⚔ ⚔ ⚔ ⚔ ⚔

Much as the Commander's demands displeased Elwytha, the thought of riding her horse lifted her spirits. The beast had been her close friend and companion ever since she was eleven—ten long years ago. If only she could ride alone, without the Commander's unwelcome presence!

Never mind, she told herself, spying the stables ahead. Her steps quickened. Perhaps on her steed she could flee from him; at least, for a little while. Her horse was the fleetest of foot in her brother's stables.

Eagerness pumped in her, and at the stable she darted ahead to find her beloved steed. There! A white head. A whinny of welcome.

Finally, a friendly face, horsy though it was. She ran and flung her arms around him. "Sir Duke," she whispered, and pressed her cheek into his white neck. Emotion choked her. He turned his head, snuffling her hair. "I'm sorry. I have no apple."

With careful, loving hands she saddled her horse and led him from the stable. The Commander waited astride a great black steed. It stood a hand higher than her own, and snorted, its nostrils flaring. The black eyes rolled, showing bits of white. A magnificent animal.

Elwytha swung astride her horse, not caring overly much that it was unladylike. Who had she to impress? And she'd ridden thusly all of her life. The Commander showed no surprise at her conduct. But why would he, since he was apparently unschooled in the finer social graces?

Sir Duke cantered sideways, toward the black beast as she gathered up the reins, and the Commander's horse skittered sideways, too. His hooves nervously danced.

Elwytha said, "Your beast is half wild."

"He's broken. He requires only a gentle word and a firm touch."

"You use no whip to subdue your animal?" Richard and the horse trainers at home approved the judicious use of the whip to break animals.

The Commander had calmed his steed and now it stood snorting, flesh quivering, a short distance away. "No." He regarded her, his mouth suspiciously twitching at one corner. "A beast is much like a human. Both can be gentled without force."

Elwytha drew a quick, indignant breath. "Are you likening me to a *horse?*"

"You speak the words. Not I. Come." He nudged his animal into motion, heading for the edge of the wood.

Fury gathered in Elwytha's bosom. He believed he could tame her like a horse? Nay. He could well think again. In fact, two could play at that game. It appealed to her as much as torturing him did. Perhaps she could wield the two together.

She smiled. Yes. He would receive nothing but unremitting torture from her until she slew him with one final, fatal blow. By then he would welcome death. Her mind spun with these pleasant possibilities as they crossed the drawbridge.

Before them rolled gentle green hills, bordered by thatches of dark forest. One stand of dense trees lay to her left. Ahead, a rutted lane lined by heather and raspberry bushes led to a tiny village. It appeared a good wind might blow the shacks over. Small figures moved about the fields, no doubt tending the wheat or barley. Elwytha saw no cattle or sheep, but knew they likely roamed the hills with their shepherds now.

The black stallion entered the wood. Fall had ripened the leaves of the ash and oak into deep golden and orange hues.

Although Elwytha followed several paces behind the Commander, in a seemingly submissive manner, her mind quickly devised an alternative plan. She itched to be rid of his company nearly as much as she desired to vex him.

First, though, to tend to the ropes of hair flopping about her head. True, they had dismayed the Commander at first. Unfortunately, he had smiled afterward, as if she were an amusing child. She untied them and slid her fingers through the plaits, freeing her hair.

Perhaps it had been a childish plan. All future plans must accomplish far more important goals—namely, retrieving her weapons and measuring her enemy's strengths. Then no surprises would remain for their final, fateful meeting two weeks hence.

She continued to smile, however, as she pulled out the last bow. Vexing the Commander had buoyed her spirits; a necessary, fortifying requirement, since apparently she'd be shackled morning, noon and night to her enemy. In addition, clever plans would need to be formulated in order to frustrate his unknown, untenable plans for her future.

There. Her hair felt better now, flowing freely down her back. A cool breeze kissed her face and slid through her tresses. The end of the treeline approached. Ahead, she spied what she sought—rolling, grassy hills.

At last, her horse cantered into open sunshine. Elwytha drew a breath of fresh, sweet air. Far ahead, a new forest stretched, which was her destination. Home lay a half day's ride beyond those trees.

The Commander slowed just as Elwytha leaned low over Sir Duke's neck and pressed her knees into his sides. "Go, Sir Duke," she whispered. With a joyful jump, her steed leaped into motion. Wind sailed through her hair as Sir Duke galloped faster and faster. Primitive joy soared through Elwytha. Home lay just beyond those woods. A place of peace, comfort, and shelter from her enemy.

She turned her head to see if she had left the Commander behind. No. His black steed followed by a mere two horse lengths. He leaned forward in the saddle, but she saw no urgency in his pose. No slapping of the reins against the horse's neck. It was as if they merely accompanied her joy ride.

She tried to ignore his presence. Instead, she focused on the sweet breeze, the rush of grass beneath Sir Duke's hooves, and the crisp feel to the fall air. Soon, the russet leaves would fall. Would she be home before then?

Would she ever make it home?

Fear drove her knees more urgently into Sir Duke, and he doubled his stride, hooves flying over the earth. Adrenaline pounded through Elwytha as fears meshed and tangled inside her soul. If only she could reach that stand of trees.... If only she could go home! A small cry gathered in her throat, but she swallowed it back. Sir Duke needed direction to keep him on course, and to keep them both safe.

Still, the Commander followed several lengths behind, allowing her to set the pace, and making no move to overtake her. Elwytha felt Sir Duke's lungs laboring and his heart pounding as they approached the wood, and knew she needed to spare her steed. She eased up and the horse slowed to a glad canter. He had enjoyed the run, no doubt.

She urged him into the sun-dappled trees. The forest here consisted of thin saplings and low bushes. Unexpectedly, Sir Duke pulled up, snorting, his flanks quivering.

She gripped the reins tighter. "What is it, boy?"

The Commander cantered to a stop beside her. Sweat glistened on the black's coat. Before he could say a word, two men on horseback appeared over the rise. Both were bearded; one was blond and scruffy, and the other was raven-haired. They bore the crest of her palace. And full armor.

The Commander edged forward. In that instant, her enemy transformed before her eyes. His face hardened into a formidable mask, and his countenance stiffened, projecting a forceful, threatening aggression. His hand rested on the hilt of his sword.

Trepidation leaped. She had never met the Commander in battle before, although she had seen him at a distance. A distance she would prefer to keep, even now.

"Get behind me, Elwytha."

"They won't harm me."

"Get *behind* me, Elwytha!" His voice cracked like thunder.

Still, Elwytha refused to comply. These were her brother's men. They owed their allegiance to her. She spoke directly to them. "Why do you trespass here, upon the Prince's land?"

One curled his lip. "Already, you pledge allegiance to the enemy?"

"I ride through the woods," she returned, easily donning her regal, authoritative tone. "State your purpose."

The blond one urged his horse closer. Unease slid down her spine, though she refused to show it. At her side, the Commander gripped his sword handle, although the blade remained sheathed.

Her brother's man edged still nearer, so now his horse sidled next to her own. He grinned at her. "The King wishes to parlay a message to you."

Something was wrong. Elwytha felt this, deep in her spirit. In the same instant, she noted the man's hand on his dagger, and the sword at his side. Quicker than thought, she relieved him of the sword, and backed her horse up at the same time.

The blade in her hand flashed in the sun that streamed through the quiet trees. "Speak your message and be gone."

The man's hand tightened on the dagger, but it relaxed when he saw that the Commander had unsheathed his sword, too. The blond man bowed his head slightly to Elwytha. Only the twist to his mouth proved his servitude a lie. "The King agrees to your match. He will attend your nuptials, two weeks hence."

Elwytha's eyes narrowed. "Give thanks to my brother for the message."

"I shall."

Beneath her, Sir Duke moved restlessly. She soothed his neck with her free hand.

"My sword?" said her brother's warrior.

Elwytha flung it, far over his head, into the wood. It landed, quivering, in a tree trunk. Exactly where she had wished it to stick.

"Godspeed," she said.

With a barely disguised snarl, the man and his companion rode to retrieve the sword. With one last, backward look of rage, both galloped in the direction of Castle Cor na Gaeth.

Elwytha's heart beat rapidly. What had that been about? The two men plotted trouble; she sensed it. But trouble for whom?

The Commander resheathed his sword and edged his horse alongside hers. He gripped her reins in one great fist. Still frowning, she gave him her attention.

The gray eyes looked silver, and as threatening as his steel sword. "You do not listen well."

"Those were my brother's men. I can handle them."

"They meant ill."

Her eyes traced the path the men had just taken. "Yes," she agreed. "But I cannot guess their true purpose."

The mutilated brow frowned deeply. "Can you not?"

Was he accusing her of treachery? Unmerited indignation swelled. Never mind if it was true; but not yet. She met his steel gray eyes. "No. We have peace, do we not?"

"Peace until the blade turns," he agreed in a quiet, warning rumble.

Her gaze steadily held his, and she offered a small smile. "You distrust me?"

"I am no fool, Elwytha. I know where your true loyalties lie."

A thread of alarm shot through her. She willfully quenched it. "I am your betrothed. That is my word to you." Never mind that she didn't actually intend to wed him. For now, she was his betrothed.

"A match I know you fully despise."

How could she deny that? "Yes."

"Yet you did not try to slay me with his sword. Why not?"

The idea had never crossed her mind. Bewildered, she suggested, "For peace? Further, I did not trust them."

"Yet you trusted me."

She frowned. "No." And then she admitted, "I knew you would not harm me."

"You chose my side over theirs," he pressed.

The treachery she planned against him twisted in her heart, stinging her with guilt. "I chose my brother's peace treaty. That is where my true loyalty lies," she told him. And that was the truth.

He nodded, but his gaze continued to assess her. "Yes. Come with me. I have a stop I wish to make."

CHAPTER FOUR

THIS TIME, ELWYTHA CONTENTED HERSELF with following the black horse.

Her brother's treacherous peace plan gnawed more deeply at her conscience as she rode. By pretending peace, she lied to both the Commander and the Prince now. She plotted to kill the Commander. After making that final, murderous choice, could she ever go back? Or would she relinquish part of her soul forever to the dark side? Could she ever again be as pure and true of heart as Richard had accused her?

These thoughts troubled her as she followed the Commander's warrior-clad person. True, he was a murderer. But could that truth prove treachery a virtue?

Elwytha did not know. And when the Commander slowed before a small, deserted church, fear filled her.

Was this a sign from God that she needed to repent?

The Commander tied his reins to a tree and slowly, Elwytha did likewise. She followed him inside, and saw that the chapel must still be used on occasion. Candles dotted tables near the altar. A few burned even now. The floor looked swept, and the pews clean.

The Commander knelt his great form before the altar.

"Why are you here?" Elwytha asked. Perhaps it was rude to interrupt, but it didn't stop her. "Truly, I know why you *need* to be here. I'm just surprised you are."

"Perhaps God will show mercy for my soul," he murmured. After a long moment elapsed, he asked, "How many men have you killed, Elwytha?"

She stiffened. "Princesses do not see battle. Besides, war is not the same as cold-blooded murder." She spat this last at his back.

The Commander remained silent, and after more long moments he crossed himself and stood. "I am ready to go."

"But you haven't asked a priest for forgiveness." She looked around. "If there is one."

The Commander moved toward the door. "My soul is too black for a priest to help."

At least he acknowledged this truth.

"Then why come?"

"I feel peace here," he rumbled, as though impatient. "Are you ready to go?"

"I would like to light a candle." She lit one for her dead brother and said a short prayer. Strange, but she, too, felt peace in the deserted chapel. As if God was near. As if it was not too late for her own soul. On impulse, she turned back, knelt, and prayed penance for her many unspoken misdeeds. Then she hesitated, wondering if she could ask forgiveness for a sin she hadn't yet committed.

But it would not be murder. All of a sudden, in the quiet peace of the chapel, she recognized this truth. She could not stab him in the back. That would be wrong. She would be no better than Thor's murderer. She shuddered. Never could she sink to such depravity.

A challenge then, face to face. He would be a formidable foe. Of this, she had no doubt. But she knew her own skills. She would win the battle. With her three daggers she could fell any man.

Still, treachery was treachery. She plotted to kill him.

Elwytha felt no better as she followed the Commander out of the chapel. Her brother deserved vengeance for his wrongful

death, she told herself. Justice had to be served. It was the
only right way.

Elwytha said little for the remainder of the morning's ride.
Thankfully, her betrothed was a man of few words, so the basic
niceties of social chatter were spared her. Instead, she wrestled
alone with her troubled thoughts.

ᚹ ᚹ ᚹ ᚹ ᚹ

After the ride, Elwytha's stomach rumbled. She had no
wish to eat in the hall with the Commander and his knaves,
however. The evening meal was torture enough to endure.
Perhaps the cook would allow her to sup in the kitchen. At
home she'd made friends with the cook at an early age.
Elwytha liked kitchens; especially their warmth and delicious
smells. She felt at home there, and already she missed that
warmth and friendliness. Was it too much to hope that she
might find a small measure of the same comfort here?

In the stone-flagged kitchen, a plump woman with a cloud
of gray hair busily stirred a pot. It smelled of soup.

"Hello. I'm Elwytha."

"Land alive." The woman dropped her spoon, startled. She
retrieved it and set it on a table. "Well, so you are." She wiped
her hands on her apron and approached. "I'm Mary, the cook.
Pleased to meet you, I'm sure." A question lurked in her eyes.
Probably she was wondering why an enemy princess had entered her kitchen.

"I would like to eat lunch in here, if you don't mind,"
Elwytha said. "I feel uncomfortable in the hall with the
uncouth..." She stopped, perceiving it may be unwise to
disparage men the cook had likely known for years. "I would
be no trouble to you."

"Of course you wouldn't. Sit," Mary invited. "I've fresh
bread and cheese. Would you like fruit?"

"Our cook at home shows me where everything is. I can
serve myself."

"Certainly not!" Mary looked affronted. "Not in my kitchen, you won't." She bustled to the larder. "Would you like honey?"

"Just bread with butter is fine." Elwytha sat at the table which Mary had strewn with various pans filled with meat, chopped onions, and other vegetables. She must be in the midst of preparing for dinner. "Don't you have help?" Cooking for hundreds of men, she knew, entailed lots of work.

"Of course. They're eating lunch now." Mary gave a merry laugh and set a trencher before her. "No rest for the cook."

"Thank you." The food tasted like ambrosia. She was famished.

Mary returned to the stove. "You're to marry the Commander, are you? If you don't mind my nosy questions."

"No. Of course I don't mind," Elwytha smiled with gratitude. She was eager to make a friend in this enemy palace, and the cook seemed inclined to be friendly to her. "And yes," she pressed her lips together, unable to hide her feelings, "I am to marry the Commander."

Mary cast her a keen glance. "He's a fine lad, is our Commander."

Doubtless, she would think so. He had led the enemy castle to many victories—against her warriors. It took her a few moments to compose a truthful reply. "He is a great warrior," she reluctantly allowed.

The cook's attention returned to the pot she stirred, but now her lips looked tight. Disapproving? Or was the pot merely difficult to stir? Elwytha felt anxious to retain the friendship they had begun to build. "I'll have plenty of time in the next two weeks to learn to know the Commander as you do," she said, in an effort to be conciliatory.

Mary smiled a little. "He does look fearsome, doesn't he? I know that can be off-putting. How is your food?"

"Delicious. As was the meal last night."

Mary smiled, further pleased. "Don't worry about the Commander. He treats all with justice. He will treat you the same way, but a warning.... He's not so kind to those who cross him."

A shiver slid through Elwytha. As she intended to cross him. Mary could not know this, and yet the warning pierced Elwytha's heart. Not that she would listen, of course. The Commander had committed a crime of his own, and she would mete justice to him.

"Thank you for lunch. May I come again tomorrow?" She stood.

"I'd be offended if you didn't," the cook returned cheerily.

With a smile, Elwytha left her new friend. She spotted the Commander as she crossed the dining hall. He headed for her, obviously intending to intersect her path.

Elwytha quickened her steps to flee, but it was a useless endeavor.

"Where are you headed in such a hurry?" he rumbled when he reached her side.

"Why do you wish to torture me again?" Elwytha asked, annoyed. She should have stayed in the peace of the kitchen awhile longer. "We spent all morning together." She strode faster toward the door that led to the outside courtyard.

"I wish to spend more time with you."

Elwytha burst into the glorious sunshine. "Why, pray tell?" she demanded. "It pleases you to torture me. Tell me the truth."

"I would like to introduce you to my men. And make you familiar with the courtyard," he returned calmly.

"How gracious you are. What courtesies you bestow upon me," she said with sarcasm. "I have no wish to meet your men."

His hand on her wrist forced her to stop.

"Do not touch my person," she hissed, and wrenched it free. His domineering ways inflamed her rebellious nature beyond all reason, yet again. "I wish to go nowhere with you. If you wish for my company so fervently, you may beseech my favor.... Not that I would grant it," she finished, her eyes narrowed.

Did amusement lurk in those clear gray eyes? The very suspicion made her bosom heave faster in indignation. He said quietly, "I do wish for your company. Now." Steel undergirded his words.

"Or what will you do? Throw me over your shoulder again? Cart me to and fro like a sack of grain so your men may sneer upon me? Nay!"

"Then cooperate. Come with me now."

Elwytha heaved another breath and clenched her fists. The brute beast. The fiendish monster. Again employing unthinkable threats to bend her to his will. "I will come," she gritted finally. "But expect me to submit no pleasantries to your heathen warriors."

Jaw clenched in frustration, she followed him about the yard as he introduced her to his various warriors. All treated him with liking and deferential respect, and all offered her a smile. They were a rough bunch. Many had tangled, greasy hair, and a few sported rows of missing teeth.

Maintaining her regal bearing, Elwytha offered a smile to each one, and inclined her head, but did not speak. And she memorized each of their names. Who knew when these facts might deliver her an advantage? The Commander did not realize—and neither had she, at first—that his little tour increased her knowledge of the castle. Vital knowledge she might need to accomplish her mission. She smiled to herself.

In all, he probably introduced her to twenty warriors, and then he explained the function of the various buildings to her. He started first with the armory.

Elwytha showed her first spark of interest. "How many weapons do you have inside?" Perhaps he would be foolish enough to show her.

He regarded her with faint amusement. "You may not enter the armory. Do not approach it, either."

"More threats?"

"A warning." Next, he led her to a grassy courtyard. Two men clashed swords as they practiced their skills. Elwytha's blood quickened as she watched. How she wished to practice, too. At home she tested her skills every day.

As if sensing her interest, the Commander remained stationary, too. "I first learned to wield a stick here," he said.

An unwitting interest sparked in Elwytha. "Really? How old were you?" She had been six.

"Seven. It is when I met the Prince for the first time."

Elwytha found this information interesting. Perhaps she'd learn more about the Prince and the palace workings if she pressed the Commander for details; at least, this was the justification she allowed for her keen interest. "How old was the Prince?"

"Five. We learned together."

"And so you became friends?"

"Good friends...as the brother neither of us had," he admitted after a moment.

Hence, the strong bond she had sensed between the two. "The Prince has no siblings?"

"The King sired none after him. His nannies wished to coddle him. He hated it, and often escaped to practice in the yard. We spent many hours sharpening our skills, and getting into trouble."

"The Prince's doing?" she guessed.

The Commander smiled faintly, but did not reply.

Elwytha pressed on, eager to make the most of this opportunity, while her betrothed spoke freely. Another question, on a different subject, had nibbled at her mind for years—long before being snared in this enemy pit. "Why does the Prince wish to be called Prince, when clearly he is the King?"

The Commander rolled his shoulders, appearing restless, and strode away from the grassy practice field. Wanting to hear his reply, Elwytha followed closely by his side. After a moment, he said, "It is something he does not speak about."

Elwytha felt disappointed. Didn't the Commander know? Or perhaps he didn't wish to tell her. Excitement energized her thoughts. What great mystery could he be concealing?

But when she searched his unreadable face, she wondered if she might be looking for mysteries where none existed.

Likely, the Prince had been called thusly all of his life, and when his father had died a few years ago, he had decided to keep the title. He certainly appeared undisciplined enough to follow his own unconventional path. Perhaps it pleased him to be different from other kings.

CHAPTER FIVE

ELWYTHA PURPOSEFULLY ARRIVED EARLY to the great dining hall that evening. It freed her of the indignity of arriving on the Commander's arm. Unfortunately, it also meant she had no buffer from the Prince, who already sat in splendor at the head table.

With reluctance, she sat on the same bench as she had the previous night, and sent the crown regent a cool, distant smile. She sniffed the air and watched servants lug pots to the tables. Stew, from the smell of it, and no doubt delicious, as Mary was a fine cook.

The Prince spoke, interrupting her pleasant meditations on supper. "You enjoyed the tour of my castle this afternoon, Princess?"

Elwytha reluctantly looked upon the Prince's sharp features and mocking black eyes. What did he mean by such comments? She did not trust him an inch. "I am pleased to be enlightened about the layout of your fortress."

The Prince gave a thin smile. "Does battle still wage in your heart, Princess?"

"No." She pasted a fake smile upon her lips. "I feel privileged—nay—astounded to be afforded such trust from my betrothed...and you."

The stew arrived, and she ladled a generous portion into her trencher.

"The Commander chooses his battles." The Prince sipped his ale. "I merely watch his back."

Elwytha's lips curled. "Truly, a practice you must be well accustomed to in this palace."

The Commander arrived and settled his large form beside her. Not so discretely, she sidled away. Luckily, the lout from last night had not arrived yet.

"Such venom, Princess," the Prince said. "You are not happy here?"

"Except for peace, I would sooner die than live within your walls, attached so closely to your brood of vipers."

The Commander regarded her with a frown, no doubt surprised to be skewered by battle words when sitting down to supper. "Elwytha..."

"Let her speak her heart," the Prince interposed. "Tell us, Princess, why you loathe the Commander so. Do you still see him as a monster?" With narrowed eyes, he baited her.

Elwytha would not foolishly unveil her hand. If they suspected the depth of her hatred, they would know the peace was a sham, and that she plotted something far more deadly against the Prince's first-in-command.

She spooned up a bite of carrot and chewed while plotting her next, subtle attack. Elwytha glanced at her huge betrothed.

"The Commander has led many successful offensives against my land. Am I to harbor warm feelings toward him?" Delicately, she sipped stew juice. "Nay," she continued, "I will pretend no love for a bloodthirsty knave such as he."

The Prince opened his mouth, but the Commander shot him a glance. The Prince tipped his head, allowing the Commander to respond to Elwytha's deliberately inflammatory remark.

In a low rumble, he said, "Speak to me with respect, Elwytha."

"I will pretend no lies."

"You wish to break the peace agreement, then."

Of course, she would love nothing better. But she frowned. "I break no agreements when I speak the truth."

The Commander regarded her. "You speak the war in your heart. It appears you do not wish for peace."

Elwytha frowned harder. How could he twist her words thusly, bending them to his meanings, to accomplish his desires? "I don't have to like you to love peace."

Steely eyes bored into hers. "Speak the reason for your hatred of me," he commanded. "I want to end this enmity between us now."

Elwytha gasped. Did he jest? Could he truly be so ignorant of the reason for her hatred? How many men had he thusly stabbed in the back, then? It must be a common occurrence, if he could dismiss it so utterly from his mind. The heathen. The unscrupulous, low-bellied snake!

She spat, "I will not comfort your ears with pleasant words, Commander. If you wish an obedient wife, perhaps a maid would serve you far better. Maybe you, after all, are the one who wishes to end the peace agreement."

The Prince drank from his cup. "I would not hold you to it, Commander."

Elwytha clenched her fists, enraged by the sly, interfering monarch's comments. She endeavored to ignore him, and instead stared at her betrothed. "Do you, then?" she demanded. If only he would end their betrothal! Perhaps she could battle him early and be done with this entire unsavory, boiling stew in which she found herself.

"No," he told her. "I do not wish to end it. You will be mine, as agreed."

Elwytha gritted her teeth and wished for nothing more than to leap up and fly on Sir Duke's back for home. But it was not to be. "As you wish. But demand no false courtesies from me, for you will not receive them." Hands regrettably trembling with emotion, she stood. "I can stomach no more of your delicacies, Prince. They poison my very marrow."

With slow, deliberate steps, even though inside she wanted to flee from their very presence, she exited from the dining hall. Tonight she would go hungry. Better that than enduring another moment of excruciating word battles with the Commander and Prince.

A thought entered her head. Perhaps Mary had a crust of bread she could eat in the kitchen. She altered her steps to see.

¥ ¥ ¥ ¥ ¥

"She hates you," the Prince said.

"Yes," the Commander agreed. He watched Elwytha glide off, her slim shoulders stiff beneath the hideous brown dress. But she was not as hard as she wanted him to believe; he knew that now. Last night, he had attributed her tears to the shock of her betrothal to him, and a first night's uneasiness within the enemy palace. But today her hot temper and the faint tremble to her hands just now had belied the cold vixen she pretended to be. As a warrior, he was trained to spot all chinks in an opponent's armor.

Beneath the hard princess's exterior lived a vulnerable woman. And, he sensed, a hurting woman.

The Prince interrupted his thoughts, "You still wish to have her, then?"

"Yes," he growled. In fact, he wanted her more now, after seeing her fiercely suppressed emotions, than ever before.

¥ ¥ ¥ ¥ ¥

"I would like to see the armory," Elwytha said the next morning, after a filling breakfast and troubled sleep. Never mind that the Commander had forbidden the possibility yesterday. She plotted something else entirely today.

Her betrothed sat writing on a parchment at a table. Again, surprise filled her that he could read or write.

His eyes narrowed. "I will not trust you in the armory."

"I am bored," she said, pretending petulance. Never could he guess her true intent. "I wish to sport."

The mutilated brow raised. "You wish to sport? Then you will sport with me."

Elwytha frowned, but inside she smiled. How blindly he had stepped into her trap. "Very well. If you insist."

He stood. "At last, then, you will admit that you are a warrior?"

"I admit to a skill with weapons practice," she said, following him into the hall. "It brightened many a boring day as a child. My brother..." she stopped as a lump caught in her throat. How could she speak of her beloved brother with the man who had murdered him—with the brutal heathen who had stabbed him in the back in cold blood? She forced herself to continue. Never could she allow the suspicion of her true feelings to bloom in her betrothed's mind. "He taught me the basics. He had great skill...and much patience with me, as a child."

The Commander opened a heavy wooden door and led the way across the grassy courtyard to a stone building. After a moment, he probed, "Your brother, the King?"

"No. My oldest brother." Elwytha looked quickly away as grief welled up. Tears crowded her eyes, but she willfully blinked them back. She would not cry again before her enemy.

The Commander said nothing, as he shouldn't, the horrible man. Rage at what he had done to her brother burned hot all over again as he disappeared inside the armory to retrieve their weapons. He reemerged with sticks. These were used as imitations for true sword play. Elwytha could not snatch hers quickly enough. How she longed to slay him now! To make him pay for what he had done.

Blinded by the wretched tears, her first two slashes swung wild. The Commander easily blocked her stick, and this calmed her as nothing else could. He would gain no victory in this match. Rage burned her tears dry.

Elwytha lunged and parried and wielded her stick with quick, deadly precision. She saw his great shoulders tense when he realized he had a true opponent.

He matched her skill, and Elwytha saw the instant he took it to the next level. His make-believe sword cut quickly to the side, but Elwytha was ready for the jab, and indeed defeated it, and twirled her weapon, nearly wrenching the stick from his hand.

All pretense of games disappeared from the Commander's demeanor. His stick moved blindingly fast, and pressed forward. She refused to fall back. Like lightning, her stick whipped, clashing with his.

Other warriors gathered to watch.

The Commander was the best swordsman she had ever encountered. Quickness and precision were Elwytha's strengths. They appeared to be his, as well. But he had an advantage she didn't. Brute strength. Although she was in top condition, he would far outlast her. Already she felt a tremor in her arms. How long had the match gone on? Twenty minutes? Thirty?

Warriors cheered now for the Commander, and surprisingly for herself, as well.

But Elwytha still had a trick up her sleeve; one her beloved brother had taught her. She quickened her tempo and pressed into offensive action, forcing him to parry her moves.

Elwytha felt hot now. Sweat trickled down her forehead and dripped inside her dress.

In swift succession, she executed the well-remembered moves. Thrust, parry...thrust, thrust, parry...then three moves, in blinding succession, designed to trick him and throw him off balance. She sensed him turn too fast and tilt on his heels, and made her final lunge. All victory, this move...or all defeat. It was her only chance. In a minute she would need to cry defeat from pure exhaustion.

Her stick thrust through the air...and bounced off his brown jerkin. It seemed to happen in slow motion. She saw the dent in the cloth, surprise flicker across his mutilated face, and then heard the approving cheers of the crowd.

Panting, she dropped her stick, her arm shaking.

The Commander lowered his stick and regarded her, his breaths still even. She could not read his expression.

He turned to his men. "The spectacle is over." His deep voice sounded mild.

With hoots and cheers, the men scattered.

Silently, the Commander held out a hand for the stick, and after a hesitation, she gave it to him. She felt uneasy. Did he feel angry about being defeated by the hand of a woman?

But she had prevailed. She was victorious. And when she battled him in eleven days' time, she would not choose sword play—or anything that required endurance—to battle him. She had learned a great deal about her opponent today, which had been her intention from the start.

Head held high, she entered the armory while he put the sticks away. Still, she sensed no emotions from him. Boldly, she challenged, "Are you angry you lost to me?"

He walked toward her, forcing her out of the armory and back into the sunlight. He latched the door behind him. "You mean a woman...or a warrior?"

She did not answer.

"Still, you deny it?" Was that contempt in his eyes?

Anger stiffened Elwytha's spine. Was he accusing her of lying? As well she had been, she admitted. Another character failing that this treachery required of her. It made her feel sick. How could she reply without admitting the complete truth, and thereby endangering her own safety?

She said, "I will give no advantage to my enemies."

He captured her hand and unexpectedly pulled her closer. Fear flared, and then settled. "Do I remain your enemy, Elwytha?" He stared down at her.

"How could you be anything but my enemy?" Anger twisted inside of her. "We've been at war all of our lives."

"Our kingdoms have. Not you and me."

Fury burned in her. How could he not be her enemy, after striking down her brother in cold blood? Did he think she didn't know? Surely he hadn't forgotten—one horror among too many for him to count?

"Unhand me," she snapped. "Pray, do not molest me."

"Have I yet?" She heard the anger in his deep rumble.

"No," she admitted. "And I will thank you to keep it that way."

"In eleven days I will claim you for my own. Perhaps you should pray for peace with me instead."

"I would sooner fall on my sword."

Shock recoiled across his features, as though she had slapped him. Satisfied, Elwytha spun and left.

⸸ ⸸ ⸸ ⸸ ⸸

The Commander felt shaken by the hatred he had seen in Elwytha's eyes. He had not suspected the depth of it—that she would sooner die than have peace with him, or allow him to be a husband to her.

He clenched his fist. Every attempt he had made to forge peace between them had hit a stone wall of resistance. Hatred simmered deep within her. Her swordplay proved it. She was clearly skilled. A warrior. One of the best swordsmen—women—he had ever battled. But he had sensed the vicious fury behind each thrust. She had wanted to hurt him. He believed she would have killed him if she could.

Was it because he had killed someone she loved? Again, he wondered who.

He shoved the heel of his hand across his prickly scalp. A stalemate lived between them. A fortified barricade towered around her heart.

If he wanted her for his wife, he would have to find the tool to weaken the foundation of her walls. And he did still want her, despite all the reasons why he should not. He liked Elwytha, and that included her spunk and fire and passion for life. If only her passion for him was not hatred.

Clearly, deep hurt fueled her anger toward him. He had done something to hurt her, but he did not know what it was. The Commander frowned, thinking. He would no longer tiptoe around the problem that she refused to explain to him. The wall would come down. He would discover the truth.

He recalled the visible emotions playing over her face as she had battled him. Yes. He knew exactly how to weaken that wall. And then how quickly it would crash.

He smiled in satisfaction and planned his next moves. As he headed for the castle, however, a few of his men reappeared and hooted and cat-called him. He should have expected this.

"She's befuddled your brain, Commander," gibed one man.

He smiled, but unsheathed his sword. His warriors needed to remember respect. With an edge of menace, he said, "I will battle any man who wishes to challenge me."

"Mayhap her sweet form caused your eye to wander," taunted another.

He rolled his great shoulders and thundered, "Pick up your sword." The men scattered, which satisfied him. Their continued snickers did not.

⸙ ⸙ ⸙ ⸙ ⸙

Elwytha sped inside the castle, intent on one purpose only—to find her blades.

"Hagma!" She spied the maid scuttling down a side hall. "Take me to the throne room."

With a questioning look in her eyes, the girl crept closer. "Has the Prince called for you?"

"I want to learn how to find my way around the castle. I wish to walk and not get lost."

"The Prince would not be pleased if I brought you to the throne room." Hagma looked disturbed.

"Bring me to its doors, and then leave me." Elwytha offered the maid a comforting smile. "I will not trouble the Prince. Never fear."

"What does the Commander say? Perhaps I should ask him what I should do." The maid wrung her hands.

Elwytha frowned. "The Commander does not need to know everything. If you won't help me, I'll find it on my own."

She spun on her heel and strode toward the great hall. When she glanced back, Hagma had disappeared. Perhaps to alert the Commander to her castle wanderings? Elwytha quickened her steps, and sped through the halls. Good thing she hadn't told Hagma her true destination.

Elwytha hurried through hall after hall, using the great hall as her starting point. She began to understand how the castle was built. The old parts were fashioned of great stones, and the newer parts were made of smaller stones and wooden timbers. The old halls were narrow, and the new wider. She knew the room where she had bathed was large, with small stones and wooden beams overhead. Likely it was in an outer wing of the palace.

Her slippers sped swiftly and silently down one hall after another, and then, quite by accident, she came across the throne room. She only knew it was the throne room because a guard slipped in through a great double door and white quartz sparkled out.

A small smile crossed her lips. Now to find that bathing room. With unerring steps, she recalled that first, terrifying journey with the Commander. Her memory did not fail her.

At last. She stopped before the familiar carved door.

Elwytha tugged on the door latch. Locked. Dismayed, she rattled the latch again. Still locked. Elwytha spun and slid down the wall to the floor. Denied. Again her weapons would be denied her. Frustration simmered. Now what would she do?

She took deep, even breaths, trying to formulate a plan. Perhaps she could check back every day, perhaps at different times, in order to see if the room was left unlocked by accident. Perhaps she could break into the armory and steal weapons at night. She needed three, in order to prepare for her final battle with the Commander. This plan appealed. Or perhaps she could pilfer the Commander's own blade from his chamber in the middle of the night.

This last plan appealed the most of all. It would be a fitting punishment. His blade had ended her brother's life. His blade would end his own, as well.

Elwytha sprang to her feet, plan fully formed. This very night the Commander's reckoning would begin for his many sins.

˅ ˅ ˅ ˅ ˅

That evening, Elwytha was again forced to endure another meal with her betrothed and his knaves. This time, however, instead of joking about her, they jested the Commander's defeat at her hands this afternoon.

"Pray, what is this?" the Prince inquired, his black eyes narrowed and amused. "Tell all, Commander."

"She's put a spell on him," hooted one man.

"Wed her soon, Commander," yelled another.

"He canna think straight," leered the lout at her side. "Nor I. I lose all sens'bilities, looking at her." To her horror, the lout edged closer and slurred, "You're s'sweet. Favor me w' a smile, Princess."

Oh, for a blade! "Remove yourself from my presence," she said, flaying him with a cold glare.

He chuckled and patted her leg. Horror convulsed through her. Unthinkingly, she jerked sideways, into the Commander. He looked at her, still scowling from the men's jests.

She shoved the man's hand off of her lap. "Leave me," she hissed. She felt the Commander stiffen, and suddenly he surged to his feet. The next thing she knew, he had dragged the lout by the jerkin from the table. The smaller man hung from the Commander's fist, feet dangling above the floor.

"You would touch my bride?" The deep rumble bristled with menace.

Elwytha cringed, waiting for his great fist to smash into the man's face. She appealed, "He's drunk. He does not know what he is doing."

This testimony did not appear to please her betrothed. He turned his glare on her and growled, "You would allow his touch before mine?"

Dismay speared Elwytha. "I wish neither. But I don't want violence done on my behalf. Throw him out. That would please me."

The Commander shoved the drunkard into the hands of two guards who had appeared. Then he settled his great form on the bench beside her. He did not look at her.

"How valiantly the Commander defends you, Princess," the Prince said, clearly mocking. "Have you captured his heart already?"

The Commander shoved his dagger into a lump of meat. "I defended her honor. Read no more into it."

The Prince smiled. "And what of you, Elwytha? Has the Commander's valor won your heart?"

He sported with them both. Coldly, she returned, "You forget your manners, Prince. It is unseemly to probe into another's affairs."

"Then you admit to an affair. I am pleased you are so well matched." A smile gleamed from the Prince.

Elwytha glared, again itching for a blade. Instead, she decided to ignore the mocking Prince. Clearly, the idleness of his mantle left him bored. He wished to annoy others only to entertain himself.

The Commander and Prince thereafter spoke of castle matters, which led to talk of the latest tribute demanded from the Northumbrian King, Osred.

"You will pay it?" the Commander asked, spearing up a final hunk of meat.

"You think I should not?"

"I do not think Osred will attack us."

"True. He has other things to occupy his mind."

The Commander nodded. "The Picts, to the north."

"Among other things." The monarch sent Elwytha a narrowed glance, as if curbing his tongue for her sake.

He needn't. Sweetly, she said, "His nuns? I hear he is a debauched, wicked young man. Perhaps your role model, Prince?"

His jaw tightened, and she felt well pleased with this small victory.

The Prince said, ignoring her, "Osred has kept his word of peace. As long as he remains ruler, I will pay. I have no wish to fight the Northumbrian hordes."

After supper, Elwytha excused herself. With a fake, gracious smile to her host, and one to the Commander, she made her exit.

In her chamber, she happily readied for bed, anticipating her mission that evening. As soon as the Commander snored into slumber, she would secure the blade. It would be the first of the three she would need for her final battle with her brother's murderer.

How shamed he would feel tomorrow morning, when he discovered his coveted blade missing. Elwytha smiled to herself. Yet another benefit to her task.

She had already decided to secrete it in her mattress. No one would find it there. She wiggled under the covers and allowed her eyes to drift closed. A small nap to refresh herself, and then she would begin her mission.

CHAPTER SIX

RAYS OF WHITE MOONLIGHT awoke Elwytha late that night. She felt disoriented, and wasn't sure how long she had slept, or how much time remained until morning. Never mind. She swiftly gained her feet and crept to her door.

Stealthily, she peered out. Was he asleep?

Yes. Moon beams outlined his still form, lying atop his bed. Elwytha slipped out and tiptoed with care across the stone floor. She heard a faint snore. Well and good. The better to monitor the depth of his sleep.

Silently, she crept about the room. First, she ran her hands through his pile of clothing on a chair. No blade. Next, she checked his boots, and then slipped over to his wardrobe. It made a small squeak as she opened the door. She froze, and whipped a glance toward the great, unmoving form on the bed. A breath gurgled in his throat, and then he snored on.

Speedily, she scoured the wardrobe. Nothing. Now she sat back on her heels, frowning. She had searched the entire room, except for his bed and his dresser. With care, she moved to the dresser. Slowly, she inched out each drawer just enough to slide her hand in and feel around inside. No blade.

She closed the last drawer and gazed about the quiet room. Where could he have secreted the dagger? Instinctively she knew he kept it near him at all times, just as she had kept hers at home. But she drew the line at searching his bed. She would serve him a knock out potion first.

Her eyes lit upon the wardrobe again. Moonbeams bathed it in pure white light. A glitter on top of the wardrobe caught her eye. Yes!

Elwytha hurried over. Standing on tiptoe, she reached up and patted along the top surface. Her fingers touched cold steel. A hiss of satisfaction escaped and she pulled the dagger down so it rested in both of her hands. It was huge, and wicked looking. Her thumb tested the blade. Razor sharp. Fear and elation mixed within her. Now to hide it.

A few steps toward her chamber, Elwytha realized the foolishness of hiding the blade in her room. If found, it would prove her involvement in its theft.

A far better plan illumined her mind. Hide it in *his* chamber. Then, when she needed it for the final battle, it would be close to hand.

Yes, a fine plot. But where?

Elwytha scanned the places she had already searched. Too easy to find in those locations. Her gaze returned to his bed, and she listened to his quiet breaths. If she hid it under his mattress, he'd likely never find it. What man changed linens? And tomorrow, when he went out, she could slip it to the center of the bed, where Hagma would never discover it.

Despite feeling pleased with the cleverness of her plan, Elwytha felt uneasy as she neared the large bed...and the man upon it. He had turned on his side now, and faced her.

She froze. Was he awake? No—the moonbeams proved his eyes were closed. She drew a shaky breath of relief. She went down on her knees and slipped the dagger beneath the mattress. Done! Success. Her hands trembled slightly. Now just to return to her room...

A hard arm clamped around her waist and she flew upward with a frightened squeak. She landed on the Commander's chest. Distress, fright, and a multitude of other emotions pounded through her. Frozen with shock, she took note of every detail of the situation, frantic to find an avenue of escape.

He wore no jerkin. Elwytha noticed this straight off. Her palms pressed into warm skin and the rock-like, sculpted muscles of his chest and shoulders.

In the pale light, his eyes watched her. She remained very still, uncertain what to do. What did he intend with this preposterous action? Did he guess her plan? Nervously, she licked her lips.

He scanned her features, and then she felt his deep rumble beneath her palms. "You wish to start our wedding night early?"

He mocked her. She saw it in the twist to his lips—the only part of his face that was not mutilated.

"N-no."

"Then why are you here?"

"I...I wished to take some air," she improvised swiftly. "Yes. I felt a vapor, and needed to stroll..."

"Crawl, you mean...to my bed."

Her face burned, and she attempted to roll off him. He foiled her attempt. Elwytha was becoming entirely too aware of his body beneath her.

"Release me," she breathed. "This is inappropriate."

"Is it appropriate to approach my bed while I sleep? What did you intend?"

She struggled again. "Not this."

His eyes, slate colored in the dim light, hardened. "You might wish to stop moving."

Her breath caught in alarm. "Unhand me this instant," she hissed.

The Commander rolled over, so at least now she was off of him, thank goodness, but now he loomed over her.

How had she managed to get in this situation?

"I would like to retire to my chamber now," she said frostily. "Pray, move aside."

"Tell me what you were doing in my chamber." The deep voice was too quiet.

"I told you. Now kindly move your oafish self." Elwytha pretended calm, but everything within her screamed to get out of his bed.

Abruptly, he sat up, scooped her into his arms and deposited her on the floor, facing him.

"Come to my chamber again at night and I'll assume you wish to sample our marriage pleasures early," he told her, his face hard. "Do you understand?"

Fright took flight within her. "Yes."

"Goodnight," he thundered, and Elwytha sprinted to her room and slammed the door. She leaned against it, breathing hard. How narrowly she had escaped that dire situation.

However, now she had one blade in place. The danger, while high, had proven worthwhile.

Elwytha crawled into bed and tried to forget how disturbed she had felt, close to the Commander, and how aware she had been of the strength of him, and the feel of his hard muscles. He had not appeared brutish and hulking without his jerkin, she realized with a flush. But rather an alarmingly virile, powerful man.

Shame shot through her. How could she notice such things about that man, her enemy? Her brother's murderer?

Elwytha pressed her hands to her eyes, confused and sick with herself. What depravity lurked in her that she would approve anything about the Commander? So he was strong...so he had muscles? So did many men.

But he had never used that strength against her, to hurt her, despite all of her provocations. In a flash of uncensored honesty, she admitted that she had been lucky he'd released her minutes ago. Few men would have done the same.

※ ※ ※ ※ ※

The sound of her chamber door opening awoke Elwytha the next morning.

"Leave me, Hagma," she mumbled. "I'm tired."

She heard a sound beside her bed and opened one eye. The frowning, squinty gaze of the Commander stared back at her.

She shrieked and jerked back, bedclothes clutched to her chin. Seeking more self-protection, she sat bolt upright and stared at the Commander, who knelt beside her bed. "Get out," she breathed. "How dare you enter my chamber?"

"Where is it?" he rumbled, gaining his feet.

Elwytha quickly gathered her wits. He had discovered his blade was missing. She pretended innocence. "What do you mean?"

He glared down at her, and unwanted fear quailed within her. She tried again. "Tell me what you seek. Perhaps I could help you find it."

"Where did you hide my *dagger?*"

Now Elwytha was glad she hadn't hidden it in her room. It would be the first place he would look. "You've lost your dagger? Why accuse me of stealing it?"

"Because I caught you crawling about my chamber last night. Where have you hidden it?" Frustration tightened his lips.

Elwytha fluttered a hand toward her room. "Search my chamber to your heart's content. I care not."

"No," he said, watching her. "It's not here."

"It is not?" she said innocently.

He clenched his great fists. "You want to make a fool of me."

"Nay. I do not sport with you." Verily, it was battle. Pure to the core.

He growled from deep within his chest, "I have been patient with you, but no longer,"

Elwytha gripped the bedclothes more tightly. Her hands trembled.

The Commander thundered, "One last time...*give me my blade*. Or you will not like the consequence."

Elwytha felt vulnerable now in her bed and sprang out, crossing her arms. Her night dress covered her adequately, thankfully. "I have no blade, Commander," she said as evenly as possible. "Feel free to search my belongings."

"No. I will search you."

"No," Elwytha gasped out. When he moved closer, she darted into his chamber, seeking escape...seeking the comfort of the blade she had hidden.

He continued to advance toward her, and she thought better of backing against his bed. She did not want a repeat of last night, and she didn't want him to suspect she'd hidden it there, either.

She turned and sprinted for the door, but the Commander slammed a hand over her head against it, preventing her escape. She faced him, chest heaving. Fright formed despicable tears in her eyes. She tried to dart to one side, but his other arm stopped her. She stared up at him and wished she had the blade now. How quickly her torture would end!

His eyes were like slate. "Remain still while I search your form."

"No!" Elwytha shuddered, and to her dismay a wretched tear spilled down her face. "Please, no. You would humiliate me thusly?"

He heaved a breath, and stared at her for an agonizingly long minute. "Do you have the dagger on your person?"

"No."

He gritted between his teeth, "Do you swear before God?"

Elwytha took a quick breath. He asked for her honor. Something she could still give him, for complete treachery had not yet rent her soul. She met his gaze steadily. "Yes. I swear before God."

"Then where did you put my dagger?"

"I don't have it. Search my room, if you please."

"Nay. You did not put it in your chamber." Comprehension dawned, and he scanned his chamber. "You placed it in *mine*."

Elwytha crossed her arms, dismayed that he had figured it out so quickly. She said nothing.

In three quick strides, he crossed the room and upended his mattress. With consternation, she watched him retrieve his deadly blade.

When he returned to her, she eyed the dagger with trepidation. What did he intend to do with it?

"Why did you hide it?"

Her gaze flickered from his fearsome face to the blade gripped in his hand. "I..." she licked her lips, "I...I wished to vex you." Quickly, she grasped for this plausible explanation. "I knew it was your favorite, and...and wanted to upset you. To make you think you had lost it."

He didn't believe her. She saw this in his flinty gaze. "Do you want me to lock you in your chamber every night?"

"No. Of course not."

"I cannot trust you. I have no other choice."

"I could have killed you." The unthinking, foolish words burst from her lips. "But...I didn't," she faltered.

He moved closer, in a deliberately intimidating manner. "I should be grateful you spared my life?"

She lifted her chin. "I told you that so you'd know I have honor. I would never stab you while you sleep. *Never* in the back." Anger rose in her. "It's the honor code of a true warrior."

"At last, you admit the truth."

"Yes," she said. "Kill me if you wish, but at least let me choose my weapon."

His gaze held hers. "You would choose the dagger."

Elwytha stilled, dismayed. How did he know? She parried, "I am accomplished with all weapons."

"True. But you favor the daggers."

How could he be so certain? Was it because she'd stolen his dagger last night? No. That didn't ring quite true.

Why did she sense that he knew something he wasn't telling her? It made her feel uncomfortable. Suspicious, too.

She shrugged, faking apathy. "You're welcome to believe whatever you wish."

The Commander sheathed his blade. "I will lock you in your room every night until I learn I can trust you."

Frustration gripped her, although she knew it was a just punishment. "May I walk freely during the day?"

"Yes. Unless you prove more treachery."

"Very well."

"I would like for you to ride with me today," he told her.

She stared in surprise. "But I don't wish to. Why don't you understand that?"

"I understand that you hate me. That will end when we spend more time together."

Astonished, Elwytha laughed merrily. "Nay, Commander. You disillusion yourself. That will *never* happen. Accept that defeat, at least."

His eyes bored into her. "I accept no defeats. Dress to ride."

Elwytha glared, clenched her fists, and without a word retreated to her chamber. That beastly man. She slammed the door. Did he think she was a servant? Would he always have his way?

No. She refused to submit. She would not do it. It didn't matter that Sir Duke would enjoy the run. Or that a tiny part of her wanted to ride in the glorious sunshine. She would not obey. The Commander had pushed her too far. He needed to learn his place. Starting now.

She quickly donned the baggy brown she had worn the second day. Hagma washed her clothes daily, so happily she could keep wearing the same horrific dresses over and over again.

Elwytha sat, arms crossed. She would refuse to leave her room.

As the moments slowly ticked by, uncomfortable thoughts began to trickle in. What means would the Commander employ this time to bend her to his will?

Would he throw her over his shoulder again? Would he drag her, kicking and screaming down the halls and out to the stables?

Humiliation burned in her at the very thought. The maids and warriors of the palace would laugh at her. And the Prince would no doubt sneer with amusement at her disgrace.

She clenched her fists in frustration. What recourse had she? She could either submit gracefully, or be made to look like a fool.

Anger trembled through her. Her brother wanted to use her, the Commander desired to rule over her; how could she escape? She felt like a chess piece, forced from one position to another. It didn't matter to either of them that her life would be sacrificed so they could obtain their selfish desires. Her wishes were insignificant.

Had she no free will? How dare they make her feel like a dog, good only for being ordered about?

Unwanted tears escaped. With angry hands, she dashed them away. How much longer could she stand this untenable position...of being subservient to her brother's murderer? She couldn't stand it now. She wanted to scream, but didn't. That man would not break her.

Trembling with anger and utter frustration, she wept.

↑ ↑ ↑ ↑ ↑

The Commander waited for Elwytha to emerge from her chamber. It was taking a long time. He would give her a few more minutes.

Why had she taken his blade? Again, he wondered. If she had meant to kill him, she could have tried last night. But she hadn't. Then what was her plan?

Nothing good, he felt certain. That's why he felt an urgency to set his plan in motion now. Today. The wall between them must come down. Courtesy, kindness, mercy...nothing worked with her. He had to get to the root of the problem.

He knew now that she wanted daggers. She'd worn them on her person when she had arrived, and she wanted them back. He would use this weakness to strengthen his plan.

Today he would allow her ample time to wander the halls, and he'd ensure that a certain room was left unlocked. She would be unable to resist investigating.

Grimly, the Commander steepled his fingers. He would have his wife. But he wanted all of Elwytha, not just her body. He would do whatever it took to get her. The danger only sweetened the battle.

ใ ใ ใ ใ ใ

Elwytha washed her face to remove traces of the brief, humiliating bout of tears. Still, the polished metal mirror did not lie. Her eyelids looked red and puffy, and so did her nose. No doubt the Commander would be pleased with her abject misery.

Stiffening her shoulders, she opened the door. She found her betrothed stalking his room.

He turned to her. "You are ready." His gaze ran down her dress, and she didn't imagine the displeased twist to his mouth. Good. At least she was allowed one meager victory.

Head held high, she marched for the door and strode out, not waiting for him to follow. Thankfully, she knew her way to the stables, and she made speed there, wishing to outrun the Commander's presence altogether.

Of course, this was impossible, but she saddled Sir Duke in peace, and then cantered behind the Commander into the bright, sunshiny day. Today she followed at a great distance. She had no wish to speak to him. No wish to be near him. He could order her about and demand her company, but he could not make her be civil. At this moment, pretending peace was beyond her.

Sir Duke ambled happily and Elwytha sniffed the fresh, crisp fall air. Despite herself, she began to feel a little better—perhaps because the Commander was far ahead. She could enjoy the scenery without being subjected to his close presence.

He waited for her now, she noticed with a bit of dismay, and Sir Duke gradually closed the distance.

"You wish to speak to me?" Elwytha inquired coldly.

"Keep pace with me," he ordered. "I have lines to inspect."

Anger flared hot again. "I am not a servant. Pray, do not treat me like one."

"You would rather I treat you like a child? Because that is how you behave."

Elwytha clenched her fists. "You order me about like a dog. I hate it! You afford me no dignity. You would have me bow and scrape to you, but *I* am the princess."

The black stallion moved restlessly beneath the Commander. "You would like me to bow and scrape to you?" he asked. "Speak the truth. This would please you."

"I want you to treat me with respect." Anger shook in her voice.

"Then treat me with respect."

"You want no respect. You desire only to wield power over me. You order me thither and yon. 'Ride with me.' 'Dine with me.' Your orders have no end."

"You wish time to yourself?"

"Yes!" She could think of nothing more glorious.

"You shall have it, then. This afternoon. But I will require you to eat with me this even."

He was attempting to be civil. "Very well," she agreed.

The Commander scanned the horizon. "We need to ride fast. A storm is coming, and I have much to inspect."

Elwytha hadn't noticed the low, gray clouds on the horizon. "What are you inspecting?"

"I search for spies."

She felt confused. "From Northumbria?"

"No." His gaze pierced her.

Shocked, she said, "You mean spies from my brother?"

"Yes. Other riders have met pairs of your brother's men, just as we did the other day."

Elwytha frowned, wondering what this could mean. She knew nothing of such plans from her brother.

"Come." The Commander urged his steed into a gallop and Sir Duke gladly matched the stride. Elwytha enjoyed the tug of the wind through her hair. At last, she felt a sense of freedom. Being outdoors helped. As had the talk with the Commander. He appeared willing to hear her thoughts. At least a little.

Perhaps she need only reason with him, and he would consider her point of view in the future. The idea amazed her. Could it be so simple? Probably not. Nothing appeared simple with the Commander. On first sight, she'd thought him an un-thinking brute, but now she knew he was a shrewd, complicated man who demanded respect from her, as well as from all of his warriors. She would need to tread carefully with him. Nothing may be as it appeared.

The morning passed without sighting any spies. Elwytha felt relieved. She didn't want to find evidence of further treach-ery on her brother's part. Had her brother formed a grander plan than he'd told her about? Did Richard want her to kill the Commander, and then he'd invade the land, using the spies' reports to infiltrate weak areas?

These thoughts troubled her, and as she followed the Commander back to the castle, rain began to drip upon her head. The sky had long ago turned gray. Now the clouds grew heavier and blacker. They still had half an hour to ride.

He abruptly turned into the trees, away from the path leading home. Wondering why, Elwytha followed, bowing her head against the great, fat rain drops. The drops fell faster, sliding like cold fingers through her hair, and across her skin. Wet splotches grew on her dress.

The Commander pulled up before a thatched shack and tied the stallion's reins to a tree. The sky chose that moment to open up. Rain poured down, soaking Elwytha as she slid off her horse. The Commander took the reins and she dashed inside the hut.

Dim light entered the small windows, and it was dry in-side, except for a far corner, which dripped rain through the thatch. It appeared to be an old hunting shack. No furniture remained, but it did have a fireplace. Old logs and kindling lay beside it.

"Look," she said, when he entered. "Do you have a flint?"

"Of course." He knelt beside her. With skill, his large hands quickly urged a spark into a flame, and then he carefully piled on small sticks, and then larger logs.

Elwytha rubbed her hands before the warmth, shivering. "How long will the rain last?"

"An hour, maybe more." The Commander pulled off his armor. He looked mostly dry beneath it, and she felt envious. She huddled closer to the fire. "Be careful," he said. "Your dress might catch on fire."

At that moment, she didn't think she'd care. Fall had come, and the crisp air she had enjoyed earlier now bit through her, chilling her through the wet dress.

"Come here."

She looked at him with suspicion. "Why?"

"If you are willing, I will warm you."

"How?" she narrowed her eyes.

"Come close to me."

Elwytha could think of nothing she'd like less. But she was freezing. "You will take no liberties?" she said severely.

Was that amusement in his gray eyes? Yes. She decided to trust him. He had never taken liberties with her before, and certainly he'd had ample opportunity.

She scooted closer; as close as she dared, and then he closed the remaining distance between them. His great arm went around her shoulders and tugged her close to his warmth. With a shiver, she pressed close, enjoying his body heat.

"You trust me," his deep voice rumbled near her ear.

"A little," she reluctantly admitted. Confusion welled within her. How could that be? How could she trust, even a little, her family's enemy? Her brother's murderer?

"A good start."

What did he mean by that?

Elwytha found it easy to lay her head on his shoulder, huddled as close as she was to him. The cloth of his jerkin felt rough beneath her cheek. His warm hand curled around her clasped cold ones. She allowed it, accepting his warmth, and his manner of care for her.

The firelight felt warm on her face. After a while, the chill left her, and she began to feel pleasantly toasty. Drowsiness made her eyelids heavy. Last night's disrupted sleep caught up with her and she drifted peacefully to sleep, feeling safe in her enemy's embrace.

\ \ \ \ \

The Commander looked at Elwytha, asleep in his arms, and a powerful, unfamiliar emotion gripped him. Tenderness?

He was amazed that such an emotion could exist in him.

With that unsettling emotion came longing. If only she would always allow him to hold her, to care for her, like this.

Though she trusted him a little now, he knew the deeper problem between them still festered like an ugly, oozing sore. He'd need to lance it before they could ever forge a true peace. While necessary, the prospect did not appeal. He had no wish to hurt her.

Her fingers felt so small and slender in his. Protectiveness surged hard through him. A more familiar emotion. But now he wished for something as he'd never wished before. The love of this woman. He raised his eyes to the heavens. Was it possible? Could it ever be possible for one such as he?

CHAPTER SEVEN

WHEN ELWYTHA AWOKE, she felt secure and comfortable. Where was she? She smelled wood smoke, and felt the warmth of a fire...and the warmth of a man's body against her and his arm about her. She took a quick breath. The Commander! She stiffened.

"I'm warm now," she said. Embarrassed, she pulled free and scooted a safe distance away. What had she been thinking? Her head still felt groggy from her nap, and she stared at him, bewildered.

He watched her, his gaze calm and level. For some reason, that made her feel even more uneasy. It was as if he'd made a decision about her that she had taken no part in. Nor would he let her.

Insufferably arrogant and high-handed of him, as usual. But as he hadn't said anything, she couldn't very well accost him for looking at her in a displeasing way. "The rain has stopped," she observed.

"Yes. Are you ready to go?"

"Of course. You promised me a free afternoon, remember?"

"Very well." He rose to his great height, and she quickly scrambled up as well, in an effort to forestall any chivalrous gestures on his part—such as offering his hand to help her up. Nay. She had already supped too closely of the Commander's nearness. Now she wished only to remain far, far from him.

The horses looked drenched and cold.

"You poor thing," Elwytha murmured, rubbing Sir Duke's face. His brown eyes looked reproachful for her ill treatment of him. "We'll get you home soon, with a warm blanket and a bucket of oats," she promised, and swung onto his back.

"Do you often speak to your mount?"

Elwytha frowned at the Commander. "Horses have feelings, too. Sometimes more than humans." She patted the horse's neck and murmured, "Right, Sir Duke?"

The Commander made no reply to this. Likely he thought it nonsense.

Leaves and branches dripped water on them as they rode through the pungent forest toward the castle. Elwytha didn't mind. She loved the smells that lingered after a rain shower, particularly in the fall. She inhaled deeply, enjoying the sweet scent of decaying leaves, damp earth, and the fresh, clean smell of rain. The cool moisture in the air freshened her spirits. She was almost sad to arrive at the stable.

The stable boy took Sir Duke and Elwytha retired to her room to change. Unfortunately, her gray dress had not been washed and returned yet—or perhaps it was still drying. So she needed to choose another frock to wear.

With a frown, she dug through the trunk. No more drab dresses remained. Only gowns fashioned out of the jewel-toned fabrics she preferred. All complemented her skin tone, or so her maid at home said.

Elwytha at last found a modest gown—it had a "V" neck, but at least her bosom would be mostly covered—and it was in a rich, royal blue damask. This shade of blue was her absolute favorite color, and it matched her eyes. She had worn it so often that the neckline had frayed the tiniest bit. It would have to do.

Quickly, she changed and left the brown dress for Hagma to retrieve later. For now, her stomach rumbled and she hurried to the kitchen for her meal.

The cook greeted her with a smile. "Elwytha. I wondered if you had drowned in all that rain. I'm glad to see you made it home safe and sound."

"It's beautiful out," she said, sitting at the table. Mary placed a trencher of bread, cheese, and fruit before her. A cup of water, as well. "Thank you."

"You were out with the Commander, were you?" asked the matronly woman.

"Yes." Elwytha unexpectedly wondered if the entire castle knew she lived in an attached chamber to her betrothed. Most likely. Embarrassment warmed her cheeks.

"He's a fine boy, is the Commander," said Mary, with a nod. She had said something similar yesterday, Elwytha remembered. The cook turned the animal roasting on a spit.

Elwytha didn't know how to respond to this comment. "You've known him all of his life?"

"Aye. Of course. I was friends with his mother, God rest her soul."

"How did he get that scar over his eye?" she blurted. And then wondered what was wrong with her. Why would she possibly care?

The cook cast her a knowing look. "You'll have to ask him yourself, miss. He's had a hard life, that one has. But the Prince has treated him well. And rightly so." She gave a nod for emphasis.

"He said they became friends as boys."

"Aye. Friends. Rivals." She shook her head, and said something Elwytha couldn't quite catch.

"What of his father?" Elwytha found she couldn't stifle her confounding desire to ask questions about her enemy. Perhaps she wanted to understand him better. That way she could identify all of his weaknesses.

Mary shook her head. "That's not a subject he'll thank you to ask. The lads taunted him, calling him all manner of terrible names. That's why he learned to battle. And a fight is how he broke his nose."

"Why wasn't it reset?"

The cook's quick motions slowed as she stirred a bubbling pot. "I'll never rightly know. The boy had lost his mother. And those who should have looked after him didn't. I don't suppose

he cared much back then. Boys don't. But it's a shame, now."
She pressed her lips tightly together, and stirred more rapidly.

Elwytha finished her lunch, feeling disturbed by these
insights into her foe. No matter what ill treatment he had
suffered as a child, she told herself, it changed nothing about
him today. Now he was a man. He made his own choices, and
one had been a wrong one—to end her brother's life.

But she did suddenly wonder how often a filthy past
tainted the present, and twisted the future. She thought about
her own family—the jealousy between her brothers; her
father's clear favoritism toward her eldest brother; and
Richard's rage and mood swings because he couldn't get their
father's attention.

And what of herself? Her father had all but ignored her. A
girl was worthless to a clan of warriors. Another reason why
she had learned battle skills—so he would approve of her. It
had certainly shaped who she was today; a warrior sent to
mete revenge on her family's enemy.

꙳ ꙳ ꙳ ꙳ ꙳

After Elwytha finished lunch, she exited from the kitchen.
The entire afternoon lay before her, gloriously empty, save to
accomplish her own purposes. The Commander had said she
could freely wander the halls. Foolish of him. Today, once
again, she'd test the door to the room that held her blades. Or
perhaps she would search out keys to the lock. In either case,
she would retrieve her daggers without delay.

"Princess Elwytha." A helmeted, armored guard with a
lance at his shoulder appeared before she had taken five steps.

"Yes?" She frowned. Had the Commander forgotten his
promise? With what further orders would he besiege her now?

"The Prince requires your presence. Follow me, please."
He turned and headed down the hall. Clearly, she was to
immediately follow.

Elwytha didn't like obeying the Prince's orders any more than the Commander's. However, she had to admit to curiosity. And suspicion. What did he want?

The guard ushered her into the throne room, where the Prince sat upon his royal throne. Did he sit there all day? She mentally rolled her eyes at his utter vanity. Did he need constant adulation to prove his worth as a man, and as a ruler?

She curtseyed. "Prince. You requested my presence?" Never mind that he had demanded it. She felt it key he understand that she had graciously granted his request.

The Prince reclined back on his throne, his pose relaxed. He inquired, "You are enjoying your stay in my palace?"

"It has satisfactory comforts," she allowed.

He smiled. "You have a cutting tongue, Princess Elwytha."

"I speak the truth."

"At all times?" His words sounded testing.

"Verily, as much truth as you speak yourself, Prince."

He smiled again and then stood, to her surprise. "I will show you something. Stroll with me."

She followed the Prince, mindful of the lance-carrying guard accompanying them. Of course, her brother had ordered no attacks upon the Prince. So he was safe from her.

"You are accustomed to fine things?" the Prince inquired over his shoulder. He opened the door to a room flanked by armed guards, and she followed him inside.

"We have a few precious objects." Elwytha would allow no detailed descriptions to pass her lips. The Prince needed no further encouragements to attack her land. She cast a quick glance about. Sunlight filtered in through slitted windows.

"We harbor prized objects, as well. As a princess, I thought you would appreciate their splendor." With a languid hand, he gestured toward a black vase, veined with gold. "From the far east."

The gold sparkled in the ebony, as did sparkles of blue. The Prince smiled as she peered at it more closely. "A treasure, is it not?" He strolled next toward a pedestal topped with a blue velvet box.

Elwytha followed, and wondered why he was showing her these prizes. For pride's sake? Did he feel no threat from her, as an enemy? Perhaps he wanted her to feel awe for the splendor he possessed. Likely, she decided. From what little she knew of him, humility did not appear to be one of his strengths.

He lifted the velvet lid. A necklace of glittering diamonds and sapphires sparkled on black velvet. Elwytha gasped, despite herself.

"You like it?" He grinned at her. "It was my father's mother's."

Elwytha was annoyed—both by her response, and for the Prince's blatant boastings. He showed her more objects of art, including sculptures and paintings. Several were of his ancestors. Last of all, he stopped before a portrait of a man in full warrior regalia. He looked huge and fearsome, with flowing black hair and eyes as black as midnight.

"This man loved battle. Unfortunately, one too many." The Prince eyed her. "My father," he said.

Startled, Elwytha looked from the portrait to the Prince. The current crown regent was a good height for a man, but finer boned than this, his sire.

He smiled. "I favor my mother."

"But you share his black hair and black eyes."

"And his affection for the ladies."

Elwytha frowned at the Prince, who watched her, his black eyes intent. Why would he shame his father with such a word? Not to mention sully her ears with such tripe? Then suspicion flared, and she frowned harder.

He laughed. "Don't worry, Elwytha. I would not steal you from the Commander."

Elwytha still distrusted him. "If you are finished boasting of your plunder, I tire."

His black eyes narrowed, clearly amused. "You mean you tire of me. Return then, to your Commander."

Elwytha glared, and stiffened her shoulders. "As much as you highly regard him, I take no pleasure in his company. Solitude serves me better within your walls."

His lips twisted mockingly. "As you wish."

Only ingrained courtesy made Elwytha drop a half, irreverent curtsey, and then she left the Prince to his prizes...no doubt ill gotten, and stolen by blood and the sword from their rightful owners. She tried to forget that her own palace harbored treasures gained in like manner.

Now, finally freed of the Prince, Elwytha sped to her next, long coveted destination. Hopefully, solitude indeed awaited her there. She desired no witnesses to the retrieval of her blades.

᛭ ᛭ ᛭ ᛭ ᛭

Elwytha swiftly found the room once again, but discovered a maid was cleaning it. Frustrated, she wandered the halls, trying to look inconspicuous as she waited for the girl to leave. If only the maid would forget to lock the door when she finished.

Many long minutes later, the maid finally took her leave. Elwytha dashed to the door. Praise be to the most high God, it opened easily in her hand. She wanted to dance for glee, but restrained herself. Looking quickly about to ensure that no one saw her, she slipped inside.

Immediately, she darted across to the rug which secreted her blades. She dropped to her knees and eagerly swept back the rug.

Nothing.

Alarm sliced through her. What treachery was this?

She pushed the rug back further, now in half. Then she caught a glimpse of steel. With a cry, she grabbed her smallest dagger and pressed it to her bosom. At last.

Then she folded back the rest of the rug, eager to find her two remaining blades. Odd she hadn't found them yet. She had been so sure she'd placed them near the stone wall. The small-est blade had been found in the middle of the rug, and the other two...

Missing. The floor lay bare.

Dismayed, she sat back on her heels. Someone must have found them. But who? The Commander?

But he hadn't accosted her with his knowledge. Surely he would have, if he had found them. Then she remembered his comment about her preferring the daggers. She frowned. Maybe he did have them. Perhaps he played some cunning game with her, even now.

Elwytha took a quick breath. She would be careful and test him to see. Luckily, he had missed this blade. Soon, she'd tuck it into a band above her ankle. No longer would she be naked and defenseless. At last, she possessed one of the three blades she needed to battle the Commander nine days hence.

The thought didn't bring the joy it should have. Treachery against that man, who had held her so gently hours ago, somehow seemed wrong.

But he wasn't that man, she told herself. He couldn't be. Gentle, caring men didn't go about murdering people in cold blood—stabbing them in the back, no less. Forgetting that fact could prove her fatal mistake. No, she would continue to collect daggers to accomplish her goal. She would be ready for battle when the time came. One down, two to go.

Elwytha left the room, looking right and left. The hall was empty. She smiled grimly to herself and headed back to the Commander's chamber. She hoped Hagma had finished drying her gray dress.

Unfortunately, Hagma hadn't. The gray dress had not re-turned to her trunk, but the wet one had disappeared.

Still, Elwytha had her knife. She felt well satisfied with this victory.

She tied a band about her ankle and fondly slipped the dagger into place. At last she felt like herself again. A woman to reckon with. She felt invincible, although she knew the deceit of that capricious emotion. She would take care at all times. No slipups. She couldn't afford to lose this dagger to the Commander, too.

† † † † †

It rained all afternoon. Elwytha whiled away the time by skulking the halls of the castle. She wanted to find more weapons, but found none. No doubt the warriors carried them on their persons. The armory would be her next adventure. Perhaps she'd sneak in while the warriors ate their luncheon tomorrow. This plan appealed. With her trusty dagger close at hand, she'd be prepared, should she meet any unsavory louts.

Elwytha returned to her room to smooth her hair for supper. Not that she cared what any of this palace's ruffians—or her betrothed—thought of her. No. For her own dignity she would retain her regal bearing.

Unfortunately, when she exited, she found the Commander in his chamber, shaving his stubbled jaw with a small blade. She spied his open trunk and smiled to herself. So, he hid knives in the box. Now only to find the key.

She fixed a pleasant smile upon her face. "Good even, Commander."

He ran the blade down his jaw and looked at her in the mirror. "Good even." Elwytha did not imagine the twist to his lips. He concentrated on his task, moving the blade carefully down his neck. No doubt he wished to employ care to avoid slitting his throat.

He had not shaved his head, she noticed. Short black hair bristled from it, nearing his resemblance to a normal man of his age.

Elwytha felt vaguely uncomfortable, watching him perform his intimate shaving task, though she wasn't sure why. After all, she had watched her brothers trim their beards on many an occasion.

"That looks hard to do in a mirror." Elwytha commented, attempting to sound relaxed and worldly.

He glanced over his shoulder. "You would be willing to help me?"

He sported with her!

Very well, she could joust as well as he. She smiled. "Truly, give me the blade, and I will finish the job."

He rumbled with quiet laughter.

Uncomfortable with the pleasant feeling lingering between them, Elwytha fished about for something else to say. Perhaps she should retire to her room. Better that than forced civility with her betrothed, the Commander.

A thought flashed to mind, and she blurted, "Everyone calls you Commander. Do you have a normal name?" Then she felt even more disturbed. Why had she asked?

He turned. "You wish to know my name?"

"No. I was only curious."

He grunted and turned away again, rinsing his blade.

"You're not going to tell me?"

"When you want to know, I will tell you."

Elwytha frowned. What sort of an answer was that? Now she burned to know it even more. The irksome man.

She took a breath. It was better this way. She didn't need to know. Why assign a name to her hated enemy? Already revenge was beginning to feel too personal, too complicated. There would be no quick felling with the sword, as in battle. How she would have preferred that. But no. Now she knew his face. His habits. The way he treated his horse, his men...her. She did not need to know his name, too.

Elwytha crossed her arms and strolled around the room, waiting for the Commander to finish. No more talk with him, she decided. It was proving treacherous to her purpose of mind.

Her betrothed finally rumbled, "I'm finished. Are you ready to go?"

Elwytha faced him, chin square, eyes level. "Of course."

His eyes scanned her form then, as if noticing her blue dress for the first time. She frowned and glanced away, in order to endure his perusal.

"Blue suits you," he said. "You look nice."

"I'm glad to please you," she said, with a hint of sarcasm.

"Have you misplaced the brown dress you favor? Or the gray?"

Suspicion reared, and she glared. "What have you done with them?"

He regarded her steadily, but did not answer.

"You told Hagma to throw them out, didn't you?" Her voice rose. "Must you strip away every bit of my dignity? I want those frocks. They are my favorites!"

"No."

"No? Pray, what do you know of women's fashion? Or what is acceptable in my eyes?"

"Speak the truth, Elwytha. You wish to displease me. That is the only reason you wore those dresses."

She glared mutinously.

"Hagma told me your remaining dresses enhance your beauty. I would like to see you wear them."

Elwytha clenched her fists. "Again you order me about, as if I'm a chattel, or a servant maid, or...or a child. I will not have it. I am a princess. You will afford me some dignity!"

"The gray and the brown enhance your dignity?"

"They are my choice," she spat. "You want to strip all choice from me. I will not have it. I will not!" Her face felt flushed, and she would stamp her foot if she didn't think it would remind him of the child she professed she was not.

"Very well," he said, his deep voice calm. "I will return your dresses if you promise me one thing."

She frowned. "What?"

"Wear whatever dress you wish during the day. At night, for supper, I ask that you wear one of the others. One that enhances your countenance."

Elwytha glared, no less displeased. "I have no wish for your eyes to ravage my form," she returned coldly. "I will need a needle and thread to fashion modest coverings for the bodices."

His lips twitched. She amused him. This infuriated her still further. "Give me your word," she exclaimed.

"Now will you accept my word?" Humor lurked in the quiet rumble.

She crossed her arms and stared at him.

"Very well," he agreed. "But Hagma will approve the fabrics and alterations."

"What does Hagma know of fashion?"

"Verily, perhaps as much as you. Now, are you ready to go to supper?"

Elwytha could not stop frowning. "Of course."

He opened the door and offered her his arm. She ignored it. "Torture me no further," she snapped. "I will only touch you when we reach the hall." She waited for no agreement. She swept out the door and down the hall, not waiting for him to catch up.

ᛉ ᛉ ᛉ ᛉ ᛉ

The Commander spoke little during supper. He brooded on the unpleasant task before him that evening; namely, prying the truth from Elwytha. Tightness formed in him, thinking of the upcoming confrontation. The things he would have to say...or do...to clear the air may prove unpleasant. He only hoped it wouldn't make matters worse between them.

ᛉ ᛉ ᛉ ᛉ ᛉ

Luckily, the Commander sat silently during supper. Good. Elwytha had no desire to speak to him. The Prince, she ignored as best she could.

"I showed Elwytha our palace treasures this afternoon," the Prince told the Commander near the end of the meal. He sipped his fourth cup of ale, and his eyes glittered, looking too sharp and too bright.

The Commander regarded him for a moment without speaking. "Why would you do that?"

"He wished to boast," Elwytha interjected. "His lust for treasure is clear to me. Perhaps it is why he continually marauds my land."

The Prince raised his cup to her. "I have agreed to peace."

"Peace," she said with disbelief. She trusted this Prince less than an inch. "Truly, you must feel desperation to agree to my brother's peace."

"Perhaps it is desperation your brother feels."

"You have lost the last five battles," she scorned. "Pray, speak truth to me."

The Prince and Commander looked at each other, and a small smile curled the royal one's mouth. "Your brother told you this, Princess?"

Elwytha felt uneasy with the unspoken messages passing between her two enemies. "Of course," she said. "He confided our victories to me."

The Prince smiled more widely now, and gulped the remainder of his ale. "Tell her, Commander. Your bride needs enlightenment."

Elwytha frowned as the good side of the Commander's face turned further toward her, revealing the mutilated, scarred side. The fearsome side. Apprehension rose in her. "Speak no lies to me, Commander," she warned.

His gaze levelly met hers. "I need to speak no lies. Your brother has lost the last five battles. Even now he sends spies into our land, although he proclaims peace." His slate eyes bored into hers. "Speak what you know of his trickery."

Confusion and alarm made her trembling hand almost spill the contents of her cup. Sadly, she didn't know whom to believe. Then she told herself that she had to remain true to her brother, her clan. Her two enemies tested her now, trying to persuade her to break confidence with her own kin.

"Nay. I don't believe you," she said. "You wish to trick me to accomplish your dark purposes. Perhaps even now you sport with my brother's peace agreement. Are you so treacherous that you would not keep your word?"

Never mind that her brother would not keep his word of peace. Best to keep a united front before their enemies.

She stared unwaveringly at the Commander, and then narrowed her eyes at the Prince. "Waste no more time with your lies. If you do not want peace, say so. I will gladly leave on the morrow."

The Prince glanced at his first-in-command. "Is that what you wish, Commander?"

"No," the giant said shortly. "We agreed to peace, and so peace we shall have."

The Prince's head bobbed; the first tiny indication the liquor had begun to addle his brain. "The Commander speaks my words for me. But if your brother proves treacherous, I will cut him down myself." The black eyes watched her, testing her response.

Elwytha swallowed. "Your words are pleasing. In my next missive, I'll assure Richard that you intend to deal honorably with him."

"Do that," said the Prince. He smiled, but Elwytha didn't like the calculating, mocking look in his eyes.

She turned away and finished her fruit. "I would like to retire," she told her betrothed. "You need not accompany me."

"I am finished." To her annoyance, he rose and accompanied her to his chamber. Inside, she made haste toward her door.

He rumbled, "I would like to speak to you before you retire."

Frowning, Elwytha turned back. "We've done enough speaking for one day. I tire of your presence."

He closed much of the distance between them. Elwytha wanted to back up, but her closed door stopped her. Besides, she would not show fear to him. Thankfully, he stopped a pace from her. He said, "We grew closer today."

Dismayed, Elwytha gazed up at him. She thought back to the hut, and the rainstorm. "No. Just because I allowed you to warm me doesn't mean we're *friends* now."

"I know," he agreed. "You hate me. Tell me why."

Did he really think she would reveal her hand to him? Never! Then he would suspect her true purpose in this castle. "Think what you wish. I care not."

"Tell me."

"I wish to rest. Leave me."

"I want to know." She saw the steel in his eyes.

"I have nothing to say to you," she gritted through her teeth. Why was he pressing this? Why wouldn't he leave her alone?

His large hands reached out and encircled her arms. "Tell me, Elwytha." She heard the plea in the quiet growl.

She tensed. "Unhand me at once."

"Nay. We will finish this now."

He wasn't going to release her. With a quick twisting, ducking motion that her brother had taught her, Elwytha tried to free herself. It didn't work. He pulled her closer to himself.

She breathed faster as fear flared. "Release me."

He took a breath, as if considering it. But then his voice came, hard and uncompromising. "Tell me why you hate me."

"No." Rage suddenly shook through her. All of his orders, all of his demands... She would not submit to her brother's murderer. Not on this issue. She would die before he wrestled the truth from her. No, *he* would die!

Viciously, she stamped on his instep. It caught him by surprise, and then she kneed him in a most painful place, and twisted free. She sprang across the room, whipping her dagger to hand. If he was determined to learn the truth, then he would know she wanted to kill him. So the battle would begin now.

He stared at her, bent double, face contorted in pain.

"Choose your weapon," she spat. "I'll give you one minute. And then we will finish this."

After several more harsh breaths, he straightened. His face looked hard and fearsome, but she allowed no fear to shiver through her. If only she possessed her other blades, how quickly she could finish this. She tried to ignore the part of her that felt sickened by her actions, and by what she was about to do. She'd given him a fair chance. It was time to finish it now.

He pulled a key from his pocket. Watching her through his squinty eye, he bent and unlocked his trunk. Two gleaming blades appeared in his hand. Her breath stopped. Her blades.

"Which is better?" he asked, his eyes like slate. "Which the better balanced?"

The breath strangled in her throat. "You found them."

"Yes."

"But you missed one," she said triumphantly. "This one."

"No." He watched her.

"No?" She felt confused.

"I left that one for you to find."

"Why?"

"So you would reveal your hand. As you have now."

"No," she gasped.

He tossed one knife to the side and advanced toward her. A trick! It had all been a trick; finding the blade, accosting her now... Indeed, he wanted to finish this. He had suspected her treachery all along, and intended to kill her now.

Elwytha focused, her heart pounding, on the vulnerable point in his neck. She only had one chance before he finished her life.

She waited as he advanced one step, two, and then she whipped back her blade. But the Commander moved far faster. His knife hurtled through the air. A scream of terror wrenched from her throat, and then his dagger hit her blade, wresting it from her fingers. Both clattered to the floor.

He advanced toward her, his mutilated face a fearsome mask. Gray eyes flashed the fury of a winter storm. Before she could lunge aside, he finished the distance and gripped her wrists, forcing them together.

"No," She struggled hard. "No, you bastard!"

His fingers tightened, paining her. He held them with one hand, while the other scooped a blade from the floor.

Horror spiraled within her. What atrocity would he force upon her now? She collapsed to her knees. He would have to drag her to her fate.

"Stand," he snarled. "I wish to speak to you."

"Nay." She wrestled for freedom with all of her strength. She had to escape. She didn't want to die...she had failed her mission. All of these thoughts mixed in one horrified jumble in her head.

Elwytha became aware that he was dragging her across the room, toward his bed. No! She sat back, digging her heels into the floor. It accomplished little. He gained his goal.

Gripping her under one armpit, he pulled her to her feet. "No," she denied, panicked. She kicked at him like a frenzied wild cat. "Nay," she moaned, as he wrestled her back onto the bed. "Unhand me!"

And then, to her utter horror, he crushed her body with his, squashing her ability to fight, to move at all. She fought to free her arms, but he held them pinned overhead. She felt cold steel against her neck. Fear and rage surged through her at the indignities he forced upon her.

"Tell me why I should not use this upon you," the Commander said through his teeth.

"Kill me then, you murdering cur," she seethed. "That's all you know how to accomplish. Death and destruction!" She bucked against him, struggling to free herself. His grip tightened on her hands. "A coward's means of conduct is all you understand."

"You try to kill me, and I must explain myself?"

"You can explain nothing," she spat. "I could never understand one as despicable as you." She heaved a great breath, hating him through her narrowed eyes. Did he sense it, the thickheaded beast? Could he feel any emotions besides rage and violence?

The fury in his eyes flickered, and then, to her shock, he tossed the blade aside. It clattered on the stone floor. What did this mean? What did he intend to do with her?

He scanned her features, as if thinking. How difficult that must be for him!

"Tell me now. Who did I kill that you loved so much?" he demanded.

Elwytha refused to answer. How could he not know, the murdering bastard? Had he killed so many in cold blood? She stopped struggling, and with a vicious glare worked the saliva around in her mouth, just as her eldest brother had taught her to do with watermelon seeds.

The Commander stared down at her intently, as if truly desiring to know the answer. Now, at the perfect moment, she raised her head and spat with all the force she could muster. Her globule of spit landed on his chin. He froze, and his grip on her wrists tightened.

"You dishonor me."

"How can one dishonor an already dishonorable man?" She worked her tongue around, trying to gather more spit.

"Tell me who I *killed*," he roared, and she swallowed her lump of spittle. Terror galloped through her again.

"How can you not know, you bastard? Have you killed so many?"

"Yes, in battle. I do not remember them all."

"Not in battle," she hissed. "In cold blood. How many men have you stabbed in the back?"

The misshapen brow and the straight brow crashed together. "What think you? I have killed none in such a manner."

"You have, you liar," she cried out. "You murdered my brother!"

Her words rang in the suddenly silent chamber.

He heaved a great breath, above her. "No."

"Your blade was found in his back."

"Which blade?"

She spat at him again, but he made no move to retaliate. "The sword with the double snakes upon it. With the seal of the Prince. All warriors knew it was yours."

"That blade?" A breath hissed out. "It was stolen."

"What?" she taunted with disbelief. "Who would steal from such a great warrior? No. You plunged it through my brother's back while he rode at peace through the woods. You ended his life with one filthy throw. That is why I cannot countenance your presence. You make my flesh creep, like worms crawl over it!"

He released her and sat up. A great frown distorted his features.

She sprang to her feet. "Now will you admit your guilt? A great warrior would speak the truth to me."

He raised his head. "I did not kill your brother." His eyes looked confused, but met hers directly. "But I promise you I will discover who did."

"You would push your filthy crime on one of your men?" she sneered. "Dishonor upon dishonor. Nay. Speak the truth now!"

He stood and gripped her shoulders with his great hands. "I did not kill your brother. I swear it."

She stared at him, her chest heaving. Why did part of her believe him? She could not. He was a murderer. And a brute beast. Look how he had just treated her.

"What does your word mean to me?" she said. "Nothing! I spit upon you."

"You are angry because I forced the truth from you. I am sorry—I had no wish to hurt you. But do not spit upon me again," he warned.

So this had all been a ruse? A game, to learn her true intentions? He had not intended to harm her, he said. But he had humiliated her. And he had killed her brother. Nothing could change that most damning fact. Elwytha narrowed her eyes, deliberately worked the saliva in her mouth, and readied for a mighty salvo.

"You do not wish to do it," he told her. "I will not allow your disrespect."

"Well, you've got it," she gurgled. A nice juicy pool had formed in her mouth.

"Stop," he rumbled. "You will not like the consequence."

She narrowed her eyes and pursed her lips. She sucked in a mighty breath and then, faster than she could react, the Commander swooped forward and pressed his mouth against hers. She gulped on the nasty glob of spit. Unthinking panic erupted in her. She beat on his shoulders, trying to push him away. Tears crowded her eyes.

"Are you finished?" he whispered against her mouth.

An unwanted tear spilled down her cheek. "Yes."

He pulled away, and his gaze traced the path of her tear. An unknown emotion darkened the gray eyes. "Do not look at me thusly," he said, and leaned toward her again. His lips brushed hers, feather soft. The gentle caress jolted through her with the force of stampeding horses.

She blinked up at him, heart slamming hard. "Do not touch me."

"I have no wish to harm you, Elwytha."

"You have already hurt me. In the deepest way possible."

"Allow me the chance to prove my honor."

"It is impossible," she told him.

"Nothing is impossible." He released her, and gathered up her daggers. "I will find the answers."

Elwytha watched him leave the chamber, feeling even more confused. He had denied any part in her brother's murder. Was he such an accomplished liar? Or did he speak the truth?

Elwytha thought back to that terrible day and shook her head. It must be a lie. She had seen his sword, deep in her brother's back. A cowardly murderer surely would not admit to his crime.

CHAPTER EIGHT

THE COMMANDER STRODE through the quiet halls, which were lit only by torches. He shoved Elwytha's blades under his belt. Anger churned in him. Nay, a furious rage soared through him. Someone...*who?*...had stabbed Elwytha's brother in the back with his sword. A knave had cut the man down and now *he* was suspected of this cowardly, dishonorable act. No, not suspected. To Elwytha, it was a fact. No wonder she burned with hatred toward him. He would find answers, and he would find them now.

Two guards with crossed swords stood outside the Prince's bedchamber.

"I wish to see the Prince," he growled in a deep, deliberately fearsome tone.

The two looked properly alarmed.

"He is...occupied," said one.

"I will not wait," he roared. The men under him knew that whip of his voice. Instant obedience was required, or immediate punishment would follow. One of the two men jumped.

"I will knock," he agreed. Tentatively, he rapped on the door.

The Commander shoved him aside and pounded on the door with his fist. "Prince! I wish to speak to you. Now."

After a moment, a maid, her hair frazzled about her head, and dressed only in a robe, opened the door. The Prince sat in his bed at the far end of the room, bedclothes drawn to his waist. He relaxed against the pillows, arms crossed behind his head.

"This had better be worth it, Commander," he said in a deceptively calm tone.

"It is. I need to speak to you in private."

The Prince shooed the maid with his hand. "Wait outside." He regarded the Commander, his eyes narrowed.

The Commander waited until the door closed. "Elwytha has accused me of a wicked crime."

"And you bellyache to me?"

"My *sword* was found in her dead brother's back."

The Prince stiffened. "You are certain?"

"Of course I'm certain."

His lips twisted. "You did not kill him, did you?"

"Of course not." The Commander barely restrained his bellow. "I wish to know whose treachery accomplished this murder. Was it done on your order, Prince?"

"You are lucky we've been friends since childhood. Your words could land you in the dungeons."

"I wish only for the truth." He clenched his fists, trying to quiet his deep breaths.

"The princess has worked her magic upon you, hasn't she, Commander?" The Prince smiled.

He clenched his jaw. "I want the truth, Prince."

"You are lucky I favor you, old friend...brother. But I tell you the truth. I did not order his assassination."

A little of the tension relaxed out of the Commander's stiff shoulders. "Who, then? Someone stole my blade and now I stand accused of the crime."

"I will discover the truth. Fear not," the Prince said. "What is your plan?"

"I will question my men. And I'll question Elwytha for more details."

The Prince nodded. "And I will send out spies into the land. We'll have our answers. And perhaps the answers will strengthen our hand. You would have a kingdom of your own, would you not?"

"No," the Commander denied. "I have told you many times, I am a warrior, not a king. I am happy to leave those duties to you."

The Prince gave him a small smile. "I will do what I can to ensure that Elwytha gives you a sporting chance. But beware. She remains our enemy."

"I wish to have peace with her."

"Peace." The Prince nodded, his obsidian eyes unreadable. "We will see."

Elwytha could not sleep that night. Her mind kept replaying everything that had happened that day...that night. So many contradictory, confusing things had occurred; the Commander ordering her to ride with him, warming her in the hut...demanding to know why she hated him. Not killing her when he had had the chance.

Why?

Had he truly conspired to wrest the truth from her? Again, why? Surely he could have guessed the reason for her anger. He had killed her brother.

And yet he had denied it. Confusion roiled within her. The blade which had killed Thor was the Commander's. Who else could have wielded the murdering blow?

He claimed the blade had been stolen.

Elwytha gazed out the window at the starlit sky. The storm had broken.

Why was she considering the possibility that the Commander spoke the truth to her? Perhaps because part of her couldn't reconcile the cowardly murderer of her brother with the man who had kissed her so gently tonight. With the man who had warmed her in the hut.

Yet tonight he had manipulated and manhandled her for the sole purpose of coercing the truth from her—he'd said so himself. Clearly, he wished only to have his own way, as usual;

his brutish side, coming through once more. The side that had killed her brother.

And the sword...what more proof did she need? No doubts troubled her brother's mind. He knew the Commander had done it. She'd seen the hatred in his eyes when Richard had ordered her to kill him.

She must trust her brother above the enemy Commander.

An idea swam to the surface. Perhaps all of this was a convoluted plot that the Prince wielded to force her hand, to test the validity of the peace agreement.

The Prince was clever. But that clever? And why had he given her as a bride to the Commander in the first place? A further test of the peace? A way to wreak further agony upon her, the sister of the man the Commander had murdered?

None of these wicked plots were beyond the Prince's scheming machinations. But they did seem just the tiniest bit implausible.

She closed her eyes, feeling more confused than ever. Her cheekbones began to ache, and she realized she'd been clenching her jaw in frustration.

Elwytha moved her lower jaw from side to side in order to relax it. Only one thing remained clear through it all. Her family. Thor. She had to stay true to her clan. Nothing else mattered. They were the ones she believed, and her brother was the one she trusted. She could believe no lies of the enemy.

As for the Commander... She thought through their confrontation again. He had insisted that he wanted only the truth. What if she had told it to him the first time he had asked? Would things have played out differently tonight?

Did it matter? Ultimately, and once again, he had forced her to bend to his will by behaving like a brute beast. He cared only about accomplishing his own goals. He cared nothing at all for her feelings.

More thoughts tangled to the surface, making her head ache.

At supper, the Prince had said Richard had lied about the battles. The Commander claimed he was innocent of her brother's blood. She also knew Richard plotted treachery through her, to their enemies.

If only she could escape this untenable position. What was the truth?

How could she ever know?

༈ ༈ ༈ ༈ ༈

The next morning Elwytha ignored the Commander as she left her chamber. She still felt not only confused, but also more than a little angry about last night's confrontation. Namely, for the way he'd forced it upon her, and for the indignities she had suffered at his hands. He cared nothing about her wishes, as usual. Now he watched her exit, and made no effort to stop her. Good. Since he'd gained his answers, maybe now he'd leave her alone.

Elwytha spent a dreary morning circling the castle grounds, surreptitiously watching the guard rotations at the armory. She still needed to assemble three blades. Her brother still trusted her with this mission, no matter what her confused feelings might be about it. She would accomplish one step at a time, and then, when the time drew near for the final battle...then, perhaps, justice would be served.

༈ ༈ ༈ ༈ ༈

Elwytha was angry with him. The Commander wasn't surprised. He strode now toward the armory. He had pushed her hard last night. If agitated enough, he'd known she would act and speak impulsively. It had been the only way to force her hand. The only way she would admit the truth of the lie between them.

He regretted handling her so roughly. But when he had seen the dagger in her hand, and the hatred burning in her eyes, he had reacted as he would in battle—to subdue his foe, no matter the cost. Thankfully, he had regained control of himself on the bed. On top of her.

No. She could not be pleased by any of it.

But now, he thought grimly, opening the door to the armory, he knew the formidable wall facing him. This morning he would begin questioning his men. He felt certain, however, that none of them had taken his sword. They respected him. In fact, several had nearly laid down their lives in battle to protect him, as he had done for them. He could not believe one of his warriors had stolen the sword, and then plunged it through Thor's back. No. Not without the order of the Prince. And he knew the Prince did not lie to him.

No. Already the Commander felt sure the answers lay in another palace.

※ ※ ※ ※ ※

After a meager lunch, Elwytha rested upon her bed, hand over her eyes. She felt the beginnings of a headache and wished only for succor. But sleep evaded her.

Perhaps she should spy on the armory still more. The thought did not appeal as it should have. Perhaps she would run into her betrothed. Not first on her list of desirable encounters, to be sure.

A soft knock came at the door, disturbing her ruminations.

"Miss, it's Hagma."

"Enter." This morning, Hagma had returned Elwytha's 'favored' brown and gray dresses, as promised by the Commander. Elwytha wore the brown. Not that it pleased her.

Hagma entered now, bearing a basket overflowing with cloth and lace.

Interest sparked, and Elwytha sat up. "What have you brought?"

"Means to alter your dresses, miss."

Elwytha spied a scrap of crocheted lace and with a gasp, lifted it gently. "But it's lovely."

"Me mum made it." Hagma smiled with pleasure. "She makes much of the lace for the palace."

Elwytha pulled out more lace confections, and then she spied strips of pale linen, embroidered with fine stitches and beads of many hues. "My goodness," she breathed. "These are the finest I've ever seen. How much does she ask for such fine work? My brother will send gold, if I ask."

"Nay, miss." Hagma looked dismayed. "The Commander told me he will pay for everything you want."

Elwytha frowned. It did not sit well, to have the Commander pay for anything of hers. She would not be a kept woman. In fact, she would not be his woman at all. "I insist. The Commander no doubt has other uses for his coin."

Hagma looked uncomfortable. "Pray, perhaps you could discuss it with him, miss. He has already paid my mother a fine sum."

Frustration swelled within Elwytha. Again, her betrothed had engineered to have his own way. Once again, she was to have no say in matters of importance to her. "Has he said which fabrics I may use?" she snapped. "How much lace?"

Hagma blinked, looking taken aback. "No, miss. He said you are to have whatever you wish."

"He did, did he?" Elwytha still frowned. Then she wondered why she was so upset. Why not take advantage of the Commander's largesse? He owed her family an unpayable debt. "Very well," she said. "Shall we get started? Perhaps you could give your opinion on these dresses." She pulled out the seven dresses in her trunk and draped them about the room. Some were made of fine wool or linen, and two were of damask.

Hagma gasped each time Elwytha pulled out a new one. "Miss! They're gorgeous, they are. Why do you wish to alter them?"

"The bodices displease me. I wish to raise the neckline thusly." She pressed the lace to a burgundy dress, raising the "V" neckline five inches.

Visible horror rounded Hagma's eyes. "Surely not, miss."

"Yes. Will you help me, or not?"

"Well yes, if you insist. But why...how could they displease you? Surely the Commander would approve of you wearing them as they are."

"The Commander is why I wish to change them," Elwytha said. "I feel...shy to have him look upon my countenance." More like she wished for armor to shield herself in every way imaginable.

Hagma giggled, obviously surprised. But she squelched it when she saw Elwytha was not smiling. "Yes, miss, I understand. But he will be your husband. He will wish to look upon you."

Elwytha wanted to roll her eyes. Certainly, he would. And this was the entire point. However, Hagma had to understand her reasoning. She'd not forgotten the Commander's demand that the maid approve all alterations. Likely, he believed Elwytha would create hideous masterpieces of her gowns if unsupervised. Not a bad idea.

"Yes, Hagma, I know that is true, but..." she heaved a breath and acquired a tortured, embarrassed whisper, "I shall have to wear them to *supper*. I do not wish to endure the ogling stares of all those knaves." She affected a delicate shudder.

Truly, if she had a blade, the knaves would learn to keep their eyes in their heads. In any case, the louts bothered her not. But Hagma need not know those truths.

Hagma giggled and nodded. "I understand, miss. How much lace were you thinking? My mother may need to make more."

Elwytha and Hagma measured lace and colored, embroidered strips on the garments, and discovered no more lace would be needed, if Elwytha raised the bodices only two inches. After trying on her burgundy gown and draping the red beaded embroidery upon it, she agreed this would be sufficient.

Hagma smiled. "It will look nice, miss. A good choice, I say."

Elwytha had to agree. She loved her dresses, and at heart did not wish to mutilate their pleasing lines. She sewed the embroidery on the burgundy, and Hagma sewed a fine lace on a green gown.

"Enough for today," Elwytha decided, when they had finished. She wanted to check the last rotations at the armory before supper, and felt refreshed now for her task.

She touched the rich burgundy fabric of her dress. "I think I'll wear this tonight. What do you think?" Suddenly uncertain, she desired the honest opinion of another female.

Hagma smiled. "It does a wonder for you. Your dark hair makes it look dramatic, it does."

Pleased, Elwytha smiled, feeling more confident in her choice. "Thank you, Hagma."

"I will return on the morrow?"

"Tomorrow afternoon," Elwytha agreed. Hagma took the basket, including the needles and scissors, with her. Elwytha didn't mind being denied those possible weapons. She found herself looking forward to wearing a colorful dress again. Perhaps it would brighten her frame of mind. Truly, she needed all the brightening possible while subjected to her betrothed's attentions.

Elwytha slipped out to the armory a few minutes later. She had guessed that the guards changed rotations every three hours. Now to verify her theory. If correct, they should change about now.

She casually strolled across the grassy courtyard, peering at the armory out of the corner of her eye. Yes! A new guard now switched with the old one. A pleased smile curved her lips. Now to find the weakness in their chain. Perhaps a slothful one, who dozed from time to time. She smiled to herself, anticipating the challenge ahead. The sport of outwitting the guards and swiping weapons appealed to her much more than sewing lace on dresses.

She dared to sweep past the armory one last time, and firmly memorized the location of the door and two windows, and the adjacent bushes.

"Elwytha." The Commander's deep voice startled her.

Jumping a bit with guilt, she glanced up at him. He stood close beside her. How had he approached so stealthily? He had done it once before, too—in the bathing room when she'd first arrived.

His hand curled around her arm. She glared at it. All of the anger from last evening swelled again with shocking swiftness. She raised a freezing eyebrow. "Kindly do not touch me."

"You're angry with me."

"How clever you are," she snapped.

"I'm sorry for how I treated you last even."

"You forced your will upon me. But that's your way, isn't it?" she stated. "You disgust me. I want nothing to do with you...a murderer, and an abuser of women."

His head snapped back, as if struck. "I had no wish to abuse you."

"And yet you did." Elwytha felt shocked by the fury vibrating through her. "I will not trust you, ever again!"

"No!"

If she didn't know better, she'd think he sounded anguished. But her wishes did not matter to him at all.

She spun on her heel.

"Elwytha." The deep voice commanded her attention. "Please," he added.

"What do you have to say to me? Verily, nothing I want to hear."

"I am sorry. Please forgive me."

She turned back, hands on her hips. "How can I forgive you, my brother's murderer?"

"I cannot prove my innocence yet. But know I planned last night for one purpose only."

"Why?"

"To clear the air between us. You hate me. I had to know why, or I could not fix it."

"You can't fix it. You can't change the past. And your brutish behavior only makes me hate you more."

"Elwytha." The word sounded rough.

She glared. "You care what I think of you?"

The great man steadily regarded her. "Yes."

She folded her arms. Why was she listening to him? Why did she care what he said? Why did his sincerity reach out and twist through her soul?

"Then do not manhandle me again."

"I will not. Unless you attack me again."

She bit her lip. "Fair enough."

"I would not hurt you, Elwytha. I did not intend to last night. I will not ever. Unless you pull further treachery upon me." The Commander's warning gaze held hers.

"All right," she said, surprising herself. "I forgive you for manipulating me last night. But I cannot trust your word concerning my brother."

"You will."

How like him to be so confident, so arrogant. She gave him a thin smile. "So, we are back to where we started."

"No. Now the truth is out. Things are not the same. And they will not remain the same." Determination steeled his features.

Clearly, he plotted still more. But what this time? She inclined her head. "I must ready for supper."

"I look forward to seeing you soon." His intense look jolted her heart. It was one a man gave a woman—his woman. Possessive. And a promise that he would accomplish exactly what he desired.

He left. Heart beating uncomfortably fast, Elwytha watched his large form stride away. He considered her his. He *wanted* her to be his—why else would he desire peace?

Why didn't these thoughts repulse her as they would have five days ago? Elwytha felt jumbled inside, and for the time being, endeavored to erase her betrothed from her mind entirely.

CHAPTER NINE

ELWYTHA DRESSED WITH CARE for the evening meal. She would not look at her motivations too closely. The burgundy dress pleased her, and she wanted to look nice for once, she reasoned. She was tired of feeling like a frumpy wash woman in drab garments.

She bathed, and then arranged her long hair atop her head, dripping tendrils down her neck. She liked what she saw in the mirror. At long last she looked and felt like the princess she was.

Taking a deep breath, she exited into the Commander's chamber. It was empty. Surprise plunged through her. Wasn't it time for the evening meal?

She heard voices in the hall, and then the Commander entered, speaking over his shoulder to someone. "At first light," he agreed, and shut the door. He glanced at her.

Surprise—no, shock—flickered across his features. He took a step closer. "Elwytha." His voice dropped to a deep timbre. Swiftly, his gaze ran down her form. "You look beautiful."

Elwytha felt pleased, but tried not to reveal it. "Thank you."

He stared at her for several long breaths, and then moved toward his wardrobe. "I will be ready in a moment."

"I'll wait in the hall." Regally, she swept out the door and closed it. She leaned against the wall. Her heart thumped hard in her chest. Why? Because of the Commander's words? How he had looked at her?

How could his opinion matter in the least? Elwytha bit her lip and tried not to think too closely on these disturbing questions. She reminded herself that he was her brother's murderer.

She stopped thinking when he opened the door. His eyes searched hers, and he offered his arm. "Walk with me?" Feeling trepidation, she did as he bid, and curled her hand under his muscular forearm.

Discomfort jangled with every step that took them closer to the dining hall. This felt too intimate somehow. It seemed too much as if, by her dress, attire, and by appearing her regal self on the Commander's arm, she was declaring that she did indeed belong to him. That she gave full assent to their marriage.

Before they reached the hall she snatched her hand away, heart pounding. "I...I can't do this."

He faced her. "Why?" An unknown emotion flickered in the slate eyes, but he waited patiently.

"I only wished to look nice tonight. I...I don't want you..." Her words faltered.

He waited, making her say it. How she hated his cold heart for that.

She said, "I don't want you to think I've changed my mind about our marriage."

"You still do not wish it."

She heaved a breath of relief. "Yes. I do not wish it."

"Would you break your word, then?"

"No. I...I just don't want you to think..."

"That you dressed to please me."

"Yes." She felt further relief that he understood.

His gaze held hers. "Didn't you?"

Her jaw dropped. "Nay! I dressed to please myself. I tire of appearing a frump."

"Verily." His hand closed around hers, and he raised it to his lips. His warm caress felt like scattering leaves on a windy day. Light, erratic pulses flickered through her skin, and her nerves. She stared at him, mouth slightly agape. She snapped it shut and tugged her hand free. Her face felt warm.

"Kindly bestow no caresses upon my person."

He smiled, but made no such promise. "Please hold my arm. It gives me pride to walk beside you into the hall."

Put like that, how could Elwytha resist?

"Very well." Her fingers curled around his arm again and they entered the hall.

Instant silence fell. No unseemly hoots or hollers. Most unlike the knaves.

Finally, a rumbling murmur swelled, and a few men whistled. Elwytha's ears burned, but she endeavored to ignore them, and lifted her chin high until they arrived at their table.

The Prince offered a mocking smile. "At last you bestow honor upon the Commander. You look a fitting bride for a king."

"I dressed to please neither of you. I felt it time to remind you, as well as your subjects," she flicked a glance at the Commander, who, with that steady, amused gaze looked like a subject to no one, "that I am a person of royalty, deserving of your honor and respect."

"Mayhap you wish us to kneel at your feet?" the Prince said.

"Only insecure fools require their subject's adulation," she stated. "I have no wish to languish upon a throne, sneering down at my subjects. Nay," she said, spooning up a bit of stew, "I would look a man in the eye and treat him like an equal."

"Thus your royal airs now," the Prince said.

"Your grace sports with me." She sent him a piercing look. "Perhaps because only games entertain your bored mind. Games with me. Games with my brother. Tell me, Prince, I confess curiosity. Why did you betroth me to the Commander? To inflict further misery upon me? Or to mock my brother's death?"

The Prince glanced at his first-in-command. "I did not mock you when I offered you to the Commander."

"Truly." Elwytha's teeth gritted. "It was a slap in the face. You knew that fact when you joined me to one of your commoners. Even worse, the one who murdered my brother."

Beside her, tension stiffened the Commander's shoulders. "You think me a commoner?" he growled in a low voice. "A bastard, and beneath your notice." The slate gaze bored into hers.

Her pulse leaped with consternation. "No. I misspoke. I wished only to know why the Prince offered my hand to you."

The Prince curled his lip, and lifted a cup of ale. "You deserve your fate, Princess. Perhaps you should appreciate my offer of peace, instead of insulting my right hand."

The Commander's hand fisted, knuckles white, on the table. He lowered his head, not looking at her, and speared up a bite of grouse from his trencher.

She had hurt his feelings.

Sorrow pierced her, and repentance. Quietly, she said, "I don't think of you as a commoner." To her surprise, she didn't. He had well earned the Prince's respect, and he gained more of hers every day. "And I don't think of you as a bastard...except in relation to my brother's death."

Her betrothed heaved a great breath, but still did not look at her. "Your words betrayed you, Princess," he said, too quietly. "You think me a monster. You have from the beginning. Do not try to whitewash the truth."

Elwytha didn't know what to say. Her royal airs and her foolish words had created a rift between herself and the Commander. What was the saying? Pride cometh before destruction? She did not like herself much these days.

Silently, she fell to her meal, and tried to swallow the lump that had formed in her throat. She didn't know how to erase her words. Both men thought she was a pompous, preening princess now. Her own words condemned her. It was ironic, for at home she felt no different than any of the palace subjects. She treated all with respect. All had been made by God. She was no better. She sipped water now, thinking on the treachery corrupting her soul. Indeed, perhaps she was worse.

Elwytha finished her meal, and said quietly, "I wish to retire. Goodnight."

The Commander let her go with barely a glance. Elwytha hurried to her chamber, feeling very alone. Inside, she slammed the door and flung herself upon the bed. Tears of remorse wet her cheeks, and she silently wept into her pillow, feeling sorrow for losing the Commander's respect.

↟ ↟ ↟ ↟ ↟

"She appears heartbroken," the Prince said, watching Elwytha hurry away.

The sore wound inside the Commander festered yet again. Elwytha had sliced right through his oldest scar; the agony of his youth, of being labeled a bastard. Of having a father who refused to acknowledge him. Who let him live in squalor. He had come to accept that, even understand it. But the taunts of the other youths...

Bastard. He had begun to think that his true name for many a year. Only the Prince's friendship had made him feel honored, and that he was worth something. A huge reason why he had become the man he was today.

"No," he said now, drinking deeply of his water cup. "She thinks nothing of me. I am worse than a bastard to her. I'm a murdering knave!" His great fist crashed on the table, surprising even himself. He shook inside, for the first time feeling helpless. Hopeless. He was a fool to think Elwytha would ever accept him as a husband. Let alone love him! What a fool he was. His grip tightened on his dagger.

"Careful," said the Prince. "Don't unman yourself. She's not worth it."

The Commander glared. "She *is*," he said through his teeth.

"She doesn't respect you." The Prince watched him.

"She hates me."

"You still wish to have her?"

"Yes," the Commander growled, hating himself for his weakness.

"Then speak to her. You are a warrior. Don't allow her to defeat you." His childhood friend encouraged him, as he'd always done. "And if she washes her hands of you, I wash my hands of Richard. That brother will get the sword he deserves."

The Commander nodded. He felt better. "Thank you. I will do as you suggest."

The Prince smiled. "Accept only victory."

ᛉ ᛉ ᛉ ᛉ ᛉ

Elwytha lay on her bed, sniffling. How could the goodwill of that man—her brother's murderer, she reminded herself—matter to her? And yet it did.

A knock sounded on her door.

Who was that? She sat up quickly, wiping her cheeks. "Yes?"

No answer.

Feeling trepidation, she arose and opened it. The Commander frowned down at her. His gaze scanned her wet face and the frown vanished. "Why are you crying?" His voice sounded surprisingly gentle.

Elwytha had no wish to pretend now. She would clear the air between them. She wordlessly waved her hand. "Because I acted pompous and foolish. I'm sorry for the hurtful things I said about you."

"You care what I think?" He sounded surprised.

Elwytha realized that his words replayed their conversation earlier today. Only then, he had admitted to caring what she thought of him. She scanned his familiar features—the bent nose, the mutilated brow. The keen, intelligent eyes. Through them, and through his actions, she saw the real man.

"Yes," she said simply. "I'm not saying we can ever have peace. But..." How could she respect this man so much? Why did his opinion of her matter? "Please forgive me," she appealed.

He smiled then, a small one, but it lightened his eyes to pure silver. Elwytha drew a quick breath. It was the most mesmerizing color she had ever seen.

"Goodnight, Elwytha."

She smiled, too. Truly, he had forgiven her. "Goodnight, Commander."

CHAPTER TEN

THE NEXT MORNING, Elwytha awoke with a feeling of disquiet. It intensified as she thought on the scenes between herself and the Commander last night. His opinion mattered too much. He was her enemy, for goodness' sake.

But she didn't know if he had killed Thor or not. Deep inside, something urged her to believe he was telling the truth. But how could that be so? Who else could have killed Thor?

Even if he hadn't killed Thor—a very big if—he was still the enemy of her palace. Indeed, he was the Commander of the entire enemy force. She was becoming too emotionally involved with him. First vicious hatred, fights...confrontations. He wanted to break through the barriers between them; she sensed that. And he had admitted as much yesterday, when he had said he wanted peace with her.

How could they have peace? He was her enemy, whether he had killed Thor or not. She couldn't forget this. She needed space from him. Things were entirely too volatile between them. Every time she saw him, another piece of her armor against him was chipped away—relentlessly—just like the man he was. And it made the tug of war between honor and the treachery in her soul even worse.

Space was what she needed. And she needed to spy upon the armory again.

Elwytha quickly ate a breakfast of toast and tea, and then dressed in the tiresome gray dress. Thankfully, when she exited her chamber, the Commander was nowhere to be seen.

She slipped outside and began her morning constitutional, walking around the castle courtyard. Her path just happened to cross the armory door with each turn about the grounds.

Elwytha walked sprightly, as if she hadn't a care in the world, and cast disarming smiles on all who crossed her path. Best for them to get used to her presence. They would come to accept it—even expect it. When it came time to do her dirty deed, no one would notice her at all. Her smiles were to garner goodwill. Her father had always told her that she'd catch more flies with honey than vinegar.

The washer women smiled this time as she passed. Pleased, Elwytha claimed this as a small victory.

She approached the armory again and slid a cunning glance out of the corner of her eye. The guard looked sleepy. Perhaps up too late last night reveling? A small smile curled her lips.

A large hand caught her wrist, stopping her. Her heart jerked with alarm, and she stared up at her betrothed.

"Kindly unhand me. And where did you come from? I didn't see you a minute ago." Because she'd been looking to avoid him!

He didn't release her. His gaze looked keen, measuring. "Why do you pace before the armory?"

"I do not pace before the armory. I am taking the air. It improves my health."

"Speak the truth to me, Elwytha." His eyes locked with hers. By her wrist, he held her close to him. It was impossible to ignore him, or the truth he demanded from her soul.

"You're paranoid. I have made no moves upon your armory."

"You love blades. Perhaps you want to steal more for your own purposes."

"What purposes?" she scoffed. "I merely walk, Commander. Surely that's not a crime." She twisted her wrist now, and he freed her. Elwytha stepped back. "You promised not to manhandle me."

"You promised no further treachery."

Guilt sparked a defensive anger. "You're a fine one to talk. You demand honor from me, when you possess none yourself."

His face hardened. "You speak of your brother's death."

"You misspeak. I speak of his *murder*."

"I told you I did not kill him."

"And why should I believe you? You're my enemy. Nay. You are the *Commander* of the enemy forces arrayed against my palace. Why would I believe any word you speak? Perhaps even now you and the Prince plot treachery against me." Her agitation increased, as these plausible theories took shape in her mind.

He heaved a great breath. "Elwytha." He sounded exasperated. "Look on me."

"I don't wish to hear anything you have to say."

"Have I ever dealt dishonorably with you?" The deep voice was quiet, patient.

Elwytha frowned on. "Besides badgering me and bending me to your will, I'm not sure."

A breath hissed through his teeth. "I have treated you with the respect and honor you deserve. Will you not acknowledge that?"

Elwytha thought on the ways he could have easily dishonored her. He had not. And the other things...the small kindnesses he had shown her; holding her in the hut, kissing her when he had regretted treating her harshly, and returning her dresses as promised. Even now, speaking reasonably when she grasped at straws for reasons to mistrust him. "Yes, you have," she admitted at last, looking down.

"Perhaps you believe I possess honor after all."

She glanced up. How could this enemy Commander possess honor? It would turn her whole world upside down to believe it. And yet... Elwytha stiffened, instinctively fighting the crack that threatened to form in her self-protective armor. For her brother and clan, she must remain clear-headed. She must face facts and discover the truth.

"Have you secured proof of your innocence yet?" she asked, knowing he hadn't. How could he? "Perhaps one of your warriors confessed to Thor's murder," she suggested with faint sarcasm. A confession the Commander would have to coerce, because it would be a lie.

"No. I spoke to them yesterday. None killed Thor. No one saw or stole my blade."

"So what happened to it? Mayhap it sprouted wings and flew into my brother's back of its own accord?"

"Nay." Frustration tightened his voice.

"How could you lose your sword in the first place?" Elwytha pressed harder for the truth. Perhaps he'd slip and reveal more than he planned. "I know little about you, Commander, but you're not careless."

"I am not," he agreed. "I lost it during a battle. One of your skilled swordsmen wrested it from my hand. I had to battle and finish him with my dagger."

Elwytha flinched at this description of the death of one of her best warriors. Yet he had died in battle. If he had not died, the Commander would have. This thought did not sit any better within her soul. In fact, she felt a sick horror, thinking on it.

His next words infiltrated her disturbed thoughts. "Afterward, when I searched for my sword, I could not find it."

"Really? Then where did it go? You say your men did not pilfer it."

"They did not. And the Prince swears he didn't order Thor's assassination."

"That proves nothing," Elwytha pointed out. "You say this, the Prince says that. In truth, your men didn't find your sword because it was never lost. You had it the whole time."

He remained calm, but his body stiffened. "I don't lie. Ever."

Again, he insisted upon honor. Elwytha didn't know what to believe. "If you speak the truth, then where did it go? Who took it? Who killed my brother?" Logically, his guilt was the only reasonable explanation. He was her brother's enemy. Who had a greater motivation to kill Thor, the enemy King?

A multitude of unreadable thoughts flickered across the Commander's face. But he did not reveal any of them. "We will continue to investigate."

"Investigate," she agreed. "But I would be a fool to believe you, unless you can provide proof. Good day."

"Elwytha." His tone commanded her to stop. "I searched for you with a purpose."

She frowned. "You said you don't require my presence until the evening."

"I have said no such thing."

"You said in the even..."

"I'd like to see you wear one of your fine dresses," he finished her statement. Annoying, that was. "I still require your company during the day."

Elwytha crossed her arms. "I am busy. I have dresses to alter." Inspiration struck. "And our nuptials to plan."

His eyes narrowed. "You wish to plan our nuptials?" He sounded disbelieving, as well he might.

Truthfully, Elwytha wished only to escape from his presence, so she could think.

He asked, "What needs to be done?"

Elwytha smiled inwardly at her success. What did a man know of planning a wedding? In his ignorance, he might believe any manner of tripe she chose to feed him. "I need to choose a dress," she began.

"I prefer the blue. It suits you, and is the color of your eyes."

It had been Elwytha's choice, as well. Graciously, she said, "I agree. I also need to speak to Mary about the food for the reception afterward." After the nonexistent wedding, she reminded to herself. Little did the Commander know the wedding would never be.

Because she would battle and kill him first.

A bolt of sickness stabbed her. She looked quickly away, her breath catching. She swallowed, trying to regain her thoughts.

"Elwytha?" Was that concern in his uncommonly deep voice? "Are you all right? Have you a pain?"

She felt even more guilty for her duplicity. Already the treachery rent more and more lies through her soul. She would not lie about her health, too. "No. I am fine."

He frowned, as if he did not believe her.

Elwytha said, "I also need to write my brother and make sure he'll arrive on the correct day. Monday of next week?"

Her betrothed continued to regard her with a faint frown. "Yes."

"Good. I will need to make sure the priest is available and the chapel readied, as well." A thought occurred to her. "Does the palace have a chapel?" She hadn't seen it yet, in all of her wanderings.

"I will see to the priest and the chapel."

She was surprised that the Commander would take this burden upon himself. Although the wedding would not take place, it did need to be planned. For appearance's sake it had to look like it would happen. "Thank you." She inclined her head. "So you see, I have much to do."

"Yes. But I wish to ride with you this morn. You can speak to Mary and alter your dresses in the afternoon."

Frustration simmered. He seemed determined to foil her plan to avoid him. That's all she needed—more time with him, which would confuse her still further. Sarcastically, she said, "You wish my presence so fervently?"

"Yes," he returned calmly.

Startled by his admission, Elwytha scanned his features. Implacable purpose and determination firmed his jaw. Surprise, surprise.

"I wish to spend time with you, Elwytha. I want to know you better."

What could she say? He spoke so reasonably. Just one velvet cloaked demand...for her presence. She bit her lip, trying to quell her instinctive desire to push him away, to protect herself. She met his gaze, trying to read his intent. To her surprise, calm patience lived there...and an unknown something else. A plea...or a demand?

She took a breath. "Very well," she said, against her better judgment. "I agree to ride with you in the mornings, as you require, if you'll grant me freedom in the afternoons."

"I cannot promise that."

Elwytha's brows wrenched together. She had tried so hard to be reasonable and civil. This was the thanks she received. "Why?"

"Because I may wish your presence in the afternoon."

"*Why*, pray tell?"

"I will give you no promises I cannot keep."

She scowled. "So I'm to be at your beck and call day and night?"

His lips twitched. "Not at night. Yet."

A furious blush heated her face. "Commander! I will thank you not to refer to such unseemly affairs." Then she blushed further, thinking on her poor choice of words. Verily, he would know no nights with her. With haste, she reminded herself of this calming fact.

He scanned her features, amusement evident. "It is why I wish to ride with you now. So we'll know each other better before our nuptials."

Elwytha muttered, "I don't *wish* to know you further!"

To her alarm, his large hand settled on the small of her back. "Will you come with me now to the stables?"

Her heart pounded. Should she bolt from his touch like a frightened filly—which unfortunately appealed too greatly—or endure it, pretending not to notice? Pride dictated the latter.

"Very well," she said. "But I require this afternoon free."

"Agreed." He did not remove his hand. Instead, his fingers slipped around her waist as they walked across the grassy courtyard. Prickling awareness warmed her skin. She struggled not to bolt. When they finally reached the stables, she gladly darted free, eager to exchange the Commander's company for Sir Duke's.

✻ ✻ ✻ ✻ ✻

The Commander's gaze traced the stiff line of Elwytha's shoulders as she greeted her horse. So, his plans to gentle her to his touch were not going so well. Patience, he warned himself, now readying the black stallion for his ride. She still distrusted him.

Truthfully, he didn't trust her fully, either. What were her plans? Why had she been sent to the palace bearing peace in her body from her brother? Richard did not desire peace; the Commander knew this in his gut. More likely, the King felt humiliated for his recent defeats...for all of his defeats since Thor had died. He wanted revenge.

Could Elwytha be a tool in Richard's plan for vengeance? She had arrived carrying knives. But she hadn't tried to kill him when she'd had the chance. Instead, she had hidden his dagger beneath his mattress. And she insisted on planning the wedding she professed to despise.

The Commander understood none of it. But he liked Elwytha. In fact, more every day. He hoped...and prayed...for no treachery on her part. He wanted a true marriage with her, even now, after all their fights and the logical reasons why he should give up. He saw in her the heart of a warrior, and the tender heart of a woman, too. Elwytha intrigued him like no other. She challenged him. He liked that.

The Commander watched her swing up on Sir Duke. Did treachery lurk in her heart? He wanted to trust her, but sensed she still hid something from him. Something far deeper; a truth only wit and cunning would draw out. He would pursue her secret. He would also seek to clear his name of Thor's murder.

He would fight for victory in the battle for her heart.

✻ ✻ ✻ ✻ ✻

Elwytha and the Commander rode the outer reaches of the Prince's land. None of her brother's warriors appeared, and

Elwytha felt relieved. Had he pulled them all in, waiting for her attack on the Commander in a week's time? Perhaps on that day Richard's warriors would lurk in the wood, awaiting a signal that the Prince's best warrior and strategist lay dead. That moment would be the perfect one to charge the palace and battle victory from their foes.

The very plot made Elwytha want to vomit. She didn't know it would happen thusly, of course. But she knew her brother well. He wanted to vanquish the Prince and capture his lands as plunder.

Why didn't the plan settle well within her soul? The Prince and the Commander remained her enemies. Didn't they?

Ahead, the Commander stopped and dismounted from his horse. They'd reached the small chapel again, and Elwytha felt dismayed. Coming here must be a practice of his; to come and seek forgiveness for his many crimes. Doubtless he needed it.

Then why was he the one going inside, while she hung back?

With reluctance, Elwytha dismounted from her horse and secured the reins to a tree. She didn't want to go inside. Guilt for her many lies and for her continued plan of treachery scorched her soul. And now...now that she had the tiniest doubts about the Commander's guilt, it seared still deeper.

Did she think she could hide from God out here?

Of course not. He saw her. And her soul testified against herself, shouting that she chose the wrong path.

Hiding out here was doing no good. She had to face her guilt. She had to kneel before her Maker and confess her misdeeds. She had to find peace for her soul.

When the Commander came out, Elwytha slipped in and slowly approached the altar. Three candles burned there today. She lit another, for her dead brother, and then knelt at the altar. The weight of the wrongdoing she'd already committed, and still planned to do, fell over her.

Unable to help herself, Elwytha wept. The treachery, the lies. All of it sickened her. And what if the Commander was innocent? How could she attack and kill an innocent man? She heaved great breaths. What should she do? Follow Richard? Avenge her brother's death?

Commit more lies, more treachery? Tears burned her eyes, and sobs choked her throat.

"Elwytha." Her betrothed's boot steps approached, and she struggled to still her shaking shoulders. What was she...a woman, or a warrior? In truth, lately, she'd felt more the former than the latter. She dragged in a shaky breath and sniffed.

"Elwytha." Concern darkened the timber of his deep voice. "What is it?" The Commander knelt on one knee beside her.

If anything, this made her feel worse. For her enemy, against whom she planned treachery, to show her kindness and compassion was too much. It sliced through her soul like a flaying knife. Wretchedly, she cringed away from him and gulped out more guilty sobs.

"I will not harm you." Anger darkened his tone.

"I know." She sniffed mightily, and wiped her tear-slicked face. "It's not that."

A silent moment passed. "Does our marriage displease you so greatly?"

With surprise, she looked at him. He possessed no clue to her treachery. He didn't know he should run for his life from their wedding. "That's not it, either," she gulped.

He frowned, his eyes concerned, and even gentle. A side she had never seen before. "Then what troubles you, Elwytha?"

In an impulsive rush, she decided to tell as much truth as possible. It seemed the least she could do, in this house of God. "I feel torn in so many directions."

He waited patiently.

"I feel grief for Thor. And I don't know what to think of you. I don't know if you're guilty or not anymore." Anguished, she whispered, "It makes everything so difficult."

He put a hand under her elbow and urged her to her feet, then led her to a pew. She sat beside him, well aware of his muscled thigh and powerful arm brushing hers. She drew a shaky breath, not sure what else to say. Wasn't this man her enemy? In truth, he was an enemy of her palace. But had he slain Thor? This made all the difference.

More helpless tears slipped down her cheeks, and she wondered what was happening to her. At home she was always so strong, so full of purpose. A warrior. But here...with all her perceptions of reality turned upside down, the rules for hatred were not so clear. Her enemies had faces and names...though she still didn't know the Commander's name.

But she could not kill him. She wouldn't.

She burst into fresh tears at this revelation. To her shock, his arm went around her, pulling her close to him, as in the hut during the storm. She stiffened, not sure what to think. Allow it? Or bolt?

"Elwytha," he rumbled. "I will not harm you."

Tentatively, and aching for comfort, she rested her head on his great shoulder. Wasn't it wrong, to receive succor in the arms of her enemy? From the man she meant to betray?

But she would not betray him. She could not.

No more, she told herself. No more lies. Unless she found proof of his guilt, she would not battle and kill him. These truths drifted up from her heart in the quiet chapel.

It would be wrong.

She relaxed infinitesimally, feeling the first bit of peace all week. It was the right choice. The right path. Her tears dripped to a halt, and she wiped them with her sleeve.

"You are all right now?" His gaze still looked gentle, and patient.

"Yes." She didn't want him to let her go, though. How could that be? But she felt such peace in his arms.

She settled her cheek against the rough cloth of his jerkin. Here, finally, she could think clearly. And she needed to finish her thought processes.

She would not battle and kill him. Not without proof. Elwytha would tell Richard that she could not kill without cause. Of course, Richard only saw the Commander as an enemy, and maybe that was enough motivation for him, but it wasn't for her. She would commit no treachery against him.

Her brother would deliver her from wedding the Commander, and that would be it.

Richard would be furious. This betrayal bothered her, too. But at least the murder of a possibly innocent man would not stain her soul. Enemy or not, death belonged on the battle-field, not at the knife of an accepted bride...an accepted peace.

Of course, she knew the Commander remained her enemy, but when Richard came, she would leave him behind; an enemy to be battled on another day, on the honorable court of battle. And he would not fall by her hand—unless of course, blood guilt stained him.

Elwytha became aware that she had leaned against the Commander's chest quite long enough. With a start, she pulled away. "I'm ready to go now."

His thumb brushed a lingering tear from her cheek.

She looked into his eyes, and her heart suddenly beat harder. "Thank you."

"You're welcome." His warm palm cupped her jaw and she knew he meant to kiss her. A gasp of alarm caught in her throat, but before she could think further, his lips touched hers.

Soaring thunder crashed through her heart. His mouth moved against hers, imprinting his texture upon her lips, and a tingling, burning warmth spread out from the point of con-tact and sped through her body. Her hand gripped his jerkin, fisting it in her hand. She had never felt thusly before, ever in her life.

Tentatively, she swayed into him, returning his kiss. She felt his start of surprise, and then he kissed her more deeply. Elwytha felt dizzy, like she was drowning in a swirling, molten vat of sensations.

With a low growl, the Commander pulled away and Elwytha's eyes fluttered open. His eyes were a deep, smoky color and his breaths came rapidly, too. Dismay settled in, and she scooted free.

What had she just done? She had allowed her enemy to kiss her. And she had kissed him back. Had she lost all reasoning capabilities?

"That was a mistake," she managed to say. "I don't want to repeat it."

"Elwytha." He reached for her hand, but she flew to her feet.

"No," she exclaimed breathlessly. How could her body betray her like this? How could she like this man's caresses?

Elwytha felt panicked. She grappled for reason, for understanding. He was her enemy. So she'd decided not to kill him? She couldn't kiss him now!

He followed her quick steps out of the chapel.

"Elwytha." He caught at her shoulder before she could vault on her horse.

"What?" She turned her confused, bewildered gaze upon him.

"You want us to remain enemies?" She heard a catch in the deep voice.

"We *are* enemies. Whether you killed Thor or not. I cannot forget that, Commander." She leaped on her horse. "Pray, take no more liberties with me."

His lips tightened, but he made no such promise, she noted. So like him. She'd have to remain on guard at all times now. Especially since her body would betray her in such a horrifying manner.

Elwytha galloped out of the wood, but she could not outrun her tortured, dismayed thoughts. How could her enemy make her feel such things? How could he warm her blood so it sang a new, wild song? It was a puzzle....Nay. An unanswerable paradox.

ϟ ϟ ϟ ϟ ϟ

The Commander galloped after Elwytha, feeling both pleased and disturbed by their kiss. Pleased by Elwytha's response. Disturbed by the depth of his. The very foundation of his soul had shaken. It scared him as nothing else could...for a scrap of a woman to wield such power over him.

He also felt disturbed by the way Elwytha had fled. Clearly, she still saw him as her enemy. Equally clear, she was confused. Doubts lived in her mind about his guilt in Thor's murder.

A step on his path to victory, the Commander realized. He would continue to pursue her...but carefully. He sensed, as he did when gentling a horse, that if he pushed too hard now, he could jeopardize her budding trust in him. And she was beginning to trust him, although she would deny it if he suggested it. Twice now, she had allowed him to hold her.

Hope grew, bright like the sunshine warming his face. Careful steps would gain him what he wished for now with deepening urgency. Could a scarred monster such as himself possibly gain the prize he sought...her heart?

CHAPTER ELEVEN

WHEN ELWYTHA ENTERED THE CASTLE—thankfully freed now from her betrothed's disturbing presence—a guard approached.

"Princess, the Prince would like to see you."

"Now, I perceive?" Elwytha frowned, for her stomach rumbled, eager for food. But the Prince could not wait. Heaven forbid that his royalness should have to languish upon his throne, fretting for an end to his boredom. "Lead on," she told the guard.

They traversed the cold, stone flagged halls until finally, with a faint bow, he opened the door to the throne room.

As expected, the Prince rested with languid ease upon his throne, his long legs stretched before him. The ridiculous, bulbous gold crown perched upon his head. Did he truly wear that all the time?

Elwytha dropped an abrupt, faintly mocking curtsey. Straightening, she inquired, "Your grace requested my presence?"

"Approach," he instructed.

Wanting to roll her eyes, Elwytha ascended the white stone stairs, nearing his pedestal. She stopped a good five feet distant. "Surely your highness does not desire me to come too near. I am, after all, still your enemy, am I not?"

He leaned forward, his shrewd black eyes fixed upon her. "Tell me if you are, Princess."

Elwytha frowned. What games did he play now? "Speak what you mean, if you please, Prince. I hunger, and your games annoy me."

He continued to watch her, and Elwytha felt uncomfortable. She crossed her arms and tapped her foot. "Have you nothing to say?" she said at last. "Have you wasted my time by bidding me hither?"

He leaned back then, eyes narrowed. "Nay." He lifted a hand. A parchment rested in it. He wiggled it in what he likely believed a tempting matter. "I received a letter this morn. Addressed to you."

Eagerness and trepidation rushed through her. "From my brother?"

"Yes. From Richard." He tapped the parchment against his palm. "I assume you wish to read its contents."

"Of course." She forced the next civil words past her lips. "If you please, I would like to have it, Prince."

"Of course." He extended it, but made no move to lean forward. This necessitated that she take several steps to retrieve it. Irritated, she snatched it with ill grace from his hand. The pompous fool. Sitting there, watching her with those sharp eyes and curled lips.

She retreated the same two steps and hastily unrolled the parchment. That's when she realized the seal had been broken. Fury soared. "You *read* my letter?" she hissed.

"Of course." Not flickering an eyelash, he continued to watch her. He lounged like a cat, looking relaxed, but ready to spring on the attack. It deepened her feeling of disquiet.

She scowled. "Pray, why would you read my correspondence, Prince?"

"Should I trust you and your brother so utterly? As the fool you believe I am, would I allow secret strategies to ferment within my walls?" he asked, clearly sarcastic. "I should allow uncensored, unchecked missives to pass freely between you, the Commander's reluctant bride, and Richard? In fact, as you will see, his letter records no pledges of peace. As perhaps none reside in your heart, either."

Elwytha quickly scanned her brother's missive.

I come on the next Monday for your nuptials, dear Elwytha. I have not forgotten you, nor the fate you have chosen. Faint not.

If I know the Prince, he fills your ears with fairy tales of his glorious wins in battle and the Commander's innocence in our brother's murder. Believe no lies of the Commander or that preening Prince. I have found a witness at last. A hunter, who verifies the cowardly act. Done in a rage, he said. Perhaps rashly. Perhaps planned in the pit of hell—the Prince's heart.

Take courage, Elwytha. You, more than many, have the heart of a warrior. Peace must come. Know your sacrifice will mean the end of warfare for our people and their children. Godspeed, sister.

Your King, and brother, Richard.

Elwytha felt shaken. A witness found? A hunter had seen the Commander kill Thor? Her breaths came very quickly, and she felt she might faint.

"Princess?" The Prince still watched her, his eyes cold. "What does your brother plot?"

She gasped, and quickly rolled up the parchment. She met his black eyes. "He plots nothing. He merely records ..."

"A witness." His lip curled. "A lie. But you know that, don't you, Princess?"

"What?" Elwytha's hand trembled.

"Your brother lies to you." The Prince's words sounded hard now, and sharp. "In what plot would he have you partake? What treachery? Speak now, and all will go well with you."

Elwytha stepped back. "The only treachery I see is yours, Prince, plotting the assassination of Thor! I'll believe no word that you or the Commander speak to me, ever again."

She turned to flee, but the Prince sprang from his throne, light as a cat, and caught her wrist. His purple edged mantle billowed up in a menacing black cloud behind his shoulders, and then settled. Alarmed, she stared up at him. Just as quickly, however, he released her. He hissed, "Speak the truth now, Princess, or you will invite death upon your head and the King's, as well."

"The Commander isn't rash." From nowhere, this thought erupted from her mind and past her lips.

The Prince's eyes narrowed. "No, he is not. And I did not order Thor's assassination."

For all of his games and sly, mocking innuendos, this time she sensed the true Prince coming through. Sharp and cunning, yes, but in this instance...speaking the truth?

She swallowed. "My brother is angry about Thor's death. As am I. But I plot no treachery against the Commander."

The Prince's sharp, discerning gaze held hers. Elwytha got the uncomfortable feeling he could look straight into her soul. It was good she had decided to abandon her treachery only an hour before.

The Prince retreated to his chair. He rested, indolent once more, upon the throne. However, his eyes remained like sharp obsidian—as if able to cut through every wall of deceit to find the truth.

Elwytha still felt shaken by the letter, but no longer knew what to think of it. Several lines disturbed her. But which? Certainly the condemning lines against the Commander. But hadn't she desired proof? Wasn't this it?

She didn't know what to think.

And now, what should she say to the Prince? Richard did plot treachery. But she did not know his true plan. Only that he wanted the Commander dead.

Elwytha felt more confused than ever.

"Princess," he said sharply. "Your thoughts tangle. You tarry too long with your response."

She licked her lips. "Prince, my brother speaks in riddles." True enough. "He's encouraging me to marry the Commander, although he knows I do not wish to do it. He's tired of war, and wishes for peace." However, likely a peace where he would be sovereign King.

Elwytha did not trust the Prince fully. Even a little, to be honest. Truth and lies tangled about her in a web so delicate a misstep would break it and the great spider would descend, eager to devour the unwitting participants. Did the spider signify her brother? Or a plot the Prince planned even now, against Richard? ...A counterplot she knew nothing about. Anything was possible.

"I'm hungry," she said. "I wish to take your leave."

"Very well." The black gaze did not release her. "But know I am watching you, Princess. My men are instructed to do the same. I will not be made a fool. Know that treachery on your part will invite the sword. You will not escape, and neither will your brother. Warn King Richard in your next missive."

Her heart thumped. This Prince was no fool, though he played at one. He wasn't a man to cross. Neither was his Commander. She inclined her head. "As you wish."

He flicked his fingers, dismissing her, and reclined more fully upon his throne. Before her eyes, she saw the Prince slip back into the cunning, mocking role he loved so well. "Do not disappoint me, Princess. Your head is much too pretty to adorn my flagpole."

With a shudder, she fled from the room, forgetting the required curtsey. That loathsome Prince! With a gasp, she shoved past the guards, out the door, and ran for the warm safety of the kitchen.

The Prince clearly suspected a plot. What a mess. She needed to study Richard's missive more closely to figure out what bothered her so much.

"Goodness, child," Mary said, when she burst into the kitchen. "You're running as if the very devil is after you."

Elwytha thought of the Prince. "Perhaps he is." She slipped onto the bench at the table, where her friend had already placed a trencher of bread, vegetables and meat. Now Mary delivered a cup of water.

The cook gave her a sharp look of her own. "Trouble, miss?"

Elwytha placed the parchment beside the trencher and reached for her spoon. "I received a letter from my brother, the King."

"Ach, did you." Mary returned to her stew pot. "Did he say something to upset you?"

Yes, he had. Elwytha spread it flat so she could look at it again. "He said he'll attend my nuptials on Monday."

"Mmm." Mary nodded. "And sign the peace agreement, as my husband reports to me?"

"Your husband?"

"Ach, yes. He's the prince's personal guard."

Elwytha wondered if she had seen him. But most of the guards wore helmets—a silly practice, and no doubt perpetuated by the game playing Prince. Perhaps he loved chess too much. "Really," she said, instead. "That's an important job."

"Me Henry is proud of it, and like to be I am, too. Except he's often home late of a night, especially when guests visit."

Elwytha could well imagine the Prince in his cups late into the night, jesting and sporting with his friends.

"Mary, I wanted to speak to you about refreshments for after my wedding."

"You want to plan the feast?" Interest sparked on the middle-aged woman's face. She wiped her hands on a towel. "Mayhap pastries? Tender legs of lamb?"

Elwytha's mouth watered at both suggestions. Too bad she wouldn't be here to partake of them. Richard would whisk her away first, abandoning the fake peace treaty. "Both sound heavenly. What of carrots with butter and a bit of honey?" One of her favorites.

"Good idea," the other woman agreed. "And plenty of ale to go round."

Elwytha smiled. "And perhaps fruit and loaves of fresh bread."

Mary rubbed her hands, and Elwytha could almost see the happy wheels turning in her head. "I'll ask maids from the village to help. And I'll need extra flour...." She trailed off, lost in thought.

"What can I do to help?" After all, it was a lot of work...for a wedding that wouldn't happen. Elwytha felt guilty for putting Mary to all that work for naught. "Perhaps it's too much. With pastries, we don't need bread as well."

"Nonsense! We will have it all. And I will not let you dirty your hands, miss," she scolded.

"But I must do something." Elwytha felt even more guilty. Would her conscience never let her be?

"Maybe you could decorate the dining hall. Perhaps leaves and a few flowers? I saw a handful of roses left in the garden. Hagma could help you."

The suggestion appealed. "Good idea."

"Just don't trouble your mind about the feast," the cook told her comfortably. "I've planned many in my day. It'll go without a hitch, it will."

Elwytha ate her food, listening to Mary happily hum. So, her wedding was planned. The Commander would deal with the priest and chapel, the food was planned, her dress decided, and she would decorate the hall. What more was there to do?

Except plan her escape route when she broke her word to the Commander. Knowing him, he wouldn't let her escape easily. Knowing her brother, he would be furious. They would both need an escape plan if Richard did something rash.

A knot settled in Elwytha's stomach. She could not foresee how it would all play out. She would take it one step at a time. But an escape route wasn't a bad idea...a contingency plan should the whole house of cards fall about her ears.

And that reminded her of Richard's letter. What bothered her so about it?

A quick read refreshed her memory.

This witness who'd seen the Commander murder Thor; who was he? Why had he only stepped forward now? And Richard's several references to her 'fate' and the 'sacrifice' she intended to make disturbed her, too. He couldn't reference her marriage, because that wouldn't take place. Then what did he mean?

These questions unsettled her spirit. As for the witness against the Commander...anger grew. It was strong proof that he truly had murdered her brother, after all. He had to be guilty. And yet how smoothly he'd lied to her. Elwytha felt sick. Again, she felt her world tilting off balance. She didn't know who or what to believe anymore.

ᛉ ᛉ ᛉ ᛉ ᛉ

Hagma and Elwytha altered more gowns that afternoon. Thoughts of the witness and the growing evidence of the Commander's guilt plagued Elwytha, resulting in several painful needle pricks as she worked. It did not improve her mood. In the evening, she donned the green dress, but made no effort to wait for her betrothed's escort to the dining hall. She would sup too nearly of his disturbing, confusing presence all evening. More, she could not stand.

The Prince rested upon his plumply cushioned chair as she arrived. She cast him an unfriendly glance and sat. Servers delivered food to the table, and Elwytha sipped water, ignoring him.

After a few minutes, she sensed the Commander behind her. He slid onto the bench and had the nerve to smile at her. "You look lovely this even, as always, Elwytha."

She glared at him, lips tight. A platter of food appeared before them and she helped herself to vegetables and broth, using her spoon to fill her trencher. The Commander watched silently as she did so. Usually he filled her plate for her, but she wished none of his false courtesies this evening.

She ate a carrot, softened by the stew juice. Delicious. After a moment, the Commander served himself, and then cut meat for himself, too. Elwytha ignored this, although she longed for meat, too. Unfortunately, she had no blade to slice off a bloody hunk.

The Commander's great hands moved slowly, assembling his meal, while Elwytha chewed next on bread. Finally, they stilled, and she felt his gaze upon her.

"Have I displeased you, Elwytha?" he growled in his uncommonly deep voice.

"Your presence displeases me," she retorted. "I cannot stand to look upon your lying countenance."

His fingers curled around her wrist, and she stared at them, displeased. "Unhand me."

"Look on me, Elwytha."

With reluctance she did so, still glaring, and he released her.

The steel gaze pinned her. "Speak what is wrong between us."

She scowled harder. "What is wrong is that you are a lying bastard."

He frowned now, which cast his mutilated face into fearsome lines. "I tell no lies. What are you speaking about?"

The Prince interjected, "The Princess received a letter from her trusted brother today." He gave a thin-lipped smile. "Truly, Princess, your heart seethes with contempt for all of your enemies."

Elwytha could not forget the Prince's earlier, horrifying threat. She clenched her fists, trembling with anger. "*You,*" she hissed down the table, "disgust me. I have committed no treachery against you, and yet you threaten to adorn your flagpole with my head. What a kind and gracious host you are!"

The Commander turned a frown upon his ruler. "Prince?" The rumble sounded too quiet.

The Prince sent Elwytha a narrow look. "I merely warned your fair princess that treachery against my crown has its price."

Anger flamed Elwytha's cheeks hot. "How weak you must be, Prince, to threaten a mere woman. Perhaps all of your preening airs have made you feel half a man. You wish to

bolster your manliness by threatening your unarmed guest!"
She shouted this last, trembling with rage.

Both the Commander and the Prince took a quick breath
and stared at her. Elwytha slammed down her spoon, but
grabbed a big hunk of bread. "I tire of you both," she told
them. "And if treachery is afoot, you, Prince, are plotting it.
And your murdering knave of a Commander will blindly and
brutishly carry it out."

She jumped up and stepped free of the bench, struggling
for majesty in her shaking anger. "I will be in my chamber,
should you wish my head this even, Prince."

Spinning on her heel, she exited from the dining hall with
smooth, regal steps. Inside, however, she longed to run from
their loathsome, frightening presences as fast as her feet could
take her.

Truly, she felt sickened and disappointed with the both of
them. She was honest enough to admit this. She'd begun to
trust...and even like the Commander. The Prince, while he
annoyed her, she'd found interesting and even amusing at
times. His verbal attack today in the throne room had hurt her,
and destroyed the fragile truce she'd thought existed between
them. Now he'd let his true colors fly. Never mind that her
brother meant treachery, and so had she. But no longer. Her
honor had come to her rescue. But no honor girded the
Commander or the Prince.

In her chamber, Elwytha burst into furious, wretched
tears. An all too common occurrence in this dark, snake's pit of
a hell.

∗ ∗ ∗ ∗ ∗

The Commander turned to the Prince with a frown.
Elwytha's hatred and fury had jarred him. He had thought
they had progressed beyond this in the chapel today. Now
things appeared worse than ever. And the Prince had
apparently played a role in it.

"You went too far, Prince."

"I must protect the palace. Treachery will be punished."

"You will not punish Elwytha. Even if she does commit treachery," the Commander said evenly.

"Really?" The Prince's eyes looked like black obsidian. "Then who will, Commander?"

"You will leave her in my hand."

The Prince watched him, and then finally gave a short nod. "As you wish, brother. But don't let her beauty blind you to her flaws."

The Commander said in a hard tone, "You scared her."

"As was my plan." He drank from his cup. "I would rather frighten her than make good on my threat."

"Maybe you should apologize."

The Prince's expression affected shock and dismay, but a small smile curled his lips. "Apologize? To my enemy?"

"Do you want her to hate us even more? What purpose would that serve—or do you intend to push her to commit treachery?"

"No. Her brother plots enough treachery for all of us."

"You are sure."

The Prince stared at him, his black eyes like coal, and all attempts at game playing vanished. "Push me no further, Commander. I will grant your request. But if you wish to know the true reason for Elwytha's distress, you must read the letter Richard sent. Don't let lust blind you to the truth about your future bride."

Fury rushed through the Commander, but he managed not to clench his fists. "Lust is not the only feeling a man can have for a woman. Don't let your jaded palate blind you."

A muscle clenched in the Prince's jaw. "You think I am so base?"

"I think you forget that women are not to be used and dismissed. As if garbage."

"I see," he mocked. "I hurt Elwytha's feelings. Do you care for her so tenderly, then?"

He clenched his fist. "Treat her with respect, Prince, or you will bring trouble on our heads."

"Your head, you mean."

The Commander took a breath. No one could win this confrontation. "Take no offense. I wish only for peace. Threats will not accomplish that goal."

"You forget yourself, Commander." The Prince's eyes were like black knives.

"I forget nothing...Prince. I ask your cooperation in this delicate matter with Elwytha. I believe if treated right, she will gladly carry through with the peace agreement. Is this your wish, as well?"

Pride stiffened the Prince's frame. His words cut like a sword, "Do not speak to me thusly again, old friend."

The Commander dropped his head just enough. "As you wish. I apologize."

His ruler relaxed infinitesimally. "I wish for no reason to scourge you."

The Commander smiled, then. "I do not wish it, either." Both knew this would never happen. The Commander was too respected and feared by his men. None would administer such a lashing to him, for fear of the consequence afterward. So the Prince would have to do it. They would battle with swords; a match which would produce a stalemate.

"I will speak to the Princess," the Prince said magnanimously, and speared up a bite of rabbit. "But only because you care for her so deeply, old friend. You must, to endanger the goodwill between us."

"I do. Thank you."

The Prince nodded, and said little for the remainder of the meal. The Commander thought about the letter Elwytha had received. What had Richard said to poison her mind against him? Tomorrow, he would find out.

CHAPTER TWELVE

ELWYTHA EXITED FROM HER CHAMBER the next morning prepared for battle. The previous night had elapsed in slow, restless misery. As she suspected, the Commander waited for her this morning.

He turned as she entered his chamber. His gaze held hers. "Good morn, Elwytha."

"Yes, truly I saw blue sky out my window," she agreed coldly. "I wish to go outdoors." Of course, she knew it would not be so simple.

"We will speak first."

"Have you concocted more lies to defend yourself?" Anger curled her lips, and she crossed her arms. "Mayhap you and the Prince stayed up half the night, plotting further lies and treachery against my crown."

"No. I would like to read the letter Richard sent you."

"You mean the Prince did not tell you, word for word?" she said sarcastically.

Patiently, he regarded her.

"Fine." She spun on her heel and retrieved it. If this was the only way she could escape his presence, then the quicker he read it, the better. It certainly wasn't a private missive anymore, not after the Prince's spying eyes had besmirched it.

Elwytha flipped it at him with her fingertips. "Take it. Read it. I await your lies." She waited, arms defensively crossed, while he did so. Again, she wondered how a man such as himself...to all appearances, little more than a serf...could read.

He finished. Grim lines tightened his mouth. "Write to your brother this morning. I want to know the identity of my accuser."

"No." Never mind if that had been her plan, as well. "You would ride on the witness and kill him. What would that prove? Except your guilt!"

He heaved a breath, and with pleasure she saw his fist clench. She'd cut him to the quick of his lying, corrupt soul. Elwytha pressed her advantage. "Nay. Your sword in Thor's back, and a witness... The evidence against you grows higher than a mountain. Why won't you admit the truth at last?"

"I did not kill your brother."

"Words, Commander. Proof evades you."

"I will learn the truth," he growled, stepping toward her. She stiffened her spine, but did not back up. "I'll speak to my accuser, face to face. And you will come with me."

Elwytha's mouth opened in surprise. "You want me to witness your atrocities? If I come, I will defend my countryman to the death."

The steel gray eyes cut into her like knives. He'd reached the end of his patience. "Write your brother," he ordered quietly. "Now."

Mutiny flared. "I will not deliver my countryman to death. I will not take part in treachery."

"I wish to *speak* to him, Elwytha." His deep voice cracked like a whip.

Her lip curled with disbelief. "You will not kill him? Tell me the truth!"

He heaved another great breath. "How little you think of me. I will not kill him, unless he pulls a blade on me first."

"And I should take your word? The word of a murderer and a liar?"

"Words. But no proof," he flipped her words back.

Tension radiated from his stiff shoulders, and his eyes were the color of cold steel. No warmth, no gentleness lurked in them today. And that was just as she wished it, she told herself. His gentleness was her undoing, and she could not allow that. She must remain strong.

Truthfully, it angered and sickened her to the very marrow that the new—no, *all* of the evidence—pointed to him being the despicable, murdering brute she had believed from the beginning. It must be true. Hurt, anger and confusion roiled within her.

"Do you plan to put pen to paper for me?" she inquired. "How will you force me to bend to your will this time?" Even more hurtful words flew to mind, and she spat them out, "Pray, what atrocities will your brutish side flay upon me? Tell me. I wish to know the fullest reaches of your depravity!"

"Elwytha!" Temper erupted and he gripped her wrists, pulling her to him. Fury burned in his gaze. "Do not speak to me in such a manner."

Alarm billowed. She had pushed him too far. Still, she dared to spit, "You wish for me to respect you? To obey all of your wishes and commands? Nay. I am a woman, not a dog. Don't treat me as such."

He stared down at her. "Elwytha," he said in a deep growl. If she didn't know better, she'd think he sounded pained. To her surprise, he released her wrists. "What will it take for you to trust me?"

An unexpected lump formed in her throat. "I need proof, Commander. Proof that you do not have."

"Allow me to face my accuser. It is the only way I can clear my name." A reasoning plea, now. Not a demand.

She searched his eyes. Frustration still lurked there, and anger...but those emotions were controlled again; tempered by his unending patience.

He was not a rash man, as her brother had accused. A rash man would not still be speaking reasonably to her now. What's more, he was far too controlled to kill someone in a rage.

More reluctant truths drifted in. The Commander had never harmed her. In fact, he had always treated her honorably. Wasn't this the least she could do...to give him a chance to prove his innocence?

"Very well," she said at last. "I will ask my brother to name your accuser. And I'll go with you when you question him."

A bit of tension relaxed out of his huge body. "Thank you."

"I will write the note now. Have you a parchment and ink?"

The Commander pulled the necessary items from a drawer, and Elwytha gathered them up. "I would like to write in peace," she said, and shut herself in her room.

Elwytha placed the parchment on her dresser and dipped the quill in ink. What should she say? How could she hint that she wouldn't battle and kill the Commander unless the witness provided infallible proof? Even then, could she? Would she?

Her quill hovered over the paper, and a great black drop sullied the center.

She would reveal nothing yet. First, the witness would show his hand. Then she would know for sure which actions she would take. As well, she needed to convey to Richard the Prince's warning. Elwytha dipped up more ink and wrote,

I received your letter, brother. I will fulfill my commitment to peace. The Prince says he desires peace as well. Beware. He suspects treachery from us both.

You speak of a witness to the Commander's cowardly act. Who is this witness? I wish to know his name. I await your answer.

I also await your arrival on my wedding morn...on the Monday you mentioned. Your loving sister, Elwytha

✝ ✝ ✝ ✝ ✝

The Commander paced his chamber, waiting for Elwytha to pen her missive. The anger and disappointment in her eyes had sickened him. And the disgust. He had thought they'd begun to make progress and grow closer together, but the letter from her brother had destroyed it all.

He balled his fists. The odds against him seemed to grow. Elwytha believed he had killed Thor. As well, their palaces were at enmity, and had been all their lives. He was her enemy, no matter who had killed Thor.

The Commander paced, frustration churning. He didn't see Elwytha as an enemy. He liked her; in fact, more every day. He longed for her, and wished she would feel the same way about him. But she felt disgust, instead. He had seen it when she'd glared at him this morning. Clearly, she still found him revolting. An ugly monster.

A low sound gurgled in his chest, and he shoved his hands through his hair...longer now, about a half inch. He'd need to shave it soon. A small part of his brain acknowledged this, while the larger part felt helpless impotence. What could he do to gain Elwytha's heart? Was it possible?

In the chapel, he had begun to hope. She had kissed him back, hadn't she? Or had it been only wishful thinking on his part?

The Commander heaved great breaths. He needed to fight. Only aggressive swordplay could release the hopeless frustration raging through him.

First, though, he would await Elwytha's missive...and he hoped she'd write plainly enough, with no hidden messages to her brother. He couldn't handle another fight with her. From the depths of his soul, he longed for peace between them, but how could he accomplish it?

The door opened and he deliberately relaxed his body posture. Elwytha exited, but her cold eyes froze his heart.

Anger arose then. Finally, the warrior surfaced and determination steeled his heart. Enough of the defeated thoughts. He would clear his name. He would fight to win, because the battle was far from over. He would try yet again...and again...to make this thing work between them.

⋊ ⋊ ⋊ ⋊ ⋊

With narrowed yes, Elwytha extended the rolled scroll to her betrothed. "You will wish to read it? And the Prince, too, of course."

The Commander unrolled it and scanned it quickly. "It will suffice," he granted, rolling it up again.

"I'm so glad to please you. Pray, may I leave now?"

He gazed at her for a long moment, as if trying to decide his answer.

She glared. "Or must I remain at your beck and call?"

"Elwytha." He moved closer, but she held her ground and refused to back up. To her dismay, he closed the distance between them. Only a spare foot separated his massive body from hers.

"Pray, what do you wish now?" she demanded. Her heart pounded unnaturally fast.

To her alarm, his warm hands closed around hers. "Peace, *ceisdein*." A demand, and a request. "I wish to have peace between us."

Elwytha's breaths quickened at his close presence...at his touch. The memory of their kiss in the chapel seared her mind. What was wrong with her? He had killed Thor! Two proofs secured this fact. Then why did she feel doubt? With difficulty, she forced out, "I feel only war in my heart."

"Do you? I know you think I killed your brother. I did *not*," he growled harshly, between his teeth.

"You have yet to prove it." She tugged free. Why did part of her believe him? How could she believe a heathen, enemy warrior? She could not!

"I will prove my honor, Elwytha."

"Until then, I do not wish to partake of your presence."

"Seven days remain until our marriage. I will spend them with you."

Dismayed, Elwytha's lips trembled. "Why won't you leave me be?" she cried out. "I've promised to marry you. What more do you want?"

"I want you, Elwytha. All of you." The fearsome face stared down at her, tempered only by the intelligence in his eyes.

Her heart thumped suffocatingly hard in her chest. He wanted her heart and soul, too—not just her body. She felt further dismay...and fear, that he might gain it. "You will not have me, Commander." He would have no part of her. She would not marry him. She would leave seven days hence, and never see him again. "I would like to go outdoors now."

He watched her for another moment, and then nodded. "I will ask your brother to send a reply with my horseman."

Elwytha took her leave. Soon they would know the identity of the witness. Soon she would know the Commander's guilt or innocence.

But for now she would seek escape routes to flee from her wedding. If she knew the Commander at all, escape would not be easy. As well, he might pursue her after she left the castle walls. She shivered at the thought—truthfully, at the thought she might want him to catch her.

Horrified, her slippered feet flew down the halls. Nay. Soon she would know the truth of the Commander's heinous crime. Then these ridiculous thoughts and feelings would die an equally brutal, vicious death. She prayed for the truth to come soon. Before it was too late.

⹋ ⹋ ⹋ ⹋ ⹋

Elwytha spent the morning scouring the castle grounds. Of course, she pretended to walk casually, as if taking the air. But her sharp eyes scanned every bulwark, every tower. She climbed the highest reaches of the castle and eyed the moat surrounding it. It wasn't deep, she determined. If worse came to worst she could swim to safety. Not her first choice, to be sure.

One thing became clear as she headed to the kitchen for lunch. To escape, the drawbridge must be lowered.

Carefully, she thought through her plan while chewing on the crusty bread Mary provided. Richard would sound his horn, indicating she was to kill the Commander. That thought shivered revulsion and horror through her. Even if she found proof of his guilt, could she battle and kill him? She feared not.

In any case, Richard would blow his horn, and the Prince would order the drawbridge lowered so her brother could enter the castle grounds. Instead, she would have Sir Duke saddled and ready, and she'd gallop to freedom, shouting for her brother to follow.

Elwytha smiled. Yes, it was a good plan. However, saddling Sir Duke and arriving at the drawbridge at the same time that her brother arrived might prove difficult. No, instead, she might need to leave her beloved horse behind, dash across the bridge and leap upon Richard's steed. Then they'd flee to safety.

Elwytha sopped up the last of her soup. Either way, she would escape the Commander and her wedding. Wasn't that her goal? To be freed of him forever? He wreaked too much disturbance in her soul. Once she fled from his presence, finally, she'd be able to think clearly again.

"You're awful quiet of a day, miss," Mary said, chopping vegetables at the huge table.

Elwytha started. "I'm sorry, Mary. I was...thinking."

"About your wedding, no doubt." The older woman's eyes twinkled. "That I can understand right enough."

A blush warmed Elwytha's cheeks. "Are you sure you don't need help with the feast? I still need to talk to Hagma about the decorations. I'm thinking we should gather up the leaves and flowers the day before? What do you think?"

"Yes." The cook nodded comfortably. "Friday would be a good day."

Elwytha frowned. "Friday? But the wedding is on Monday."

Mary blinked. "But the Commander spoke with me this very morning. Saturday, he said."

Saturday? Instant fury fulminated in Elwytha. She sprang to her feet. "I'm sure it's only a misunderstanding. I'll speak to him now."

"Let me know, lass. I'll need a few days to prepare."

"I'll tell you this afternoon," Elwytha promised. "Don't worry."

Seething, she exited. Her betrothed should certainly worry. She'd blister his ears with rage. How dare he change the wedding day? He'd agreed to Monday. She'd told Richard Monday. What was he thinking? Did he suspect her plans to bolt? Did he intend to plot in advance to thwart all of her moves?

Elwytha had worked up quite a steam of rage when a helmeted guard unexpectedly stepped before her. "The Prince would like to speak to you."

Elwytha glared, hands on her hips, at the gray mustached man. Could this be Mary's husband Henry, she wondered unexpectedly. But never mind. "I must speak to the Commander," she denied. "Tell his royalness I will attend to him later." She tried to move around him.

The older man's lance blocked her way. "I'm sorry, miss, but his highness said now."

Of course he had. Further fury gathered in her bosom. She heaved great breaths, trying to get a grip on her temper. What could that vile, game playing Prince want now? "Lead on," she said through gritted teeth, and strode after him to the throne room.

The man led her in, and then bowed deeply before the Prince, who for once sat upright on his padded throne. "Your highness...Princess Elwytha." The guard backed away, and Elwytha stepped forward. She made no move to curtsey.

"You summoned me, your imperial highness?" She didn't bother to hide her anger or scorn.

"No curtseys today, Princess?" The Prince regarded her from on high, for she made no move to ascend the royal steps.

"You wish for no deceit. I will give you no false adulation."

"You tread on dangerous ground, Princess."

"Are you more royal than I? Nay. A curtsey is a gesture of respect. You have lost all of mine."

He relaxed a little, and crossed his legs. "Because of my threat to hang your head upon my flagpole?"

Elwytha did not bother to reply.

"Your Commander took me to task for that thoughtless remark."

With surprise, she said, "He did?"

"Would it help if I apologized?"

Her eyebrows rose. "You would apologize to me?"

"I wish for peace. Commit no treachery within my palace, Elwytha, and all will be well between us."

This didn't sound like an apology to her. She bowed her head in an equally disingenuous manner. "Your warning is heeded. However, your humble apology evades me."

He smiled then, obviously pleased with himself. "You need not fear me, Princess. I leave you in the Commander's capable hands. Should you commit treachery, he will mete out your punishment."

Nerves fluttered through her at this revelation. The Commander had earned a reputation for brutal efficiency on the battlefield. All of his enemies usually fell by one vicious thrust of his sword. He could end her life just as quickly.

Faintly, she said, "I intend no treachery." Except to abandon her nuptials and the peace agreement. Neither was a crime worthy of the sword.

"Good," the Prince said. "Then you are ready to attend your nuptials on Saturday."

"Monday," Elwytha frowned.

"No." The Prince inspected a fingernail. "I convinced the Commander that Saturday would be a far better day."

Temper bubbled. So the change was the Prince's doing. "Why would you lower yourself to interfere in my wedding?"

He gave a small, thin-lipped smile. "Does Saturday displease you...or does it displease Richard?"

"I wish to have my brother attend my nuptials, Prince. How dare you deny me this right?"

"Richard may attend. But he will be notified on Friday evening. If he truly desires to attend his beloved sister's wedding, he will arrive on time."

Elwytha heaved an infuriated breath. "I am not ready to wed the Commander so soon. I have much to do. I..."

"No, Princess." He flicked dirt from beneath his fingernail. "Don't try to fool me. All is planned. Perhaps you wish the wedding anon, instead?"

Elwytha clenched her fists, feeling a helpless fury. How she longed to smack the Prince's implacable, mocking face.

"So we are agreed," he said. "Saturday it is."

Elwytha's lips felt numb, for she clenched them so tightly together. "If you have nothing further to say, I will take my leave," she ground out. In fact, immediately she would pen a new letter to Richard, warning him of the change. Somehow, she'd find a way to deliver it to him.

"You do not appear eager for your nuptials, Princess. Perhaps not for peace, either?"

How could she reply to this question? Elwytha wished only to escape from marrying the Commander. But by fleeing, she'd break the fragile peace. "I do wish for peace," she countered. "But the price is high."

"Has the Commander told you his name?" The Prince relaxed back, his sharp eyes watching her reaction to this bewildering subject change.

"No. But what has that got to do with anything?" Elwytha wondered then if the Prince had taken leave of his senses. Perhaps too much alcohol addled his brain. But no, his eyes looked too sharp, too keenly black. She crossed her arms and waited for him to unveil the new game he played.

"No? I will give you a hint, then. In the Bible, the balm of his name is referred to for the healing of the nations." He watched Elwytha.

She felt puzzled. "Are you suggesting his name is prophetic?"

"A priest told his mother that he'd had a vision. As a result, he gave her the Commander's name."

"Truly?" Elwytha said, amazed. "He's said nothing of it."

"No. But you haven't asked, have you?"

"Yes. Once..." But she hadn't really wanted to know. Or at least, she'd told herself that. "What is his name?"

"Ask him." The Prince refused to say, which didn't surprise her.

Elwytha returned to his earlier comments. "What do you mean by a balm of his name? How can a balm be made of a name?"

"His name was a country. In that country was a balm that the Bible suggests could heal the nations."

"And you're suggesting this balm...the Commander...will provide healing between our two lands?"

"The balm only heals if it is applied to the wound."

"The wound between our lands is deep, Prince," she said grimly.

The black eyes held her own. "Are you willing for restoration?"

"I do wish for peace."

"Your marriage will provide that peace. The future lies in your hands, Princess."

Much as she didn't want to admit it, the Prince spoke the truth. If she abandoned her wedding, she would abandon peace. More battles would commence. More death, more hatred...this was their chance, now, to end it all.

If her brother would allow it.

"You have much knowledge, Prince. Perhaps your idleness reaps some rewards. Maybe you have other pearls of wisdom to enlighten my mind?" She said this mockingly. Really, she wanted to escape from his presence and think on what he had told her.

"One more truth may capture your fancy."

With a sigh, she said, "I eagerly await your brilliant words."

He smiled, just the tiniest bit. "His name also means a mass of testimony."

"A mass of testimony. So he...the Commander...is a testimony?" This seemed farfetched to Elwytha. Likely, the Prince enjoyed too much leisure. How else could he cobble together such abstract ideas?

He shrugged. "Perhaps."

She decided to play along. "A testimony of what?"

"Of a past failure making right the present. A testimony between my father's land and yours."

"You speak in riddles," she told him. But a hidden message lived in his words. She sensed it, and she saw it, lurking in his black eyes. Still another game? Or a veiled truth? "Does it please you to play games *all* the time?" she wanted to know.

"My games are deadly serious, Princess. Surely you realize that by now."

"I realize you are not as simple as you might appear." Elwytha hesitated, waiting for the Prince to grasp the full depths of her scurrilous charge. His eyes hardened, and his lips thinned. She felt pleased. Her insult had scratched his black heart of stone. With a smile, she continued, "Nothing is simple with the Commander, either."

"True. The Commander says what he means. Perhaps to a fault...much like you."

"I believe you value plain speaking as well, Prince. It is better than lies, don't you think?"

He eyed her, his expression cool and menacing. "You do not wish to get on my bad side, Elwytha."

A little fear warned her to watch her words, but she did not heed. "Truly, I didn't know I had seen your good side."

"You are dismissed, Princess." His tone was sharp and cold. "Let the Commander enjoy your barbed tongue. He possesses far more patience than I." With a curt motion, he ordered the guard to escort her out.

Elwytha went willingly. She was glad she had irritated the Prince. It was the least he deserved after all the games he played. Not to mention his flagpole threat and presumptuously changing her wedding date.

Her wedding was only five days away. Elwytha felt a small bit of panic. She would write Richard now. Her steps slowed as she approached the kitchen. She should tell Mary the news, as she'd promised. Reluctantly, she stepped through the doors to do so.

True, the Prince would have his way, but she would still escape his Commander. What difference did two days make? None, as long as she got her missive to Richard in time. She didn't trust the Prince to tell Richard by Friday evening. No. She would not leave her fate in the hands of that capricious ruler.

CHAPTER THIRTEEN

ELWYTHA SLIPPED PARCHMENT and ink from the Commander's drawer and quickly wrote her letter to Richard. Then she carefully replaced all the items and slipped the missive into her pocket. Neither the Commander nor the Prince could know of this letter, or they would destroy it. She'd carry it until such time as she found a trustworthy messenger to send it. Where she might find one in this palace, she did not know. However, she would be prepared at all times.

Hagma appeared soon after, and they finished altering the last of the dresses. Elwytha asked if the maid would help decorate the great hall.

"Of course," Hagma gasped, hand to her throat. Clearly, she felt honored. "What will we do, miss? Have you ideas already?"

"Mary suggested leaves and flowers. What do you think?"

"Lovely," Hagma agreed. "And what of bowls of floating candles? We could place the flowers in them, as well. The roses would look ever so lovely lit like that."

Elwytha smiled. "I knew I should ask you. You're so creative, like your mother."

"Oh, no, miss." Hagma cast down her eyes. "It will be fun. I'd like to help make your wedding beautiful." She added shyly, "You've both been so kind to me."

Elwytha could not think of any kindnesses she had bestowed upon Hagma. "I haven't..."

"But you have," Hagma interrupted, and then bit her lip. "You treat me as an equal, and the Commander...I always thought he was fearsome. I was scared to work here. But he's ever so nice to me. He looks a bit rough, but he's got a heart of pure gold, he does, miss. You are so lucky."

Elwytha's heart twisted at Hagma's words. She believed them, too. But what of her brother? How could the Commander not be guilty of his blood? How could he possibly prove himself innocent?

Elwytha dropped her head and bit off the last piece of thread. She lifted her blue dress. "The Commander should like these alterations, don't you think?" she asked with a small, uncertain smile. She had replaced the old, frayed embroidery for new, and she'd allowed the modest hint of bosom to remain.

Hagma smiled. "Perfect for your wedding, miss."

Elwytha nodded and folded it away. Her wedding. The Prince contended it would heal their lands. Elwytha felt torn and utterly confused. Should she marry the Commander? ...Only for the sake of peace, of course.

Not that she would marry a murderer. First, she would see what the witness said. Only afterward could she choose. Moreover, if she did decide to marry him, she would need to convince Richard to agree to the peace.

The whole messy situation seemed impossible to set right.

Elwytha forced her mind back to planning her questionable wedding. "Shall we gather the leaves on Thursday?"

"Nay, miss. I have another idea. My mother has several warrior friends who will gather them for us. Perhaps they can gather them Thursday? Then we can decorate on Friday."

"Good idea. We can gather the flowers on Friday, too," Elwytha suggested. "Perhaps in the morning, and we can decorate in the afternoon."

Hagma nodded. "A fine plan." With a pleased smile, she took her leave.

Elwytha viewed her dresses, packed in her trunk. All were altered now. All modest. None would cause a knave's eye to wander...or the Commander's either. Good. Just as she wished.

With a sigh, she pulled out a deep purple gown and changed for the evening.

ᚹ ᚹ ᚹ ᚹ ᚹ

Elwytha heard the Commander enter his chamber. He had left her alone all day. It was the first time ever, and while this should please her, it troubled her. Perhaps her words had been too sharp this morning?

But what if they were? Wasn't he a lying knave?

Or was he? Elwytha just didn't know. She felt so confused. And while she'd prefer not to see him tonight, it was a fool's wish, as was her perplexing, illogical desire to trust him. Neither would be granted her.

After allowing him time to change, she exited from her room. Already her stomach rumbled in anticipation of the evening meal.

Confoundingly, her heart leaped when she saw him. The Commander stood with his broad back to her, facing his highly polished metal mirror. On the table was a basin, and he held a shaving blade in his hand.

He lifted the blade to his wet black hair.

"Leave it," she blurted, horrified at the thought of him shaving himself bald again.

The Commander turned, brow raised in surprise. He ran a palm over his prickly looking dark hair. "It pleases you?"

"Why do you shave it?" Why was she interfering, would be a better question.

"I've done it since I was a boy. My mother said it was easier to wash. The lads thought it made me look fearsome."

"And you wish to look fearsome."

"It's an advantage on the battlefield." He gestured to his mutilated face. "It's not hard to convince others." After a hesitation, he lowered the blade to the wash stand and wiped his fingers on the towel.

"You won't cut it?" Elwytha felt amazed, and also uneasy. "Don't change your habits on my account."

"I will leave it, if it pleases you."

She blinked at him, wondering yet again why she had spoken. Why should she care one way or another?

He pressed deeper. "Does it please you?"

Elwytha took an uncertain breath, unwilling to surrender an inch of ground to her foe. "It makes you look more human," she said flippantly. "A man like any other." That was a lie. The Commander was like no man she had ever met, hair or no hair.

He regarded her with patience in his eyes. "Then I will leave it."

She turned away. "Please yourself. I wish to sup now. Are you coming?"

Though he did not answer, she felt his presence close behind her as she headed for the door.

≬ ≬ ≬ ≬ ≬

At the evening meal, she allowed the Commander the courtesy of filling her trencher. Silently, she ate beside him. A glance took in the Prince, eating quietly, which was unusual. She wondered what plots roiled in his troublesome head now. Perhaps in her secret missive to Richard she should warn of possible trickery on the Prince's part.

Elwytha ate little, although she'd felt hungry earlier. Her troubled, conflicted thoughts and feelings made her feel vaguely sick. She longed to know the truth about the Commander once and for all. Was he a fearsome, murdering monster, or the gentler man she had come to know? Gentle on occasion, but not soft. There was nothing soft about the man at her side.

He regarded her now with concern in his eyes. "Have you a pain? Why don't you eat?"

"I'm fine." Elwytha forced herself to take another bite of bread. The sound of running footsteps caught her attention.

An armored man, parchment in hand, dashed across the hall and stopped behind the Commander, breathing hard.

"The return message you required, sir," he said, handing it over.

"Good work. Go fill a trencher. You must be hungry."

"Yes, sir!" The lad rushed off with a glad smile for the praise.

Elwytha saw her brother's seal on the rolled parchment. It was the return reply to her letter. "That was fast," she said, amazed. They'd sent it this morning, and here was the reply this even. She had expected it sometime tomorrow at the earliest.

The Commander's gaze held her own. He pushed the parchment into her hand. "Open it."

"You will allow me to read it first?" Elwytha felt further amazement. Of course, she knew he would read it next. Quickly, she broke the seal and unrolled the parchment. Her brother had penned few words.

Why do you wish to know, sister? But since you ask so prettily, I will tell you it is the hermit Daniel, who lives in the far mountains. I require your allegiance, Elwytha. Believe no lies of the enemy. Richard

The hermit! Unthinkingly, Elwytha passed the missive to the Commander. She had thought Thor had been murdered closer to the Prince's land, to the south. Perhaps the hermit had been wandering at the time?

After reading it, the Commander passed the scroll to the Prince. He turned to her, elbows on the table, massive shoulders leaning forward. "You know of this hermit?"

"Yes," she admitted. "Sometimes in the summers we would vacation up near the loch. My family has a small house there." Small, in that it was a two story thatched hut with ten rooms. "I've spoken to him several times."

The Commander's gaze held hers. "Is he a man of character?" he rumbled quietly.

Elwytha thought back. "I don't know. He was nice, but easily spooked. He's old," she explained. "I'm surprised he's still alive."

"We will visit him on the morrow."

"It will be a hard ride," she warned. "At least six hours from here."

"Then we will stay the night. Will your house be open?"

"Yes," she faltered. "But no one will be there. We close it up for the winter."

"All the better," he said grimly. "Pack a warm cloak. I'll see to provisions."

Elwytha felt uneasy on a number of levels. Going on a journey with the Commander and staying overnight in an abandoned cottage, alone with him, was not the least of it. But something else about the whole situation disturbed her.

"You look uneasy, Princess," the Prince said. "Pray, share with us your misgivings." The black eyes looked sharp.

She glanced at the Commander. She had no wish to walk into a trap...and no desire to deliver him into one, either. She licked her lips. "The loch is in a valley. There are only two ways in—over the mountains, or through the pass. It's shorter through the pass."

"You suspect a trap," the Commander said at once.

"No." Elwytha shook her head. "I don't suspect anything. I just feel...uneasy. And my brother was killed far south from there. At least, I thought he was." Troubled, she fell silent.

"A trap, Commander?" the Prince said. "Would you secure your honor at such a high cost?"

The Commander glanced back at Elwytha. "I would."

Misgivings roiled inside her. "We will go over the mountains," she decided. "I know the way well. Often, I rode alone on horseback during the summers. I believe I know a safe route."

"You will place your life in Elwytha's hands," the Prince remarked. "Do you trust her so greatly?" Clearly he would not, if that sharp, cynical look in his obsidian eyes was any indication.

"I will be armed," the Commander said, and that was the end of the discussion.

Elwytha fell silent, and picked at her bread. Surely her brother didn't plan a trap. Did he suspect her reluctance to kill the Commander? Perhaps so, for she had demanded the witness's name. She had demanded further proof of the Commander's guilt. If Richard suspected she was unwilling to kill her betrothed, would Richard take it upon himself to do so? And what would she do if her own countrymen attacked them while they traveled in the mountains? Who then would she fight for? Her brother, or the Commander?

One week ago that question would never have entered her head. The fact that it did now, disturbed her greatly.

CHAPTER FOURTEEN

THE NEXT MORNING, Elwytha packed a small bag with the basic necessities, fastened her thick woolen cloak with a ruby broach, and joined the Commander at the stables after breakfast. He wore a thick jerkin of leather armor, studded with metal—but no helmet, she noted, watching him saddle his horse. The black snorted, releasing white puffs into the cold air. Elwytha was glad of her fur-lined cloak. Cold nipped her nose and cheeks. Winter had at last arrived.

A stable boy had already saddled Sir Duke, so she tied on her leather bag and swung astride. She noted a pouch hanging from the other side of her saddle. A water skin and rations, she assumed.

Now the Commander swung astride his own steed. He looked huge and fearsome in the armor. His long-sleeved tunic and pants were black, and matched his hair. He wore his dagger and two swords hung from his belt, one on each hip.

No armor for Elwytha, but she should not need it in her own land. Then why did she wish for weapon?

She felt nervous about the trip ahead. Little slumber had relaxed her mind last night. Troublesome worries tangled her thoughts. No answers. Only questions. Perhaps today the greatest of her questions would be answered—the truth of the Commander's guilt.

Again, she wondered if he would go to all this trouble to prove his innocence if he were guilty. Riding into the enemy land, he could be a lamb to the slaughter, for all he knew.

But he would not be, Elwytha determined. She would protect him from her brother's men. She would receive an answer to her questions.

How she longed for a sword!

The horses clopped across the drawbridge. Elwytha drew alongside her betrothed. "Why don't you wear a helmet?"

"I never wear a helmet."

"Thus your scar?"

"Thus my scar," he agreed. "I cannot see well with a helmet on. I want to see every enemy. And every attack before it hits me."

Elwytha smiled. How like him to be aware of every situation...to plan and finish battles in his mind before they ever began.

"Shall we race to yonder stand of trees?" she asked with a grin.

He smiled.

She leaned forward and pressed her knees into Sir Duke's sides. With a joyful leap, he sprang into a gallop. The cold wind sliced icy fingers through Elwytha's scalp as she stretched low on Sir Duke's neck, urging him on with soft words. Hooves thundered, and she felt a wild, primitive joy surge as they sped across the plain.

The Commander's steed raced beside her, and she slid a glance at his rider. A small smile edged his lips as he cast her a glance, too. He sported with her. Just as she realized this, the black charged ahead. Sir Duke seemed to sense the game, for he doubled his stride, his great, valiant heart straining for the win. They closed a little of the distance.

All too soon the trees approached, and Elwytha pulled up on the reins. A race through the forest would prove too dangerous. She couldn't risk Sir Duke breaking a leg. They trotted up to join the Commander.

"A fine steed you have," Elwytha said, graciously conceding the win.

"As is yours."

She smiled and patted Sir Duke's neck. "Never a better."

The Commander set a quick pace through the forest, and then they cantered through the grassy hills on the other side, steadily heading toward the mountains ahead.

By lunchtime they had reached the foothills, and they dismounted by a fast flowing burn to feast on lunch while the horses nibbled grass.

They ate silently for a time, while Elwytha cast about for things to say. It wasn't hard. Questions bubbled within her. She wanted to know more about the man beside her; ill-advised as that may be.

Her teeth crunched into a red, juicy apple, and she licked her lips when juice dripped. "How did you learn to read?"

His lips curved a tiny bit. "You wish to know about me, Elwytha? You want to be friends now?"

"Have we ever been friends? But I confess curiosity. Tell me how you learned."

"I wished to learn," he said. "As a boy, I saw the King reading missives. I wanted to do the same. One day, at sword practice, I mentioned it to the Prince. He told me to come the next day to his school room."

"The King allowed it?"

"He knew nothing about it. Not then. The priest didn't want to teach me, and complained to the Queen. She ordered me back to the stables."

He fell silent, and Elwytha again felt compassion for the boy he had been; fatherless, mocked, and denied the education he desired. "So what happened?" she encouraged.

"The Prince spoke to the King. He decided to allow it."

Amazed, Elwytha said, "Why?"

"It pleased the Prince. And the King approved of my sword skills. He thought me a fitting companion for the Prince to sharpen his sword against."

"Who is better, after all these years? You, or the Prince?"

He smiled. "We are evenly matched. Both the best in the land."

Elwytha well believed this, after battling him with sticks the other day. "Was the Queen displeased to be overruled?"

"Yes. But her health was failing, so she said no more. She'd always been frail. She died a year later."

"So that's why the Prince has no brothers or sisters."

The Commander turned to pluck an apple from his sack. "Yes," he said in a low voice.

"Interesting," she said, and finished her own apple.

"What of you, Elwytha?" he said. "You are learned as well. Unusual for a woman. Were you a fine student, or did you skip letters to practice with the daggers?" His gray eyes met hers, and they lightened to pure silver when he smiled.

Elwytha couldn't help but grin back. "How well you know me after so little time, Commander. In fact, my brother Thor is the one who insisted I learn from the priest. I enjoyed it, but escaped at every opportunity I could to battle my brothers in the yard."

"Your father allowed it?"

Elwytha waved a hand. "He didn't care. I could be an imbecile for all his notice. He did approve of my battle skills, though. So I tried to please him with that." She tossed her apple core to Sir Duke. "And I learned my letters at the same time. I couldn't allow my brothers to be more learned than I."

"A pure motivation."

"Sneer not at me, Commander. I am as well learned as any man. Perhaps more so than you," she added slyly.

"The Prince's tutor taught me everything he knew," he returned mildly. "I determined to learn it. I wished for every drop of knowledge."

"How pure of heart you are, Commander. And, I grant, far cleverer than I thought when I first met you."

He smiled, then. "You approve something about me."

"Yes, I respect you. I think you know that."

His gaze held hers. "Now I need only to clear my name?"

Her breath caught at his implication. "And I would be your willing wife?"

"Would you?"

Elwytha's heart beat faster and she looked away. "I don't know. I can make no decisions until I know the truth."

His calloused fingers touched her chin, urging her to meet his gaze again. She stared at him, not knowing what to say. Tumult swirled through her heart. Her hand closed around his wide, strong wrist.

"I will make no promises I cannot keep," she whispered, and tugged it down to her lap. She glanced down at his hand, with hers over its top. His was large and brown and well sculpted. Hers was smaller, and a lighter brown. Upsetting the balance, his fingers curled over hers, dwarfing them. She felt secure and protected with his warm hand holding hers. Unsettlingly so.

She tugged hers free. "It's time to ride. Or we won't arrive until sundown."

Ⓧ Ⓧ Ⓧ Ⓧ Ⓧ

The horses picked their way to the top of the mountain. The wind bit, strong and icy at the top of the ridge. Below them lay the dark blue loch. In the distance, she glimpsed her family cottage in a spot cleared of trees. Other huts dotted the far shore, but no smoke rose from any of them. Snow would fly soon, and no one wanted to be trapped in that private cove with no avenue available to deliver supplies.

Except for the hermit, of course.

Huddling inside her cloak, Elwytha took the lead, following an old, remembered path down the other side of the mountain. If she remembered correctly, it would pass near the hermit's hut. Perchance he would be home. Otherwise, they would need to search for him on the morrow.

Her ears began to hurt from the freezing cold, and she tugged her hood tighter under her chin. "Good boy, Sir Duke," she murmured to her champion steed. "You remember the way, don't you, boy?"

Gray clouds wisped on the far horizon, and Elwytha shivered. At these temperatures, it could snow. It was still early for it, but one never knew. If it did snow, they'd have to leave through the pass. The mountainside would be too treacherous.

They dipped down now, to the tree line. Ash, birch and oak trees blocked a little of the wind. Elwytha's fingers were red and cold now, and her nose dripped in a most unladylike fashion.

So far, she'd seen no sign of anyone. No hermit. No tracks of warriors laying a trap. All was silent in the wood. Russet leaves drifted to the ground, and the crisp, pungent scent of earth smelled heavenly.

In a level area, the Commander moved alongside her. "How much further?" His ears looked red, as did his bent nose. At least now he had a little hair to warm his head.

Elwytha gestured ahead. "Down a few more turns. Then right at a huge boulder."

He nodded, but continued at her side, scanning the woods as they rode. She sensed caution in his posture, and she sharpened her ears, listening as well.

Nothing, except a few chattering red squirrels and the twitter of a bird high above.

The boulder was exactly as she remembered it, Elwytha was glad to see. As high as a horse, it sat like a huge, squat triangle. Leaves decorated the top.

"Now just a little further," she said, and again took the lead. Here was a faint trail, worn by the hermit. She saw no horseshoe prints. No tracks at all, except for those of a wild goat.

At last, ahead, she saw the familiar corrie, and then the dilapidated, leaning hut tucked into the hollow. Smoke curled out of the chimney, and relief filled her. He was home.

Elwytha dismounted and tied Sir Duke to a branch. "Daniel?" she called. "It's Princess Elwytha. I've come to visit you."

Silence. The Commander dismounted, too. His massive presence beside her gave her a feeling of security in the uneasy silence.

Elwytha stepped closer. "Daniel?" The Commander put a hand on her arm, stopping her.

"Let him come out. Go no closer."

It seemed like a good plan. She had no desire to enter that precarious hut.

Elwytha heard a faint sound behind her, and spun. She saw the flash of the Commander's sword, and then a high cry as an old man huddled against a tree. His arms covered his face, and white hair stuck out in all directions. He wore ragged, filthy clothes. A dagger gleamed at his belt.

"We wish peace," the Commander said, resheathing his weapon.

Elwytha spoke soothingly. "Daniel? Do you remember me? It's Elwytha."

The old man peeked over his crossed wrists. One eye looked a rheumy blue, and the other, a dark brown one, stared off in a completely different direction.

"Princess Elwytha? Truly, it is you!" The hermit lowered his arms and grinned, revealing one snaggly tooth. "It's been too long since you visited your old friend."

"True. We couldn't make it up here the last few years, because of the wars." She glanced at the Commander. "And then Thor died."

"Aye, Thor." The old man ambled closer, clutching a walking stick in one gnarled hand. She moved aside and the hermit continued toward his hut. "Would you like a hot cuppa? I've a nice bark tea this year." He cast a wolfish grin over his shoulder. "But only for those with a stern stomach. Perhaps not for you, Princess?"

"We can't stay. I need to ask you about Thor's death."

"Eh?" The hermit continued his snail's pace to the door.

"Daniel, I need to ask you a question. Please stop," Elwytha entreated.

With seeming reluctance, the old man did as she asked and turned to face them again. "Ask your question, then, Princess."

"Did you see him killed?"

The old man rubbed the knob of his walking stick. "Aye. Who wants to know?"

"I do," Elwytha said, not allowing the Commander to speak. She cast him a warning glance. "Where did he die?"

"Yonder." Daniel waved vaguely toward the south. "I hunted for squirrels. That's how I came across them."

"Who?" she pressed.

"Your brother. And his murderer. A great hulking man, he was. Fearsome and bald as the moon. He stabbed Thor in the back, vicious as a snake. Thor never saw it coming. Never saw it coming," he muttered.

Elwytha glanced at the Commander. "Would you recognize the man if you saw him again?"

"Oh, rightly so. Rightly so." The old man glanced at the Commander, but no recognition flickered.

"You're sure?" she pressed.

"Sure enough." He fluttered an impatient hand near his ear, as if irritated. "Why all the questions? Leave an old man in peace. Come have tea." He turned back toward his hut.

Elwytha wanted to partake of nothing in that filthy hut. "Thank you, but we can't. The sun will go down soon. We need to find shelter."

The hermit turned slowly, and this time he fixated upon the Commander. "Take good care of our princess, young man. These woods aren't safe. No. No, they're not." He frowned, and his good eye slid to and fro, as if testing the forest, looking for evil.

"I will," the Commander rumbled. "We will take your leave."

"Thank you, Daniel," Elwytha said softly. "Take care of yourself."

The hermit pushed a hand toward her, as if to shoo her off. "Don't worry about me none, Princess. I keeps my place. And happy I am if I do as I'm told. Go home now. And Godspeed with you." He turned and staggered into his house and slammed the door.

Unease filled Elwytha, and she turned to the Commander. "Maybe we should head back now. We still have an hour of light." She suddenly didn't want to descend to the loch. It felt like a pit. A trap.

"It may snow tonight. No shelter awaits us over the mountain."

"I feel that something is wrong," she whispered, and looked up at him pleadingly. "Can we not go home?"

"We would go to your home, the cottage." He regarded her. "Or is it your home no longer?"

Elwytha had meant home as the Prince's palace, where she felt safe. Why didn't she feel safe in her own land?

She touched his arm. "Commander." She could give no words to her feelings; for her desire to keep him safe and alive. "Please."

"Do you know of shelter over the mountain?"

"I know of a cave."

"A cave." His steely gaze weighed her words, considering them. He was fully the Commander now, assessing the situation. Choosing the best plan. "Where?"

"On the other side of the ridge. Further north a half hour, maybe."

"It would be dark before we reached it."

And treacherous. He didn't have to say it. And the cave would be cold, especially if it snowed. They had no blankets.

His gaze gentled. "I will not let you freeze to death. We will go to the loch. But we will stay in one of the other huts, and make no fire until dark."

Elwytha nodded. She didn't like it, but saw no better option.

* * * * *

The Commander selected a hut on the far side of the loch, remote from the others. Elwytha inspected the shack while he led the horses deep into the forest, which would help shelter them, should it snow. He had brought horse blankets for them as well, Elwytha was glad to discover. She could rest easier this night, not having to worry about Sir Duke's comfort.

The shack consisted of one room with no windows. It reminded her of the hunter's cottage where they had sheltered from the rainstorm last week. Discomfort poked at her, remembering the closeness they had shared on that occasion. It would not happen again, she told herself.

Logs were stacked next to this fireplace, too, and she assembled kindling in readiness for a fire later. Crude shelves held a pot and spoon. Blankets were stacked in a corner. It contained none of the fine comforts of her family cottage, but it would shelter them for the night.

Elwytha still felt uneasy. They had encountered no one as they had descended the mountain in the deepening twilight. No signs of horses or men in the peat at the loch's edge. The Commander had led them around the loch by threading through the forest. Hopefully, few prints would betray their passage. Soon it would be too dark for anyone to track them. And still she'd seen no one.

If her brother's men came, they would traverse the pass, she knew. And here, at the far end of the loch, they were far from the pass. If men came, hopefully birds or other noises would betray their presence before they came upon Elwytha and the Commander.

Were her brother's men coming? Why did she feel so suspicious and uneasy? Didn't she trust Richard?

Not really, she had to admit. Treachery lurked in his heart. In fact, she had agreed to participate in one of his treacherous plans. He could plot still more. Elwytha wished she knew what her brother was thinking.

The Commander entered the dim cottage, and immediately the small room felt even smaller. He left the door open to allow light to enter.

"I've readied wood for a fire," she offered, retreating to the stack of blankets she'd dragged near the fireplace. She sank onto them now, and wondered about their cleanliness. Perhaps she'd sleep with her cloak next to her body, with the dubious blankets on top.

The Commander sat across from her and pulled food from his pack. "We'll leave at first light," he told her.

Elwytha ate as well, leaving food for breakfast the next morning. Outside, night closed in. She could barely make out the Commander, a few feet from her, and already the cold bit into her bones. She sat huddled, arms crossed, burrowed down in the blankets.

"Will you start the fire now?" Her teeth chattered.

After a moment, she saw a dim movement as he moved toward the fireplace. He seemed to move reluctantly.

"Don't you want a fire?" she asked.

"I wish for warmth. But I don't want the smell of smoke to give away our location."

"Do you think anyone would search now, at night?"

Again the small hesitation, which didn't inspire comfort. "Likely not." A light flickered in the darkness, and then an orange flame licked up from the bits of brush she had laid in the grate.

"You've laid a fine fire," he said quietly.

Elwytha felt pleasure at his words. "Thank you."

The fire burned brighter, and he added one log at a time, building its stability and heat. Elwytha huddled closer, relishing the warmth.

"How many blankets have you?" he asked.

"Oh!" With a start, Elwytha realized he was probably cold, too. Kneeling on the floor, she pulled them to the space between them. "Four," she said with satisfaction. "Plenty for each of us." She took two and draped them about her shoulders.

The Commander didn't touch his. Instead, he tended the fire, and nudged the burning logs with a stick to keep the spark showers confined to the stone hearth.

He looked at her, and firelight cast his fearsome features into shadows. "Have you found your answers?" he asked, his deep voice calm.

Elwytha's heart jerked a little faster. "Daniel described you, and your vicious blow that killed my brother."

"No. He did not recognize me, and I stood right before him."

"You have hair now. Maybe that is why."

"Maybe because the man he saw wasn't me. If indeed he saw anyone at all."

"You suggest he was lying?" Although Elwytha sounded incredulous, the thought had crossed her mind as well.

"He spoke too quickly. As though he had memorized his part well."

A breeze blew through the open door, and she rose to shut it. "Speaking quickly is no proof of a lie," she pointed out.

However, she did recall hearing Daniel mutter that he'd be happy if he did as he was told. Could someone have told Daniel what to say? It seemed farfetched. Indeed, it strained the reaches of credibility. Who would do such a thing? And why? And why would Daniel comply? Unless he'd been threatened to do so.

The door flapped open after she'd closed it. She shoved it shut once more.

"Still, you will not believe in my innocence?" Frustration growled through the deep voice. The door slammed open again, and he rose to join her.

She did not answer, but hugged the blankets tighter to herself as he tested the door. He took the spoon from the shelf and jammed it underneath. Now it stayed shut. Elwytha moved closer to the warm fire.

"Why does proof evade you, Commander? Maybe because none exists. Perhaps you should give up."

"I will never give up," he growled. "I am innocent. I wish for you to believe me."

"You want me to trust you."

"Yes." In the firelight, his gaze held hers. Part of her did believe him. Why couldn't she say that?

At last, she admitted. "I found Daniel's testimony questionable, as well. I will consider the evidence, and tell you what I decide."

The Commander looked away, and again it was one of those rare times when the mutilated half of his face became blacked out in the shadows. She saw only his good side, with its angles and planes, light and shadow...the thick black hair, now a finger width long, the dark slash of his straight brow, and his eye in shadow, black as midnight. His expression was grim, and fearsome.

A stab of recognition shocked through Elwytha. It was as if she knew him—or he reminded her of someone she'd seen before. But who?

Her heart pounded as she stared at him. Something told her it was critical not to miss this. Who was he?

Then he frowned and fully faced her, and he was the Commander once more.

"Why do you stare at me in such a way?" he rumbled.

Jolted from her perplexed trance, she blinked. "No reason."

"Still no honesty between us, Elwytha?"

His displeasure bothered her. "You just reminded me of someone, for a moment. I don't know who," she said. "See? No big secret."

He moved closer. "You do not know who?"

She frowned. "Should I?"

"No," he said after a moment. "You should not."

She frowned harder. What riddle was this? "Verily, speak the truth to me."

"I want to be your husband," he said evenly, with a dark touch of an unknown emotion. "What more do you wish to know?"

She wanted to know nothing about him, she told herself.

"Your name," she said. "I want to know your name." A mistake, she knew it, as soon as the foolish words departed from her lips. The situation was too intimate now, with the two of them alone together. But she did not retract her words.

"You wish to know my name." He moved still closer, but she did not back away.

"Yes," she returned, her eyes narrowed. "Just tell me. Is it so awful? Is that why you won't tell me?"

He stopped a mere breath from her, and she looked up at him. A little of the old fear flared for this big man. She topped his shoulder, but only just. His size was massive, but consisted of only pure muscle. No fat would dare find purchase on his intimidating form.

His hands closed around hers, feeling warm and solid. Alarm skittered through her, but she wouldn't look away from him.

He said, "You say you distrust me. Then why don't you flee from me?" His eyes looked a dark, smoky color.

"I'm not scared of you." A lie, but she remained still, determined to show it as the truth. For it to be the truth.

"My name is Gilead."

"From the Bible? The Prince hinted that to me."

"Yes. A priest had a vision. He told my mother my name should be Gilead. It means rocky and strong. A mass of testimony."

"That story sounds like a testimony of its own. Your mother must have had high hopes for you."

"She envisioned me leading the warriors."

"And you do."

A shadow flitted across his features. "She never saw."

"I'm sorry." And she was. "My mother died in childbirth when I was one year old. The babe perished, too. Do you have any other brothers or sisters?" she asked on impulse.

"My mother bore no more children."

"Oh." What a lonely childhood. At least he'd had the Prince for a friend. Doubtless others, as well.

She realized he still held her hands. She tugged at them. "It's late. I...I wish to sleep."

He did not release her. Instead, he leaned forward and kissed her. The sensation burned, like popping, fizzling rain on hot metal. Her pulse accelerated. She swayed into him just as he broke the contact.

Alarmed, she blinked up at him. He watched her, appearing to measure her response. Heat bloomed on her face, and she tugged her hands free. "I would like to retire. Goodnight."

"Goodnight, Elwytha." His deep tone resonated through her soul, following her as she huddled into her blankets, on the far side of the fire. She closed her eyes, trying to pretend he wasn't there.

What was wrong with her? She had enjoyed his kiss yet again.

Wasn't he Thor's murderer? Again, she reminded herself of this disturbing possibility.

Then why didn't she believe he'd done it any longer? Why would her heart blind her mind to the truth?

Confused, she buried her face in her arms. The fire crackled nearby, and she heard the soft movements of her betrothed wrapping up in his blankets and settling down for the night.

Complication after complication twisted through her relationship with the Commander. Gilead. She rolled it around in her mind. It suited him, in an odd sort of way.

She recalled his kiss, and his hands holding hers, gentle as always, although clearly he felt frustrated with her this evening. Because no proof had been found to vindicate him. She thought back over the days she had known him. He had never hurt her, except for when she had struggled to gain her weapons or attack him. Even then, she knew from experience that he had exerted only the minimum force needed to protect himself.

She thought about the way he treated his men. The honesty ingrained, deep in his soul. Even her clear half-truths displeased him. Could he be more honorable than she?

No. Wasn't he a heartless killer?

Or was he?

Could he be telling the truth about her brother's death? If he was, then who had murdered Thor? And why had the Commander's sword been used? And why would Daniel lie?

Elwytha found no answers to these troubling questions. She remained awake long after the fire burned low in the hearth.

CHAPTER FIFTEEN

ELWYTHA AWOKE TO FREEZING COLD and soft, muffled movements. She blinked her eyes open. The Commander's large frame filled the open doorway.

She sat up a little. "What is it?"

"Snow," he rumbled.

Snow! No wonder she felt so cold this morning. Of course, the fire had been dead for hours. She arose, blankets still wrapped around her shoulders, and joined him at the door. In the dim light of the partially cloaked moon, a wonderland met her eyes. Pure white snow covered the grass, and coated the tree branches in the forest. It was at least three inches deep.

"It's beautiful," she whispered, hugging the blankets tighter against the bite in the air.

"It is dangerous." The Commander wore his full armor this morning, with both swords at his hips. "We will leave now," he told her. "I'll get the horses. You gather the rations."

The unease from yesterday fell upon Elwytha, stronger than ever. Quickly, she gathered their supplies. It took only moments, and she waited in the doorway with the bags at her feet. Still, she clutched the blankets to her. Perhaps she'd take them with her. It felt far too cold for her cloak alone. Of course, the Commander did not appear chilled. She wondered if small things such as heat or cold ever bothered him. He was so uncomplaining...always ready to choose the best plan of action, no matter the price to himself. Look how he'd gone into the snowy forest to get the horses. Now she wouldn't have to tramp through the snow, wetting her footwear and possibly her skin.

Trepidation rose as she waited for him. Was it taking longer than it should? Was he all right? Anxiety bloomed. When would he return?

Finally, his great form and that of the two horses emerged from the woods. She hurried to join them, and gave Sir Duke's cold nose an encouraging rub before handing a bag to the Commander and securing her own. Blankets still about her, she swung into her saddle. The Commander already waited atop his horse. When he saw she was up, he sent the black stallion trotting through the fresh snow toward the pass, twenty minutes distant.

Hopefully, if there was a trap, the snow would deter it. Who would be about on a dark, snowy morning like this one? She'd much rather be in her warm bed with a hot cup of tea in her hands. Were men such different creatures?

Perhaps they could escape the valley before they were ever detected. And who was to say a trap was laid? Perhaps her unease was only her imagination, run wild. Too many suspicions of plots and treacherous subplots tangled through her mind. Richard's...and what of the Prince? Surely he was no innocent in the intrigues snarling between the two kingdoms.

Elwytha nibbled on bread before they reached the pass, fortifying herself for the possible confrontation ahead.

Finally the narrow pass loomed ahead. Sheer, rocky walls closed in on either side. She knew from experience it would take fifteen minutes to traverse, and the most dangerous section was on the opposite side. There the sheer cliffs lowered to rocky jumbles. Perfect for warriors to hide amongst and spring an attack.

The Commander went first. His hand rested on his sword hilt as they moved forward. He felt the danger, too. And yet he'd chosen to place himself in this position by visiting Daniel and staying at the loch; all just to clear his name, and to keep her from freezing last night. Elwytha had no doubt that if alone, he would have returned over the mountain last night. So both of the reasons he was here, in this perilous situation, was because of her.

"Commander," she called. He glanced back. Here, at last, it was wide enough for two horses to ride side by side, so he slowed so she could catch up. Overhead, the sky had lightened to a dull gray. Low, heavy clouds still obscured most of the sky. Little light reached their deep, dark crevasse, however, and the Commander's face was hard to make out.

She said, "The treacherous part is five minutes distant. If you will trust me, give me your extra sword. I'll fight, should we be attacked."

"Against your brother?"

Her breath caught. "My brother would not be in a snowy pass before daybreak."

"You know whereof I speak." He sounded grim. "Your brother's men."

"They wouldn't attack me." Elwytha hoped this was true. But she accompanied the Commander. She may be a side casualty if they were determined to take his life.

"But with pleasure they would attack and kill me," he returned.

"No." The word blurted before Elwytha could stop it. "I will not let that happen."

"You would protect me at the cost of your own life? If you fight for me, you will become their enemy, as well."

"It will not come to that," Elwytha insisted. "And why do we speak of something that may not occur?"

He rode silently for a few moments. Then he said, "You feel it too, Elwytha. Danger. It lies ahead."

"Then I will ride first. If a trap is laid by my brother's men, I will reason with them. They will not harm me."

"If an attack is laid, they will not rest until I am dead." He spoke with cool, faultless logic.

True. "Then give me your sword."

"No. If you have a sword, they will attack you, too."

"You do not trust me," she accused. And why should he? She had been sent to kill him, for heaven's sake. Not that he knew this. Neither did he know that she would never again consider committing such a heinous act.

"You would choose your enemy over your own brother?" Disbelief undergirded his words.

"I choose justice. An attack on you would be murder. I cannot countenance that, especially as I have no proof of your guilt."

"Nor proof of my innocence."

"An attack would be cowardly and dishonorable." Somehow, she had to make him see. But see what? Would she truly choose his side over her brother's? Would she fight for the Commander to the death? For honor, she had said. But was that all there was to it?

The end of the pass approached, looking dim in the blue shadows of brightening daylight.

Anxiety ratcheted higher in her heart. "Give me your extra sword," she insisted. Fear simmered. "Please, Commander." She threw the blankets backward, off her shoulders, so they rested on Sir Duke. Then she unclasped the broach holding her cloak together and lowered it, securing it to her waist. Cold air bit into her skin, making her shudder. But if battle lay ahead, she'd need her arms to be free. She'd need full movement to defend her life and that of the Commander's.

Ready at last, she looked at him, eyes direct, jaw tight with resolve. It was time for battle, and she needed her weapon. The Commander's steely gaze held hers, and then he unsheathed the sword on his left hip. Metal glinted as it flashed through the air. She caught it by the hilt.

"Thank you, Commander. You are ready for battle?"

But she didn't need to ask. His face had settled into a grim, fearsome mask, and aggression tightened his frame, like an extra suit of armor he donned to face battle...and possible death.

Together, they rode through the last feet of the pass. Rocks loomed high above, and Elwytha cast alert glances from side to side. At last she felt like a warrior again; at home in battle, where she had first earned her father's approval. Would he approve of her now, about to fight her brother's men?

She saw no movements in the rocks as they rode past, and then saw why. Ahead, blocking their path just beyond the pass, were six horsemen. Each held a lance and sword. Each was helmeted. One carried her brother's flag.

Fear and a little sickness squeezed through her insides. So, they would attack openly. Perchance they would negotiate. She rode forward, but stopped short of lance range. Her brother's men remained motionless, as if waiting for an unknown signal.

"I am Princess Elwytha," she announced. "We travel in peace. We wish safe passage to the Prince's land."

No response. The men—none of whom she recognized—stared at her like ominous specters of death.

She demanded, "Have you no words for me? I entreat you in the name of King Richard to move aside."

Still no word, but now they began to advance toward her. She sensed the Commander at her side now. Fear rose, but she froze it, steeling her mind into battle mode. How she wished for armor. She still kept her sword at her side, exhibiting no aggression. The Commander, she noticed, did the same.

The men continued their advance. Faster. And suddenly their snorting horses charged. Simultaneously, the men drew back their lance wielding arms. Three weapons flew through the air, and Elwytha's sword deflected two. The other flew wild. Then the lance wielding warriors were upon them.

Elwytha fought as she had never fought before. She could not keep track of the Commander's movements, for she desperately battled to save her own skin.

Her sword flashed, unhanding one lance—another, she deflected. Sword wielding horsemen wheeled around and followed behind the lance bearing ones, pressing the attack. She whipped her sword in a blinding fury. How dare these men attack her? She was Princess Elwytha. But they pressed on, faces masks of hatred, battling to kill her...to kill *her*. Some part of her mind recognized this. They seemed as determined to kill her as the Commander.

Silent, pure snow drifted down from the sky; a jarring contrast to the unholy battle.

With quick precision and well-rehearsed skill, Elwytha unhanded sword after sword, but after one man was disarmed, another took his place. The men gathered up their swords and the attack pressed on. She could not continue forever. They would not stop until she was dead. She would have to kill them. Her brother's men...she would have to battle them to the death.

A deadly calm fell over her then. Elwytha parried and thrust harder and faster, focusing...waiting...for the chance to pierce through the gaps in their armor. Armor she knew well. She knew exactly where their weaknesses lay.

Her foe made a foolish move, and his sword flew high.

Elwytha whipped back her sword and kicked Sir Duke forward. The blade skewered her opponent. Faster than thought, she whipped out the bloody blade and faced her next opponent. She barely saw the first man topple from his horse.

Two men attacked her at once. Two blades against one wasn't a fair fight. Then one retreated. Why?

Viciously, she fought the remaining man. He lunged forward, sword aimed at her head. She lifted her sword to deflect it, and out of her side vision she saw something hurtle through the air. Blade still up, she instinctively tried to deflect it. A tremendous weight smashed against her blade, and then slammed into her head. Pain screamed through her mind and then only blackness fell, soft as the snow.

$$ \text{\textdagger} \quad \text{\textdagger} \quad \text{\textdagger} \quad \text{\textdagger} \quad \text{\textdagger} $$

The Commander had killed two men and battled the last one. Out of the corner of his eye he saw Elwytha, fighting valiantly. He had only to finish this last one, and then he'd help her. The warrior's horse pranced to his left, affording him a quick glance of Elwytha's foes. She battled two at once. In all his days, he'd seen few warriors as valiant as she.

Suddenly, one of her attackers fell back and a huge, spiked mace spun through the air. Horror slammed through the Commander. Elwytha's blade flashed, but not quick enough. The deadly weapon smashed into her head.

Silently, as if in slow motion, she toppled from her saddle. Terror seized him.

"Elwytha!" he roared. He felt the knick of a blade on his arm and turned on his opponent with vicious fury. With brute strength, he unarmed the man and finished him. He charged on Elwytha's foes, wielding his sword with murderous skill. One fell, and the other, seeing his comrades' dead bodies littering the ground, turned tail and galloped south, in the direction of Richard's castle. In war, the Commander would have chased and finished him, but not now.

He wheeled the black back and galloped up to Elwytha's still form. Sir Duke stood over her, as if protecting her with his body. The Commander leaped off his horse and crouched on the snowy ground.

Elwytha lay silently, her face as white as death; her body as still as death.

"Elwytha," he moaned, and gathered her lifeless body into his arms. He looked heavenward and cried out from the depths of his soul, "God Almighty! Please," he whispered, and pressed his lips to her hair. "Please!" he groaned aloud. "Elwytha."

Tenderly cradling her in his arms, he staggered to his feet. He didn't know where to take her. He didn't know where he was going. For the first time ever, his battle sharp mind felt blurry, fogged with grief.

Silently, the horses followed him. She lay so still, so white in his arms. A ragged sob wrenched from his throat. "*Annsachd*," he whispered, and helplessly kissed her. Warm breath touched his lips.

Warm...breath?

She lived? A great bolt of incredulous joy energized his soul. She lived? How could it be possible?

Carefully, he examined the matted hair on the side of her head. Blood had congealed, but no fresh blood flowed. Holding her with one arm, as if she were a babe, he gently brushed his fingers over the wound. No crushed bone. Her blade must have deflected more of the blow than he'd thought. But clearly she was unconscious, and just as clearly she needed tending. He could not do it here, on enemy land.

Hope and fear gathered in his heart. She could still die. She needed rest and warmth, and the wound cleaned. He would provide it all. Everything she needed. But first they would need to ride to safety.

He gathered up Sir Duke's reins and climbed on the black, holding Elwytha carefully. Then he gave both horses their head to gallop for home.

CHAPTER SIXTEEN

ELWYTHA FLOATED THROUGH the clouds. It was peaceful, and free of pain. And then she heard a faint roar. A voice. It sounded familiar. And then she wrenched back to earth. Pain exploded through her head.

Moaning, she slowly drifted to consciousness. Something rhythmically bounced her body, worsening the pain. "Stop," she mumbled. "Stop!"

"Elwytha." It was the Commander's voice. It sounded oddly urgent.

Her eyes fluttered open to stare into his anxious gray ones. He held her in his arms, she realized. More, they rode a horse. Hence the unbearable bumping.

"Stop," she begged. "Please stop."

"Stop?" he sounded bewildered.

"The bumping. It hurts," she whispered. Tears ran out of her eyes, depositing cold drops in her ears.

"We're not safe. We are still on your brother's land."

Elwytha shut her eyes again. Agony hammered through her head. "How much...longer?"

His arms tightened around her. "I wish to carry you home, to the Prince's castle. Where you will be safe."

More helpless tears trickled out as the agony in her head intensified. "I can't bear it. Please...I can't." The warm blackness of unconsciousness beckoned, and gladly she reached for it. Her body relaxed, becoming limp, as her mind swam for that peaceful nothingness.

A low sound wrenched from his chest, tugging her back to the pain. "Stay with me, Elwytha." And then she felt his warm breath as he pressed a kiss into her hair. "I know a place. Only a half hour distant. Sleep no more. It's dangerous."

"It is?" she said faintly. A thought sparked in her brain. "More so than you, Commander?"

She felt the faint movement of his chest. A laugh. "Verily, as dangerous as the peace between us."

She smiled, but the blackness beckoned again. "Speak to me," she whispered. "Say anything. Tell me of...your childhood. Your father."

She felt him stiffen, and then he relaxed. "My father is dead."

With effort, she fought through the blinding pain to respond, "You knew...who he was?"

"Yes. I knew." He sounded quiet and grim. "He left me a bastard, and married another instead of my mother."

"H'rrible," she muttered. "Why?"

A small silence elapsed. "My mother served him. She was a bastard like me. My father felt she was good enough to warm his bed, but not to marry."

"I'm sorry."

"It's life. I came to accept it."

"He was a noble?" Faintly, she pressed this out. Conversation was becoming more and more difficult with the searing, pulsing pain in her head.

"Noble in title. But he performed few noble deeds."

Silence fell, and she found it harder and harder to combat the darkness.

"Elwytha?" His voice wrenched her back yet again from the brink. "Are you asleep?"

"Nay," she whispered feebly. "Talk...about anything. I can't..."

So the Commander talked about his childhood. About the battles he'd fought. His rumble comforted her, as did the strength of his voice. He would take care of her. She would be all right. How, she did not know, but surely he would make it so. She heard the splash as horse hooves traversed a stream. They picked at a slower pace through the water for a long time. To cover their tracks, she realized in some deep part of her mind.

After what seemed like hours of agonizing pain, the Commander's horse stopped. Elwytha roused herself enough to cling to his neck as he dismounted. He carried her as easily as a child in his arms. She heard him knock on wood, and then an old voice that sounded like creaking branches welcomed them in.

He lay her on a cot. She felt his warm breath on her cheek and groggily opened her eyes. He said, "Mistress Fern will attend to your wound. I will see to the horses."

Elwytha caught at his hand before he could depart. "Stay," she begged, terrified, incapable of other words.

With a glance at the wizened old woman beside him, he nodded and knelt again beside her.

"Sip this," the old voice creaked.

The Commander helped her lift her head, and Elwytha swallowed a bitter potion. She wanted to retch, but hadn't the energy.

"That will help the pain," scratched the old voice.

Elwytha lay still, suffering through the gentle cleansing of her wound, and the sting of ointment smoothed on her scalp.

"Not bad. Not bad at all," cackled the old woman. "I've seen worse. Much worse. Rest now, but don't sleep."

Elwytha nodded slightly. Already the pain felt a tiny bit better. What potion had the old woman given her, she wondered.

"Go see to the horses, young man. She'll be fine for a spell."

Elwytha released the Commander's hand, which she realized she still held, and heard his boots recede from hearing.

"Your betrothed, is he?" Mistress Fern wanted to know.

"Yes," she whispered, shifting her head slightly to ease the pain.

"When will you be married?"

"Saturday."

"Mmhm." The old woman cackled. "With rest, you should be up for it. I'll leave you now, but no sleeping. We'll try a nice broth soon."

The morning drifted by in a haze. Elwytha scanned the small hut in bits and pieces. It looked clean, with mended curtains at the windows. Herbs wrapped in string hung from the ceiling. The old woman must be a healer of some kind.

Elwytha drank broth for lunch, and Fern seemed pleased she kept it down. The Commander sat across the room and she felt his frequent glances. He was worried about her, that was clear enough.

After dinner of a bit of bread and soup, and the application of more ointment, Elwytha's head felt clearer.

"You should be ready to travel tomorrow," Fern said. "Drink more of the potion, so you can sleep."

The pain had begun to intensify again, although Elwytha had said nothing. Obediently, she drank the wretched brew and lay back again. "I can sleep now?"

"Sleep," agreed the old woman. "Tomorrow you will be right as rain."

Gladly, Elwytha relaxed. Only this time blackness did not call to her. Just the soft comfort of sleep.

⟨ ⟨ ⟨ ⟨ ⟨

The Commander watched Elwytha slip into sleep. Peace relaxed her features and at last the worry eased in his heart.

"She will be all right?" he asked Fern.

With an eye roll, the old woman swatted his arm. "Of course, Commander. Just as you lived to see many a battle. Fear not."

Fern had tended him after a fierce battle years ago. She'd found him prone and bleeding on the forest floor not far from her cottage, and with her sharp tongue and prodding stick, had provoked him to his feet for the small walk to her hut. Now, later, he realized he could have died from the deep wound in his side. But the old lady had healed him. As now she had healed Elwytha.

"Thank you," he said simply. He could not speak the depth of his gratitude.

"That's Princess Elwytha, is it not?" the old woman inquired, handing him a cup of tea.

"Yes."

She cackled. "And she would marry one such as you? Mind, I know the soft heart of a kitten lives inside your thick warrior skin. But one as refined as her...and you? Does she know?"

The Commander felt uncomfortable, and did not answer directly. "She agreed to marry me for the sake of peace between our lands."

"Did peace administer that blow to her head? Or your cuts?"

He frowned. "Nay."

Fern's dark eyes looked sharp and wise. "Then why partake of such a treacherous peace?"

He did not answer.

"You love her. That's why." The old woman cackled, as though satisfied with her keen insight.

"Yes, I wish her for my own." He would admit no more. But who was he fooling? Certainly not Fern. And certainly not himself. "Peace is still possible, with careful steps," he contended. "King Richard claims I killed Thor. Once that dispute is settled, peace will be possible."

"Who will tell the girl?"

The Commander understood what the discerning old woman meant. "She will find out on her own."

"Who will tell her who killed her brother?" the old woman pressed obstinately.

"I will not. The truth must come from someone she trusts."

"Not you, Commander? Would you build a marriage on so shaky a foundation?"

He looked at Elwytha, sleeping peacefully. "I build the foundation one stone at a time."

"Is she willing?"

Fear and dread tightened like a vise around his heart. "I do not know," he said quietly.

The old woman patted his hand. "You deserve the best, lad. Don't ever forget it. If your kingdom would be her heart, God grant you your one, dearest wish."

† † † † †

Elwytha awoke the next morning feeling much better. Pain still ached in her head, but it compared not at all to yesterday. Mistress Fern pronounced herself pleased with the healing of the wound, and said Elwytha was well enough to ride. After partaking of a meager breakfast of bread and tea, Elwytha climbed up on Sir Duke in the crisp air, cloak about her.

"Thank you," she told Fern. "I don't know what we would have done if you hadn't been here to help us."

The Commander agreed. "Your kindness will not be forgotten."

Fern smiled. Her scratchy voice said, "The best thanks would be your happiness." She said this to the Commander, but her smile included Elwytha. "Blessings be upon you and the family you will have."

Elwytha felt a catch in her heart and glanced quickly at the Commander. Who knew if their marriage would take place...let alone if she would bear him children.

His eyes smiled, settling on Elwytha, as if pleased with Fern's prediction. "Are you ready?"

"Don't forget the herbs if the pain returns," Fern admonished. She patted Elwytha's leg. "Many happy days, child." The dark eyes flickered with compassion. "Faint not."

Elwytha wondered what that meant. Nothing good, most likely. Perhaps the healer sensed trouble coming her way? In truth, Elwytha saw it all too clearly herself, coming in the form of Richard for her wedding, the day after tomorrow. Would the Prince allow Richard in the castle after this attack on the

Commander? Not to mention the attack upon her, although she doubted this would trouble the Prince's mind.

Elwytha rode at an easy gait beside her betrothed through the woods. He asked, "Your head is well?"

"It's fine." She'd drunk a small sip of the healer's potion that morning, and already the dull pain she'd awoken with had diminished. Today the sun shone, and the earth was wet from the melted snow. Small patches of white still clumped in the shadows of rocks.

They rode in silence for a while longer, and then broke into sunshine and grassy hills. Sir Duke increased his gait. Doubtless the warm sun on his ears brightened his spirits, as it did Elwytha's.

The Commander directed the black stallion closer to Sir Duke, and Elwytha guessed he wished to speak to her. She sent him an inquiring glance.

"Tell me, Elwytha," his deep voice rumbled. "Does Richard desire peace?"

Alarm skittered through her, but it was a reasonable question after the attack yesterday. What could she say? "Richard hates you," she admitted.

"And you, too?"

She frowned. "What do you mean?"

"Richard's men attacked us both yesterday, Elwytha."

She looked away uncomfortably. "I know. I don't understand it."

"Does he see you as a threat to his crown?"

She felt indignant. "I wouldn't steal it from him."

The Commander pressed deeper. "Does Richard understand your honor enough to trust you?"

"We're the only ones left of our family—except cousins. He loves me! He would never hurt me." Elwytha could not accept this horrible possibility—that Richard would betray and kill her, just to secure his throne from the potential threat she posed. Richard would never think she'd kill him to gain power, either. It was preposterous. "I would *never* hurt him," she exclaimed. "He knows this well."

"Filial love beats strongly in Richard?"

"He is loyal to our family," she insisted. "It is true, he can be self-absorbed. And deceitful." She bit her lip, afraid she had said too much. Richard was her brother. He'd never betray her, and she would never betray him, either. Honor to clan was the highest code she could uphold. "As I said," she reiterated evenly, "Richard hates you for killing Thor. Likely he wished to ambush you to mete out justice. His men probably saw me as a threat since I carried a sword, so they attacked me as well."

More silence stretched as they rode. "Will you uphold the peace, Elwytha?"

Her lips parted, insulted. "I did not slay you with the sword," she said with asperity. "What further proof do you require?"

"You fought well. But maybe you intended only to defend your life?" The steel gaze pierced into her, as if trying to read the truth in her heart.

Elwytha felt ridiculously hurt and ever more offended by his questions. "I told you I would fight with you. I kept my word. Does that count for nothing, Commander? You tossed me your sword. Do you then trust me so little?"

"I want to trust you, Elwytha. But your brother's peace feels like no peace at all."

As it was not. What a tangled web! And she felt like the trussed insect, right in the center. What words wouldn't betray Richard, but would tell no lies to the Commander? She wanted to protect him from her brother. If the Prince allowed Richard in the castle for their nuptials, she would need to form a plan to protect the Commander. How, she did not know. If only she could convince Richard to agree to peace. How simply this whole mess would straighten out then.

"Elwytha?" His deep voice recalled her attention. "Is it peace?" A demand lurked...velvet cloaked...for an answer.

She gathered her thoughts. "I wish for peace, Commander. And if Richard has doubts, then I will attempt to convince him that peace would be best for everyone."

"He respects your opinion so highly?"

"Yes, Richard respects me," she agreed. "I can best him with the sword. He will consider my words." But for how long, was the question. Once Richard set his mind upon a plan, he was difficult to reason with.

"And yet he feels no threat from you." Elwytha heard the faint disbelief in her betrothed's words.

"I cannot read Richard's mind, Commander. When he comes, I will attempt to speak to him. More, I cannot promise."

"Warn your brother that treachery will end in blood. His blood." A fearsome mask hardened the Commander's face and his eyes felt like steel daggers, piercing into Elwytha, warning her.

Fear trembled inside her. How quickly the whole false peace could crumble. And if it did, not only Richard's life would be in jeopardy, but hers, as well. For she had no doubt that Richard would reveal her part in the whole wretched plot. Elwytha quailed at the thought of the Commander's fury unleashed upon her.

She said, "I will send him a missive about the new wedding date. If you wish, I will convey your warning, as well."

He nodded. "Agreed."

They rode on silently. The closeness they'd shared at the loch and at Fern's hut seemed gone now. Elwytha felt very alone, as if already the Commander's anger lashed upon her soul. But she would not betray him. She would not. To her dismay, she wanted him to believe her. To trust her. To like her. To look upon her with favor.

And yet she deserved his warning words. Hadn't she come to the Prince's castle intending to kill him? How he would hate her if he knew that now. That thought made her shudder. No. He could never find out. It all had to work out peaceably. It just had to.

"You are cold?" His tone had softened, and she looked at him quickly. "You shudder inside your cloak."

"Nay. The sun is warm." But her heart felt cold...and she realized with dismay that only his smile could warm it.

They rode in silence for a long time, and ate bread for lunch while still riding. As they passed the hunter's cot where they had sheltered from the storm, Elwytha realized they finally neared the castle. Her thoughts turned to their wedding—the wedding that may not be. And then her mind turned back still further, to that first day she had arrived at the palace, thinking to marry the Prince, of all people. She snorted at that horrifying thought. Instead, she had been given to the Commander.

Now she looked at him, riding silently beside her, and a question occurred. "Why did you agree to marry me so quickly when I first arrived?"

He took some time to form his response. "It seemed like a good plan," he said at last. "I wished for peace, and I wished for a wife."

"Any woman would have done, then?" she inquired, feeling ridiculously slighted.

"I thought so. But I was wrong."

"Wrong? Not you, the Commander of all the Prince's forces? Pray, don't you always make sound, strategic judgments?"

A low chuckle rumbled in his chest. "What I mean, Elwytha, is I did not know I would desire you. You, alone. A woman with much spunk. Any other would not battle me like you do."

"You like our fights?" she asked with some surprise.

"I like your spirit," he said. "I like the way we are together."

Elwytha glanced down, feeling shy as he spoke these words of passion to her. Her cheeks felt warm, but then she forced herself to meet his steady gaze. "I did not know I pleased you so well. Mayhap I should think up new arguments to vex you, if you like them so well."

"Or new hairstyles to pain my eyes," he agreed with a grin.

Elwytha laughed out loud. "Nay. For verily, they pained my head still more."

At last, they reached the castle. Already the drawbridge was lowered. Guards must have watched for their approach. Stable boys took the horses to feed and care for them, and Elwytha and the Commander stopped by the kitchen for a tasty morsel to last them until supper. Elwytha's stomach rumbled mightily as they entered the warm kitchen.

Mary fluttered her hands in the air. "Land alive! We were worried to death about the two of you. Come in. Sit. You must be hungry."

Speedily, she assembled a feast of fruit, cheese, and bread. Then she settled across from them. "Tell me what happened," she urged. "I've only a minute."

Elwytha told much of the tale and Mary looked properly horrified. "And your head. Are you aright?"

"Thanks to Mistress Fern, I'm fine."

Mary looked at the Commander. "The same Mistress Fern who healed you all those years ago?"

He nodded, and Elwytha wondered what had happened to him.

Mary spoke up, since her betrothed didn't look like he would. "She snatched him from the brink of death, she did. If not for her, our Commander wouldna be here today. The King left him for dead. They all did, as the life bled out of him." She shook her head. "It's a miracle, it is. A right miracle. And glad we are you're with us today. Aren't we, miss?"

The Commander glanced at Elwytha, as if wondering about her response. She couldn't help but smile. "I cannot imagine my life here without him in it."

Mary clucked. "You need to rest, miss. Perhaps a hot bath before supper. Go along, now. You take good care of her, lad."

"I will," he said quietly, and as they left the kitchen, Elwytha felt his large hand on her lower back. It felt warm and possessive. For the first time, she didn't wish to flee from him.

How could that be? Did she believe him innocent of her brother's death? Did she trust him so completely now? No logical answers existed, but in her heart...in her heart she longed for it all to be true.

CHAPTER SEVENTEEN

"YOU LIVE," THE PRINCE GREETED the Commander. He sat at a round, highly polished wooden table in his sumptuous living quarters. Red and blue tapestries lined the walls, and polished wood warmed the floors. Late afternoon sunlight streamed in a narrow window, lighting the room, and a fire burned in the grate. "Sit. Do you want a drink?"

The Commander sat, but refused the drink. The Prince regarded him. "You walked into a trap." It was less a question than a statement.

"Yes. I knew it, and prepared for it."

The Prince took a sip of ale and stared at him directly, his lips faintly curled. "Did your princess betray you?"

"No. She fought valiantly. Almost to the death."

He raised an eyebrow. "She chooses you, then?"

The Commander heaved a breath. He still did not know. "I would like to believe so."

"We will see, will we not?"

He nodded.

"What happened?" the Prince demanded, his voice as cutting as a fine blade.

"An ambush awaited us outside the pass." He described the battle and Elwytha's valiant fight, and her injury.

"Six horsemen." The Prince dwelled on this for a moment. "And they attacked Elwytha as well." His eyes narrowed. "Maybe her traitorous brother reveals his hand?"

"I believe so," agreed the Commander. "But Elwytha insists she wishes for peace."

"She will convince her brother to love peace as well?"

"She says she will try."

The Prince nodded. His dark eyes blackened to obsidian. "You will be prepared?"

"Yes. And you?"

He smiled. "I have been prepared from the beginning. If Richard betrays us, we will have peace—with one thrust of the sword."

"And what of Elwytha?"

"Allow her to play her hand fully, Commander. Let her true character shine forth. And if she fails you..."

Alarm tightened in his chest. "You will leave her in my hand," he thundered.

The Prince eyed him. "I will. I trust you to choose wisely."

The Commander did not know if his foolish heart could subscribe to wisdom where Elwytha was concerned. He could only hope—and pray—that she would not betray him.

\ \ \ \ \

Elwytha rested in the tub, clean at last. The warm water felt heavenly, and relaxed all of her sore limbs. The ride, the deadly battle...all now ached through her body. She hadn't noticed the pain before—perhaps because she'd imbibed of Fern's noxious potion earlier today. But her head didn't ache so much now, so she'd decided to forgo the nasty stuff.

A towel supported her head and she closed her eyes, seeking further rest. To her dismay, the battle against her brother's men sprang to mind, as vivid as if it were happening now. They had come for her. They had attacked *her*. Elwytha remembered this afresh.

Had Richard ordered them to kill her, as well as the Commander? Or had his men fought her because she carried a sword?

No answers settled well within her mind. It made no sense. Why would Richard order her killed? Did he see her as a threat to his crown? Would he murder his own sibling so coldly?

Had he murdered Thor?

Elwytha gasped and sat straight up. Water sluiced down her shoulders and cold air puckered her skin. No. She beat back the treacherous thought.

Never would Richard commit such a heinous crime. He didn't lust for power that greatly, did he?

And yet he had hated Thor. All during their childhood Thor had been their father's prized son. The perfect example. Honorable and just. The best swordsman. A new fact whispered up. Someone would have had to stab Thor in the back to kill him, for he'd have defeated a direct attack.

Who, except those in her own castle, knew this fact?

Elwytha gulped and reached for her towel. Shivering, she exited the tub and rubbed her body hard, trying to shove these traitorous thoughts from her mind. Richard would never kill Thor.

And Richard loved her. He would never hurt her, either. Both had received little of their father's love or attention. This had formed a fragile bond between them. Honestly, however, Elwytha had never been close to Richard. He'd been far too moody. She had loved Thor best, and understood why her father had lavished such praise upon him. She could not resent it, for she loved him, too.

Slowly, Elwytha dressed, unable to stop her horrible thoughts. After her father had died in a hunting accident, Thor had ascended to the throne. He had reigned for two years. Battles between their land and the Prince's had not flagged, although toward the end Thor had mentioned peace. He wearied of war, and suspected the Prince did, as well.

But then the Commander—or someone—had killed Thor, and that was the end of peace. Richard desired more land. More tributes from the peasants. He was a hard man; a fact she could not deny. He beat his horses, and she'd heard of men killed because they failed his orders. He wished for absolute power, and absolute subservience from everyone—including herself.

Elwytha padded back to her chamber and distractedly tugged a comb through her wet hair. She picked at the snarls, paying them little attention, and stared at her blue eyes in the mirror. Eyes the exact color of Richard's. Surely the man who shared her blood could not commit such an unspeakable act...and surely he had not ordered the attack upon her, as well.

But Elwytha felt her world slowly tilting off balance. Once thought, the suspicions could not be bottled up. The fact remained—someone had killed Thor. But had the Commander murdered him, or had Richard ordered it? Neither option was palatable. What was the truth?

Still not paying close attention, her comb nicked her scalp wound. Pain pierced her and she cried out. Ready tears spurted down her cheeks. Did everything have to be so painful? So unbearable?

She pressed her fingers to the wound and fresh blood came away. The comb had broken the scab.

A knock thundered on her door. The Commander. She attempted to wipe up her tears. "Come in."

He opened the door. A frown contorted his brows. "Have you a pain? I heard you cry."

Her lip trembled, but she willed it to stop. Wasn't she a warrior? The battle had reminded her of this truth. Now the battle to find the deepest truth required her to think straight, and logically, to find answers.

He sat beside her on the narrow bed, and she looked at him in surprise. "Your wound pains you?" he asked gently.

Weak tears welled higher now. How could his kindness so quickly strip away all manner of her armor?

"I...I was foolish, and poked it with the comb." She stared wordlessly at the blood on her fingers. She made to wipe them against her dress, but his hand closed around them, stopping her. She looked at him, even more surprised. What did he intend by this action?

His gray eyes held hers. "I would like to attend to you," he said quietly.

Warmth leaped inside her. "Oh, but you don't..."

"I wish to."

Her heart beat faster. "I'm fine," she attempted to deny.

He crossed the room to her basin of warm water. He dipped a wash rag in it, wrung it out with one strong fist, and returned with the ointment in his hand.

Elwytha felt further warmth as he sat beside her again. Her heart beat ridiculously fast. She would not be able to stop him. She knew this well enough, so she carefully lifted her hair out of the way to assist him. Then she felt his fingers, gentle on her chin, holding her head steady, while the warm cloth dabbed at the wound. It barely stung. Then she felt a soothing coolness as he applied the ointment to her scalp.

"Thank you," she managed, and allowed her hair to fall free again. Quickly, she cast him a glance. An unknown emotion heated her, making her feel flustered. "I appreciate your...kindness to me." Unable to stand his nearness any longer, she sprang to her feet, took the cloth and the ointment from his hand, and deposited them where they belonged, across the room. She wiped the blood from her hand, back still to him.

She said, "I would like to dine in my chamber this evening, if you do not object." He would think she was tired, and while that was true, it wasn't the full truth. Attempting to firm her chin, she turned to face him. "I wish to retire early."

After assessing her features for a moment, he nodded and rose to his feet. "I will tell Hagma."

Elwytha was relieved. Her feelings for this man continued to grow, springing outside the carefully sealed chambers of her heart. He was a danger to her; now, more than ever. "Thank you." She attempted to smile.

Again his gaze raked her face, discerningly, unnervingly intelligent, as usual. "You are troubled." A statement.

No sense denying it. "Yes," she allowed.

"Why?"

Helplessly, she waved her hand. "It's as I've told you before. I don't know what to think...about anything. You. My brother. It's all such a *mess*," she gritted this last.

He advanced toward her. "Can you not be loyal to me, and to your brother, too?" His hands closed around hers, and she gazed up at him wordlessly.

"I wish for peace," she insisted brokenly.

"And we shall have it. Our marriage will provide that firm foundation."

A marriage she meant to flee? But what if she didn't? Could peace truly be served? Conflicted thoughts twisted through her heart.

"Do you wish it?" he persisted. Another velvet cloaked demand for the truth from her heart.

A reply evaded her, for she did not know.

"I wish it," he told her, and kissed her. His lips burned like fire across her own. The brief contact ended, and she stared up at him, feeling dizzy and weak at the knees. Why did she want to melt into his arms now? His nearness befuddled her, playing tricks with her mind—at least, this is what she tried to tell herself.

After a moment, he said, "Have you written your missive to Richard? I will send it at first light."

Elwytha had written one several days ago, but now she wanted to destroy that one and pen a new one. "I will write it now."

The Commander released her hands. "I'll get the parchment and ink."

After he'd left these items, he left her alone, closing her door behind him. Elwytha gazed at the parchment for a long time, searching for the best words to sway her brother to peace. To warn him to eschew his treachery. Finally, she dipped up ink and wrote.

Brother, my wedding is moved to this Saturday hence. I pray that you come early. Could peace be so evil? Again I ask you, would the sacrifice of honor serve either of us well? Leave your sword at home, brother. What benefit lies in the enemy's pit? Your loving sister, Elwytha

There. The clearest hint possible that she wanted to commit no treacherous act. And a veiled plea to rescue her early and forget his bloody plan. He was a smart man. He'd read between the lines. If he came bearing his sword, he would leave with it buried deep in his heart. She shivered at that grotesque, horrible thought, and delivered the letter to her warrior betrothed.

He read it and nodded approval. "Your words cut as sharp as your tongue." Was that a faint smile?

"You approve, then?" she inquired, eyebrow raised, and suppressed a sudden grin. "Or would you love more words?"

His smile edged up. "For me, you mean."

"They please you so well. I wish only for your approval."

He grinned with quiet, appreciative amusement. "Do you flirt with me, Elwytha?"

Her face burned. "No! I merely inquired if my missive meets your exacting standards."

His eyes smiled, pure silver now. "I would like to continue this conversation. But it might be better finished after our marriage feast."

Her mouth opened and her heart pounded hard in her breast. "You overstep your bounds, Commander. Good even."

Hastily, she retreated to her chamber and closed the door. She leaned against it, breathing quickly. What in the world had she just done? In truth, she had flirted with him. Had she taken all leave of her senses? The wallop to her head must have addled her brains. She needed a good night's rest to clear her thinking abilities. In fact, the sooner she retired, the better.

CHAPTER EIGHTEEN

WHEN ELWYTHA AWOKE, DIM LIGHT filtered into the room. She felt sleepy. Another cloudy day. Perhaps it might rain. Or snow. It was the perfect gloom to precede her fateful wedding to the Commander on the morrow.

It was the wedding Richard may stop, and the wedding she may flee—unless she decided to pursue peace, and convinced Richard to agree to the same. Would she marry the Commander to guarantee peace between their lands?

Would she marry him under any circumstance?

Elwytha did not know the answer to any of these questions. She lay still on her bed, listening to the noises outside. A faint, spitting sound. Rain? What of the flowers she and Hagma still needed to cut this morning?

Again, for the wedding that may never be.

Elwytha was tired of lying still and doing nothing. She needed to get out and about, and allow her mind to breathe, and her body as well. Perhaps she'd don her cloak and take a turn around the grounds before the earth became too soggy.

This plan appealed. She quickly dressed, fastened her cloak about her, and silently left the room. Hagma had not arrived with her breakfast yet, so it still must be early.

Even so, the Commander was not in his room. This did not surprise her. What did he do with his days? Practice sword play with his men? Train the warriors? Plot battle strategies with the Prince? She knew the Prince already suspected treachery. He had said as much a few days ago. Now, after the attack at the pass, these suspicions would be strengthened. More reason to convince Richard of peace.

Swiftly and silently, she sped down the cold stone hallways to the door leading to the courtyard; to the flower garden where she had fled that first night, fleeing from the mocking Prince and her frightening, murderous betrothed. Or so she'd believed at the time.

She stepped into the light, sprinkling rain. The dampness chilled her, but she pressed on, for the ground was not muddy yet. And the flowers...she saw none. Where were they? Just two weeks ago, lush bushes had bloomed. She had sniffed their sweet scent and they had soothed her anguish and fear.

How her perceptions had changed in so little time. True, the Commander was still huge and fearsome, but not the brutish monster she had believed. Intelligence, gentleness, and discernment tempered his natural tendency to command, dominate, and aggressively insist upon obedience to his orders.

An unusual combination in a man.

Elwytha hurried on, warming a little now. The rain felt cold against her face, but the fresh air smelled sweet and heavenly. Few people were about. She approached the armory. No one was outside, and the door stood open. Could the Commander be inside?

Without thinking, she stepped to the door and peered in. Dim light revealed swords, daggers, lances, armor—every conceivable weapon of war. But no Commander. No one was inside.

Two weeks ago, this opportunity would have filled her with giddy delight. She'd have dashed in and pilfered three of everything she could carry. At the very least, three daggers. Temptation beckoned now. Would her daggers be in the pile? What harm would it do to merely look?

Feeling as though she were taking wrongful steps, Elwytha approached the daggers. A shiny pile of them filled a bin. All sharp. All wicked looking. A quick perusal proved that none were hers.

The Commander was right. She did prefer the dagger. She loved the look of them, and the feel of them.

She spied a small, slender one with a rapier thin blade. It bore no jewels, but a design of leaves was battered into the hilt. It balanced perfectly in her hand. Again, with a blade in hand, she realized how naked she'd felt lately with no dagger strapped to her person. At home she always wore one. Thor had taught her to be prepared at all times, for any manner of attack. Maybe he'd been afraid one of the warriors would assault her, she realized now. But still, she loved the blade. Reverently, she stroked the weapon. A fine piece of craftsmanship, this.

A huge hand gripped her wrist, and with a twist, forced her to drop the knife. With a gasp, she faced the Commander. Her heart beat hard. His eyes looked like steel in the dim light. "Again you would steal a blade?"

She drew a quick breath. "I was tempted," she admitted, knowing he would only tolerate the truth. And she did wish to be truthful to him.

"Can I still not trust you?" Displeasure tightened his features. This wounded her far deeper than a blade ever could.

"I planned no treachery." She had to make him see. "I feel...unclothed without a blade." Discomfort warmed her cheeks. "At home I always wear one. I have since I was twelve. Thor insisted I needed protection at all times. And so now..." she gazed up at him wordlessly.

"You need no blade here. I will protect you." He held her very close to him, and still he read her features, unsmiling.

"I'm sorry," she said. "But know if I had really planned to steal a dagger, I would not have stared at them for so long. I did not intend to betray you."

He pulled her with him outside, into the sprinkling rain. His hand slid from her wrist to her hand, engulfing it, and he led her toward the castle.

Now the rain felt cold, and Elwytha shivered. "Where are you taking me?" She hurried to match his long—probably angry—strides. He did not answer, but instead led her past the dining hall to a small room beside the kitchen.

The open door revealed a chamber lined with sumptuous tapestries and warm, wooly rugs. It held a polished wooden table and two chairs opposite each other. Fresh baked honey buns spilled from a basket. The sweet scent assailed Elwytha's nostrils. A platter of eggs and bacon lay in the center of the table, and cups of spiced cider marked the two place settings.

She stared at the Commander as he closed the door behind them. "What is this?"

"Breakfast." His gaze didn't look much softer. "I wanted to surprise you this morn. Tomorrow I will not see you until the ceremony."

Elwytha looked at the delicious feast upon the table, and then wordlessly back at him. No wonder Hagma had brought her no breakfast this morning. He had planned this—likely last evening.

"Thank you," she said softly. "It looks delicious." If only she could mend the breach between them. If only she hadn't entered that armory!

How could she convince him that she'd meant no treachery?

"Commander..." She bit her lip, not sure what to say, only knowing that she wanted all to be right between them.

"Sit." He moved toward his chair.

"Nay." With boldness, she reached for his arm, stopping him. His eyes narrowed in surprise. "I wish for things to be right between us. Please believe me. I did not mean to steal a blade. I will not betray you."

His gaze bored into hers. The grim line of his mouth softened, ever so slightly. "Verily?"

"Yes. Truly," she told him from her heart.

He dipped his head and tension relaxed out of his great shoulders. "I believe you."

"You do?" Relief rushed into her heart and Elwytha impulsively flung herself into his arms and hugged him tight. His arms closed around her, secure and solid. Alarm and delight skittered through her. He smelled clean, of soap, and his jerkin today was made of worn, soft leather. He felt nice...solid and warm; safe, yet disturbingly dangerous to her fluttering nerves.

"Umm." She pulled back, feeling flustered and jumpy. His gaze looked warmer now—gentle, just the way she liked it. Further relief rushed through her, and she smiled at him. "Thank you." Uncertainly, then, she tugged away. He let her go.

She was glad he had released her, she told herself. "The honey buns smell delicious," she said, and busily filled her trencher with fluffy eggs and thick, chewy bacon. If possible, everything tasted even better than it smelled. She sighed. "Mary outdid herself this time."

"She's a fine cook."

"She's planned quite a feast for tomorrow." Elwytha again felt conflicted. Was she lying to him now, pretending that she would marry him on the morrow, when in reality she planned to flee?

Of course it was a lie. And one he'd hate her for. Discomfort squeezed her heart and she reached for another honey bun. She didn't want to lie to him. The whole thing made her feel sick.

He spoke, thankfully pulling her mind from her troubled thoughts. "Your missive will reach Richard this morn. I sent my fastest horseman."

"Thank you. What time will the ceremony be?"

"At noon. Hagma will bring you to the chapel."

Elwytha nodded. Plenty of time to escape, should she desire to do so. A hysterical part of her wanted to laugh. What a fine farce her wedding might prove to be.

"Elwytha." His deep voice commanded her attention and she gave it. "Again, you are troubled. Will you tell me what is wrong?"

Surprise leaped. How easily he read her. So, what could she say? *I don't know if I should marry you or not?* He trusted her now, she saw it in his eyes. She wanted to keep his trust and respect. "I have nerves, Commander." She bit her lip. "Don't you?"

His hand covered hers and it comforted her. "Elwytha, I have no doubts and no nerves. I wish to marry you. I cannot wish for anything more." Passion undergirded his words, and sincerity. He spoke from his heart, and the force of it impacted Elwytha's very soul.

"Truly?" she whispered.

"Truly." Passion and gentleness, determination and need flickered plainly over his features, intensifying his gray eyes to a deep, smoky color. He lifted her fingers to his lips. "I wish for nothing more than for you to be my wife."

His lips sent electric tingles racing over her skin, and she stared at him breathlessly. Then he kissed her fingers, each knuckle, and Elwytha felt a spinning, delicious feeling inside. All warm prickles and leaping excitement.

"Do you want me?" he asked quietly. "Do you wish for me to be your husband?"

It was a question, a need, from his heart to hers, and it smashed through the walls Elwytha had built around her heart. The truth lay there, under the last stone, but she would not turn it over to find it.

"I do, more than I did in the beginning," she admitted, pulse hammering. "You have gained that victory, Commander."

Disappointment flickered across his features, and she felt guilt and pain for hurting him. But she would not lie to him. Hadn't she lied enough already?

He released her hand and she felt bereft. And a coward for not turning over that last stone in her heart.

"Thank you for breakfast," she said too quickly. "I should go. Hagma and I have much decorating to do today." She stood, clutching her cloak in hand.

"I will see you this even," he said quietly. He chewed on the last of his bacon.

Elwytha stood still for a moment, watching him and feeling terrible, and then hurried out. She would tell him no more lies. Wasn't that for the best? Wouldn't he thank her later?

She believed none of it as she hurried for her chamber to return her cloak. What was wrong with her? Why did she have so many conflicting emotions for that man? She splashed water on her face and combed her hair again—carefully, this time. Her head didn't hurt today. A good sign. She smoothed on a little more ointment and left her chamber.

Soon, she would have to make a decision about their marriage. But today was a day of reprieve. She would decorate the hall. Tomorrow Richard would arrive. This fact did not cheer her. Truthfully, it depressed her.

Didn't she want him to come? Elwytha searched her heart.

No. Honestly, she dreaded it. Was it because of the evil he still might want to accomplish? Or because he would stop her wedding? Discomfort and dismay tightened in her at this thought.

Warily, her mind touched the disturbing question—did she want to marry the Commander after all?

Nay. Of course not. Her breaths came faster. The last, unturned stone beckoned her to turn it, to reveal the truth. But she could not.

Of course not, she told herself again, hurrying for the dining hall and the huge decorating job before her. She did not want to marry the Commander. She wished to be freed from this palace prison as speedily as possible.

Elwytha struggled to forget the way he had looked at her this morning. And how she had felt in response.

She did *not* wish to marry the Commander. Peace or no peace. She did not.

✷ ✷ ✷ ✷ ✷

The Commander fisted his hand and stared at it. The remains of breakfast held no appeal for him. Clearly, Elwytha still did not want to marry him. Perhaps she never would. But she didn't hate him anymore...at least, he hoped she did not. Could that be a firm enough foundation for a marriage?

The great warrior feared not, and buried his fingers through the unfamiliar hair at his scalp. What more could he possibly do? He had chosen to trust her when she'd pled innocence at the armory. He treated her with gentleness and kindness...in truth, he would treat her no other way.

Was he still so repulsive to her? He fingered his bent nose, his disfigured brow. Would she always see him as the monster he appeared on the outside?

He heard a sound in the doorway.

Mary asked, "Are you finished, then? I saw Elwytha leave a moment ago." She frowned as she came closer. "Are you aright, Commander?"

"I will survive, Mary."

The cook patted his shoulder and gave him a kind smile. "Don't give up, lad. You're a warrior. Never stop fighting for what you want. You may yet gain the victory."

She cleared the table and left him with those wise words.

It wasn't in him to give up. Yet again, the Commander acknowledged this truth. He would fight, for it was all he knew how to do. He would fight...and maybe he should pray. He needed the help of someone far bigger than himself to reach Elwytha's heart.

※ ※ ※ ※ ※

Elwytha stood at the last table. Pottery bowls with floating candles adorned it. She looked throughout the great hall and wonder filled her heart. All of this was for her and the Commander. For their wedding.

Tiny white flowers scented the air with vanilla and mingled with the faint sweetness of the last wild roses, which Hagma's friends had harvested yesterday. That was why the bushes had appeared plucked clean this morning. It all looked fresh and beautiful.

A part of her wished the marriage feast would take place, and she could partake in it. For a moment, she imagined it.... The smell of roast lamb and fresh baked bread. All of her favorite foods on the tables. People happy and laughing... The Commander, standing next to the head table, waiting for her to arrive. No longer her betrothed. Her husband. Her heart jumped at that thought. She imagined him smiling as she approached...and his wonderful eyes turning to silver.

Elwytha's fingers tightened on the basket of flowers. Just for a moment, in that impossible fantasy, she had wanted to reach for him. Her mind allowed her to go no further. She would not marry him. He would not be her husband.

Elwytha tried to ignore the emptiness this truth brought her. No. He would not be hers. Biting her lip, she finished decorating the last table for a wedding feast that would never be.

"Elwytha?" Hagma approached, her basket of flowers empty. "Are you all right? You look about to cry."

She swallowed the ache in her throat. "I'm fine. The hall looks beautiful, don't you think?"

Hagma smiled. "That it does, miss. Mary and I and my mum...well, we've got something for you, after we've finished here."

"You do?" That reminded Elwytha of a favor she needed to ask. "I've asked enough of you already, Hagma. But I wondered if I could ask one more thing."

"Of course." Still looking a bit concerned, the other girl smiled.

"I've no one to stand with me at the altar. I'm not sure if Richard will come in time. Would you consider being my maid of honor?"

Hagma gasped, and her hand flew to her throat. "Nay, miss. I could never do that. I'm not nearly grand enough. Heavens! How could you ask?"

How could Elwytha say that the wedding probably would never take place—but if for some strange reason it did, she didn't want to stand up there alone. "You and Mary are my

only friends here. I'd be honored if you would do this for me."
And she hoped Hagma wouldn't be too upset if Elwytha ran
out on the whole thing.

"Well," the maid sounded doubtful. "It doesn't seem right,
miss. Are you sure?"

"Please," Elwytha said simply.

Hagma watched her, and then nodded. "Very well. I'd be
happy to. Now, come with me. That table's as good as done.
Mary's waiting in the kitchen." Giggling, Hagma urged her to
hurry to the warm kitchen. The smell of fresh baked bread
permeated the air, and Elwytha's stomach rumbled.

"She's here, Mary," Hagma called, darting ahead. "Sit
down," she told Elwytha.

She sat at the great kitchen table as told, and Mary
arrived, wiping her hands on the apron around her waist.
Hagma carried a burlap covered object. She set it on the table
before Elwytha.

"There you go, miss. From all of us here." Pleased, the two
looked on as Elwytha reverently touched the package.

With wonder, she said, "For me?"

"Open it, do," Mary said, with a jolly laugh.

Carefully, Elwytha pulled aside the layers of rough cloth,
and then she gasped. A white linen garment lay there, carefully
folded. Fine embroidery and beadwork of amber and gold
sparkled down the bodice and all the way—she shook it out—to
the floor. A beautiful nightgown, soft and beautiful, and hand
finished with crocheted lace.

Elwytha burst into tears. She deserved nothing so fine.
She'd come with treachery in her heart, and even now plotted
to leave the Commander at the altar.

"Miss. Miss." Mary hurried over with a cloth to mop her
tears. Comfortably, she sat next to Elwytha. "Now miss," she
said softly. "What troubles you?"

In that moment the cook seemed like the mother she'd
never had. Elwytha longed for comfort, but knew that was
impossible. "It's...I don't deserve it," she whispered. "You are
both much too kind to me."

"You're our friend, you are, miss," Hagma said.

"Mayhap she's nervous of her wedding day," Mary said with wisdom.

Elwytha sniffed. That was certainly true.

Hagma took the gown from her and folded it back up again neatly. "Now you go and put it in your trunk, so it will be ready for tomorrow night."

Wordlessly, Elwytha nodded, and then impulsively hugged Mary, then Hagma. "Thank you so much. I don't have words to tell you how much...what it means to me."

Mary smiled. "We can see. And we wish you all the best. The Commander is a fine man. He'll make you a fine husband."

Hagma looked on in smiling agreement.

They may well be right, Elwytha finally admitted in her heart. He was a fine man. And she couldn't believe that he had killed her brother. He was an honorable man. In fact, he possessed the deepest integrity of any man she had ever met.

"You're right," she said softly. With a faint smile, she hugged the precious gown to her and left her two friends.

Would she marry him if Richard didn't come? Could she?

Elwytha's heart beat faster, considering it. She could choose to do it. She bit her lip and fled faster through the corridors. Heart pounding, she burst into the Commander's chamber. She had expected it to be empty, but her betrothed knelt there, locking his trunk.

"Elwytha." He stood, tucking the key in his pocket, and she stared at his fearsome face...half of it. The other not. His eyes looked concerned, and he caught at her arms when she made to dart past him. "Elwytha." The deep voice commanded her to look on him. "You look like a frightened doe."

"I..." Wordlessly, she hugged the gown tighter to herself. She tried, faintly, to pull free of his grasp, but he didn't let her.

"Would you still run from me?" Pain flickered.

"No." Truthfully, she ran from herself. From her feelings for this man. The last stone in her heart shuddered, turning over by itself.

Lord help her, she *did* want to marry him. To be his.

She gazed up at him. How could this happen? How could she want to marry the enemy Commander?

"Speak to me," he told her.

"I...I've been thinking about our wedding."

"And?" He waited, his eyes looking dark now.

She heaved great breaths. Her lips trembled.

"Do you still despise it so much?" His voice sounded harsh.

She gulped. "Nay!"

His expression gentled. "Then what is it, Elwytha? Why do you still flee from me?"

"I..." She heaved another great breath. "I...wish to tell you..." All of a sudden it became clear. No less frightening, but clear. The Prince's voice in her head. Words of peace between their lands. But more, her feelings for this man. "I will marry you on the morrow. I will no longer flee."

"Verily?" He seemed to sense the momentousness of her statement, although surely he had had no inkling that she'd planned to leave him at the altar.

"Yes." Her eyes met his now, her heart thundering like galloping horses. "I will marry you, Commander. Tomorrow."

He stood very still. "Willingly?" Apprehension and the barest hope flickered.

"Willingly." She added in the barest whisper, "I don't believe you killed my brother."

Startled, he searched her eyes, as if not daring to believe it. "You don't?"

"No." At last she admitted this truth to him and to herself. This man would no more commit that cowardly, heinous act than he could jump over the moon. This she knew, deep in her soul.

The Commander grinned, a great, wide one. "Thank you, Elwytha. Your faith in me means everything."

Gently, he drew her close and kissed her. His kiss seemed to seal his possession of her, but more, it hinted of tenderness and passion...of a promise that their life together would be good. Overcome with emotion, she melted into him. A tremble overtook her. She hoped he was right. She hoped she was making the right decision.

The Commander kissed her again and pulled back. A frown lowered his brow. "You look pale. Are you aright? Does your head hurt?"

"No. It's been a long, busy day." Busy working through thousands of different emotions. Worrying, wondering how Richard would take her betrayal. What if he would not agree to peace? Would the Commander still want her? That thought scared her. She touched his arm. "I wish to retire early this even, so I will be ready for the morrow."

He nodded, and scanned her features. "You have made me happy, Elwytha," he said in a deep, quiet voice.

She smiled back, and then slipped into her own room. Elwytha rested her head against the closed door. She would marry the Commander. Had she taken leave of her senses?

No. She wished for it, as she'd wished for nothing in her life. And she believed that he was innocent. But what a tangled mess it still was. Should she warn him that Richard may spit on the peace? That Richard wanted him dead? But he must already guess that, after the attack at the pass.

No. She would say nothing to further endanger her brother's life. It was up to Elwytha to convince her brother to accept peace. If not, then to prevent bloodshed. In truth, the wedding may never take place. Even though the Commander said he wanted to marry her, would he still feel that way after Richard came and ripped the peace to shreds?

Elwytha closed her eyes and said a silent prayer; for peace on the morrow. It was the only wish in her heart.

CHAPTER NINETEEN

ELWYTHA AWOKE THE NEXT MORNING to clear sunshine blazing through her window. Her wedding day. She would marry the Commander at noon.

Had her brother arrived yet? But surely his horn would have awoken her.

A knock came at the door, and she called for Hagma to enter.

Her friend hurried in with a huge smile. "Aren't you excited, miss? It's your wedding day."

Elwytha found she did feel excitement—and trepidation. "Has my brother arrived?"

"Nay, miss. But a few hours remain until the ceremony. Plenty of time for him to arrive."

Hagma's words of comfort did not make Elwytha feel better. In fact, she hoped Richard wouldn't come at all.

Did she wish to marry the Commander so dearly?

She did, heaven help her. Heart skittering faster, thinking on the marriage ceremony ahead today, she joined Hagma in giggling over the food, her dress, and ideas for her hair.

Elwytha bathed after breakfast and dressed in the blue gown, and then Hagma did her hair. She peered at it in the Commander's large mirror. Doubtless he would appreciate Hagma's artistic hairstyle far more than Elwytha's previous attempts at hair design. Her hair fell in gentle waves, and tiny white flowers were pinned about the crown of her head. Her cheeks looked flushed, and her blue eyes luminous.

"You look a fairy princess, you do, miss," Hagma said with satisfaction. "Now, on with your cloak. We need to ride to the chapel."

"Ride to the chapel?" Elwytha was confused. "But isn't it here at the castle?"

"Not the one the Commander has chosen for your wedding."

Could it be the little chapel they'd visited in the woods? Where she had felt convicted of her treachery and amended her ways? Where the Commander had first kissed her?

Wonderment and emotion overtook her as they cantered smoothly, so as not to disrupt her carefully styled mane, and stopped outside the tiny chapel in the wood. The black stallion, a white stallion, as well as a few other mounts stood quietly tied to the trees.

Elwytha and Hagma slid off their horses. The maid had donned her finest dress, a light blue, for her duties as maid of honor. Her eyes sparkled. She seemed just as excited about the wedding as Elwytha.

"Are you ready, miss?"

"You go first. I need to catch my breath."

The maid nodded and slipped inside. Elwytha looked at the tiny chapel. In just a moment, she would marry the Commander. Her brother had not arrived yet. Nothing would stop it now. Just as her fluttering heart wished.

The Prince exited. His black eyes were slightly narrowed. "Are you coming, Princess?"

"Yes, of course."

Something glittered in his hand. It was the sapphire necklace he'd shown her. His grandmother's. Astonished, she stared at him.

His lips tilted in a half smile. "A loan." He moved behind her to put it on, and she lifted her hair out of the way. The cool necklace draped around her throat. His quick fingers fastened it. As she lowered her hair, he said in her ear, "Do not hurt him, Princess. Or you will pay."

She whirled. The black gaze held hers in steady warning. She frowned, for his words had pricked at her happiness. "You possess few social graces, Prince. But you do possess a suspicious mind."

He smiled. "Deal honorably with the Commander, and all will be well."

"I would not hurt him," she said in a low, vehement voice.

His smile edged higher. "See that you don't." The Prince opened the door for her.

She gasped when she saw the interior of the chapel. Rose petals were strewn over the floor and their delicate scent wafted through the air. Candles burned on the altar. Beautiful white bows adorned the ends of the pews, which were mostly empty. Only a few armor clad warriors sat on them. And straight ahead, down the aisle, stood the Commander. The Prince edged by and strode to take up his position beside his friend. But Elwytha had no eyes for anyone but the Commander.

He wore a black jerkin of the finest cloth, and black breeches and boots. It matched his growing black hair and the black slash of his brow. The clothes had been made to fit him. For once, his broad, strong shoulders didn't strain at the cloth. They fell in crisp lines down his form. Her heart beat faster. He looked handsome. Not a brutish warrior, but a man.

He smiled then, just for her, and she melted inside. This man wanted to marry her. He would be her husband this day.

With a trembling smile, she slowly stepped down the aisle to meet him.

The priest, a short, thin man with receding hair, began the ceremony. Slowly it progressed; the ancient rituals, lighting the candles, listening to the priest's words, facing each other... The Commander's eyes held hers as his deep voice promised to love and cherish her all of his life. Tears gathered in Elwytha's eyes as she gripped his hands and pledged her life to him. In fact, in this sacred place, she felt the vows went so much deeper. As though she pledged her very soul to him.

They exchanged rings. Hers was a beautiful twisted white and yellow gold. His was a plain band. The priest pronounced them man and wife. Then the Commander grinned and kissed her with soul stirring passion. She blushed as they parted, hearing raucous cheers from the warriors. The louts. But she speedily forgot them as she smiled up at the Commander, her husband.

Her wedding had been all that she had ever desired, and more.

The guests showered them with rose petals as they left the church, and then they all rode back to the castle. The Commander rode close by her side, and she kept glancing at him, unable to believe they were finally married.

Elwytha still saw no sign of her brother as they clopped across the castle drawbridge. Stable lads took the animals, and the whole company entered the great hall. It was filled to overflowing with warriors and maids and all the people of the palace.

A great cheer went up as the Commander and Elwytha entered. Flushed with excitement, she took his hand and let him lead her to the head table.

"A toast," the Prince said, raising his cup when all were seated. "To my right hand and his bride. May they enjoy many years of peace...and passion."

Elwytha's face flamed. Embarrassed, she sipped from her cup. The Commander smiled at her. He didn't appear embarrassed, and she looked quickly away. She knew he anticipated their night together. Her fingers trembled as she lined up her spoon even with the edge of her trencher. Richard would not arrive to rescue her from her fate. And indeed, wasn't this what she wanted?

Still, her heart raced with nerves and anxiety. If only she could run, and fly as free as a bird from the tallest tower. But that could not be, and indeed, in her heart, she did not wish for it.

She glanced toward the closed doors leading to the castle gate. No Richard. A relief, but troublesome, too.

"You are disappointed your brother didn't come?" the Commander asked, with his usual perception.

Elwytha glanced at him, startled. "I...I am disturbed. I hope all is well."

"Never fear," the Prince interjected. "Rats are not easily killed."

Elwytha was shocked, and for a moment words escaped her. Then she cut back, "So speaks wisdom from the lips of a serpent."

"Prince," the Commander said mildly. "It is our wedding feast."

The Prince smiled. "Then I will toast Richard's absence, and the peace that has begun." With a mocking head tilt to Elwytha, he drank deeply from his cup.

Elwytha wanted to roll her eyes, but instead she ignored him for the remainder of the meal. As the Commander had said, it was their feast. A time for celebration. The beginning of her new life. But how long would it last? If Richard arrived on the morrow disdaining peace, would the Commander want to keep their marriage vows? Or would he reject her, as Richard would probably reject the peace?

These thoughts brought no cheer, so Elwytha endeavored to ignore them. She savored the tasty roast lamb, the honey glazed carrots, and the fresh bread. Delicate tarts were served for dessert. Mary had outdone herself. In the background, Mac à Chruiteir strummed beautiful notes on the clàrsach, adding a final, delicate note of beauty to the perfect day.

More rounds of jovial toasts circled the room afterward, and Elwytha realized again how well respected and liked her husband was. His men revered him. She had no doubt that many—if not most—would lay down their lives for him.

The Commander smiled, and under the table reached for her hand. "Are you ready to say good even?" he asked quietly. Her heart leaped with anxiety and excitement as she met his gaze. It steadied her. She nodded, unable to trust her voice.

When they rose, ribald laughter and advice peppered the air.

"Carry her, Commander, as you did when she first arrived," shouted one lout.

Elwytha closed her ears, unwilling to hear any further mortifying jests. She held the Commander's hand tightly as they left the dining hall. The quiet halls soothed her nerves a little, and they walked slowly toward his chamber. He seemed to be in no hurry, and that helped calm her a little, too.

At last, they entered his chamber, and the door closed the world out. She stared up at him and licked her lips. "I...I would like to change," she whispered.

He nodded. "Take the time you need."

She hurried into her room and closed the door, heart pounding. She could find no name for all of the tumultuous feelings battering her. Fear. Excitement. Anxiety. But mostly, overwhelming, heart pounding nerves. Slowly, she changed into the beautiful white gown Hagma and Mary had given her. Then she pulled the white flowers from her hair and brushed it. That's when she realized she still wore the Prince's necklace. Carefully she unclasped it, and then opened the door to the Commander's chamber.

He sat on the edge of their marriage bed, thankfully still fully clothed.

Hesitantly, she moved closer and held out the necklace. "Would you return this to the Prince?"

"Yes." He placed it on the table next to his bed.

She stood very close to him now, at his knees, and looked down at him. His large hands settled on the curve of her hips. She drew a breath of surprise. She liked it...even savored it.

He looked up then, into her eyes. His lips were pressed tight, as though apprehensive. Nervously, she stared back, but offered him a faint smile. His eyes lightened to a clear, wonderful silver. "I don't repulse you?" he asked quietly.

Wordlessly, she shook her head.

His hand closed around hers and he urged her forward, onto his bed, to lie beside him. Elwytha's heart beat faster to be so close to her husband.

Leaning over her, he kissed her slowly, and then rained kisses down her throat. She liked his touch, and found herself longing for more. The Commander whispered, quiet and warm against her neck, "I wish to please you."

Elwytha didn't know what he meant. But she did know one thing. His touch thrilled and pleased her to the very core of her being. She whispered, "You are."

He drew back and looked at her, lips curved a bit. "Verily?"

With a trembling smile, she said, "Yes, truly."

When he kissed her again, she shyly kissed him back. A new emotion swelled in her heart then, and with amazement, her mind touched it.

Love.

She loved the Commander...her husband. Shock and wonderment filled her, and Elwytha pulled back to gaze at his beloved face. Her hands cradled his jaw and she looked into his silver eyes, at his bent nose and his beautiful mouth. And his brow—so straight and dark on one side and so slashed and cruelly misshapen on the other. She lifted her head and kissed it, wishing that by her touch and love she could heal it. At least, perhaps, heal his heart.

He watched her, unmoving, with hope and a dark bit of wonder in his eyes. "I don't repulse you?" he asked yet again.

"No," she breathed, stroking her thumbs over his cheekbones. "You don't repulse me at all."

A low, aching rumble sounded from his chest. He kissed her then with a barely checked, searing passion. Elwytha's blood lit on fire, and she melted against him.

After long moments, she hesitantly touched his shoulders, and with an inarticulate sound, he removed his tunic. Now she felt his warm skin, hard and alive with muscle beneath her fingers. Her cheeks flushed with the bold liberties she took with him. Clearly, though, he did not mind. His low growl said she pleased him.

Hot languor stirred in her blood when he kissed her throat, and a wordless, aching longing grew in her. She longed to be closer still to this man she loved.

Elwytha felt self-conscious when he loosened her dress, but not for long. How could she feel embarrassed when his silver eyes told her that she was beautiful, and his every kiss, every touch cherished her? Love surged in her, frightening in its intensity. Elwytha wanted to give herself to him, completely and utterly. Forever.

Soon all her mind saw were sparks and light, and finally, when she could not stand the separation between them another moment longer, the Commander took her as his own. Elwytha shuddered with the beauty and fulfillment of being one with the man she loved.

Later, when she lay quietly, replete and full of wonder, she wondered how it could have happened. How could she love her enemy...the man she'd thought had murdered her brother?

But he hadn't killed him. She knew it now, more deeply than ever. For the Commander was a man of honor. It was a fact she had learned well. He would never stab a man in the back—in battle, or out of battle.

More disturbing thoughts followed. The peace agreement. Why hadn't her brother come? Did he want her married? Did he view her as a threat to his crown? Did he want her out of his palace, and was this his way to rid himself of her?

Elwytha did not want to believe any of these things, but she also did not know what to believe after living in the enemy's keep for two weeks. One thing she did know. She loved the Commander, and she would go to any length to protect him from her brother's plots.

CHAPTER TWENTY

ELWYTHA SLEPT ALL NIGHT CUDDLED in the crook of the Commander's arm. She felt comfortable and safe. The blast of a horn cruelly awoke her from this peaceful rest.

Her brother! It blasted again.

Elwytha sat straight up, clutching the bedclothes to herself. The cold air nipped her shoulders. He had come.

Dread rose. She wished he'd go away again. She wished she didn't have to see him.

Beside her, the Commander rumbled, "Your brother has arrived." His hand curled around her elbow, urging her back to him.

"Yes." Gladly, she snuggled back into his strong, warm arms.

"He can wait a while longer to see you." He smiled, and she grinned back.

"Yes," she whispered, and her husband kissed her, luring her mind to passion again.

Later, after a sumptuous breakfast that had been left outside their door, they set out to find Richard. They found him in the Prince's private study, sipping ale in a comfortable chair. Two guards stood close by.

The Prince and King Richard looked for all the world like good friends, talking and enjoying a drink. Except when Elwytha stepped through the door she felt the thick tension thrumming through the room.

Richard rose when he saw her. "Sister." He allowed her to kiss his bearded cheek. Cold blue eyes regarded her. He was not happy, she discerned immediately. "You look well."

"As do you, brother." She glanced at the Prince, who lounged in his chair, long legs languidly stretched before him. He watched Richard as a cat who'd found a mouse. Apprehension crawled through her.

"Richard," she said, "this is the Commander, my husband."

Richard's lips curled. He stared at the Commander, but made no effort to acknowledge him. He turned to the Prince. "I wish to thank you for your hospitality. Also for the feast tonight to celebrate our peace. Now, I will take your leave."

The Prince nodded. Beside Elwytha, the Commander now radiated an ominous, tightly leashed aggression.

As Richard passed Elwytha, his eyes met hers. The message was clear. *Meet me later*. She nodded imperceptibly, and he was gone.

The Prince spoke. "Princess, you brother promises the oil of peace. Now we will see—will it smooth our differences, or will it burn?"

Elwytha feared she knew the answer to that, and the Prince knew it. His sharp eyes cut into her. Silkily, he pressed, "Don't hesitate to rush to your brother's side. As the Commander's wife, you have his full trust, and the full run of the palace. Pray, do not disappoint."

Elwytha frowned uncomfortably, and wished to escape the annoying Prince, but she made herself sit, along with her husband, and listen to the two discuss armory repairs. While she found this interesting, most of her mind dwelt upon Richard and what he might be plotting. Even now, she shivered with the horror of what she had planned to do only two weeks ago; and over what she knew her brother expected her to do, even now. She had to speak to him. Reason with him. Argue for peace. And warn him, if all else failed, that the Prince suspected a trap.

Feeling edgy, she fidgeted until the Commander noticed. He turned to her. "You can visit your brother. I'll be along soon. He's in the guest quarters."

Elwytha smiled at him, unable to hide her love. She hadn't told him yet. It still felt so new...so precious and tender. Did he love her, too? She was afraid. What if he did not? What if Richard ignored her pleas and broke the peace? Would the Commander still want her for his wife? Or would he despise her then?

She forced herself to rise. Despite the Prince's unwelcome presence, she longed to stay with the Commander. Fear soured her stomach. What if, after she spoke to Richard, the peace fell apart and things were never the same between them again?

"I'll see you soon," she promised; more to herself than to him. She would see him again. All would be well. It had to be. She felt too shy to kiss him in front of the Prince, although she longed to.

The Commander felt no such qualms. He walked her to the door and kissed her before she left. Joy warmed her heart and leant wings to her feet as she sped toward the guest quarters.

۲ ۲ ۲ ۲ ۲

Elwytha knocked on her brother's chamber door. By now, her spirits had settled. Soberly, she marshaled her thoughts. Time to figure out her brother's plots. Time to convince him of peace, if possible.

"It's Elwytha."

"Enter."

Elwytha entered her brother's large suite. Soft white pelts covered the stone floor, tapestries decorated the walls, and a large bed, draped in red fabric, looked imposing in the far corner. Twin, high, slitted windows let in the bright morning sunlight.

Richard looked fit, and his beard appeared to be freshly trimmed. He always trimmed it before a new offensive. This clue to her brother's mindset did not quiet her fears.

"Are you welcoming me to the enemy castle, sister mine?" he inquired, approaching her. She could read no emotion on his hard face.

"Are you here to sign the peace agreement, brother?"

Richard gave a small smile. "I am here to achieve my goals." He came still closer. "Do you still pledge loyalty to your king?"

An odd energy radiated from him. Uneasily, Elwytha replied, "You are my brother. Would I abandon you?"

He eyed her, his blue eyes so dark and hard they appeared to be stones. "You tell me, sister."

Uncomfortably, Elwytha changed the subject. "I expected you yesterday. Didn't you receive my missive in time?"

"I did," he acknowledged. "But it displeased me."

"Why?"

His lips curled higher, revealing gritted teeth. "Your warnings for peace, and your pleas for honor disappointed me. Tell me, Elwytha. Did they force it from your hand, or did you write it from your heart?"

Elwytha frowned and opened her mouth to speak, but Richard raised his hand. "It matters not to me. But if you would pen...nay, *love*...their words so much, I decided a night in the monster's hands would serve you well."

She gasped. "You wished for me to suffer?" Never mind that she hadn't. It had been her brother's evil intent. She could scarcely believe her ears.

Richard smiled. "Did you suffer, sister? Or did you enjoy it?"

Outraged, Elwytha swung to slap him, but he caught her hand. "Tell me the truth," he hissed. "Are you for me, or against me?"

Elwytha wrenched her arm free and glared. Clearly, no peace lived in his heart.

Dread gathered. Still, she would press for information in order to divert the plots Richard clearly intended to carry out. And she had other questions for him to answer, too. "Why did you order an attack on us at the loch?"

He barked out a laugh. "Now we address the truth. Yes, Elwytha. Answer my question first. Do you love the monster so tenderly? I hear you fought to the death for him." His brow lowered, looking menacing, and his eyes were cold. "What of my crown? I'm your *brother*. You owe fealty to me. Do you serve me, sister?" He gripped her arm again, and to her shock, she felt the prick of a blade at her neck.

Elwytha gasped. "You would kill me, brother? Did you send those men to kill me, too?"

"My men are fools," Richard hissed. His bearded face came closer. "Are you, as well?"

Elwytha's heart beat rapidly, but she struggled to think rationally. Richard threatened her because he doubted her loyalty. She must convince him of it—what good would it do the Commander if she were dead? In fact, what good would it do her?

"Brother," she said, as evenly as possible, "I have followed your plan, even though your men attacked me. What further proofs do you require of my loyalty?"

To her surprised relief, he released her. But for how long? Fury still burned in his blue eyes. She would need to be careful...and very, very convincing. "Really?" he said smoothly. "Then why does the monster still live?"

"You did not come, and now I'm married to him," she retorted, struggling to slip into the role of upset sister, rather than disbelieving, distrustful sister. "Wasn't that your wish?"

"So kill him, and be rid of your unwanted husband."

"I waited for your arrival. For the speedy rescue you promised. Is it still promised?"

Her brother's eyes narrowed. "You doubt me?"

"I have no wish to die," Elwytha told him. "As soon as the Commander is found dead they will come after me."

"Silly sister. You will have hours to make your escape."

"What do you mean?"

"Tonight, after you satisfy him, he will sleep. Kill him then."

Her face flamed and horror sickened her. "You want to use me as a murdering whore!"

"No. A murdering wife." He smiled, a nasty one.

Fury arose, but Elwytha heaved a breath, trying to calm herself. Trying to plot a game to trick her brother. To secure the Commander's safety.

He said, "Kill him, and so seal your fealty to me. Then I will promise you continued protection within my castle walls. If you do not..." He left the warning unsaid.

"Are you threatening me yet again?" she asked in a low voice. "Did you want me to kill him at first light this morning, when you sounded your horn? When I had no chance of escape? Do you want me dead, brother? As you wished our brother dead?"

Her brother went quite still. "You accuse me of treason," he hissed.

"We both know you hated Thor. I ask for the truth. You want to barter my life for a false peace. For the death of the man you say killed our brother."

"Ah. The monster has filled your head with lies."

"No, he hasn't."

"Don't tell me you desire him." His words twisted, sounding ugly. "Or do you admit allegiance to a murdering heathen over your own brother?"

Elwytha looked away, heart pounding. She had almost slipped. "No! Of course not."

"Yet you question me."

In keeping with her act, she spurted, "I question why you did not come as you promised. I wish to know my avenue of escape tonight. Are these unreasonable questions?"

"Your attitude belies your servitude to me. Your pride will be your downfall, sister, if you do not repent."

Unwisely, she countered, "You mean if I do not submit to your orders."

"Kill the monster," he spat. "Or I will. But know that if I do it, you will have no place in my castle. On the other hand, if you kill him, you will enjoy many years of peace and safety."

Her flesh prickled. Elwytha did not trust her brother's promises. For the first time, she accepted this truth. The Commander may be their enemy, but he always spoke the truth to her. He treated her with respect; not as a pawn to be played to further his goals, and then discarded when he felt threatened. And she loved him.

No love lived in her brother's eyes. Only an appetite for murder and a lust for power. If she resisted him—if she refused to submit to his demands—he would kill her, even now. The realization—the fear of it—sickened her.

If she was armed, Richard would not be so bold, but right now, he knew he held the advantage. And he felt threatened by her. She read it in the barely suppressed rage in his eyes. The Commander had been right. She must tread carefully now, for the future—her future—lay in her hands. As well as the future of two kingdoms. Peace or war? Life or death?

Sounding as cold as she could, Elwytha said, "As you wish. I will kill him this even. Plan my escape at midnight."

Her brother's lips curled up. "Good. And I will take care of the Prince."

"What do you mean, you will take care of the Prince?"

Richard's glance slid away. "I will protect you, should he try to bar your escape, of course." Her brother flicked a glance over her face. "Fear not, sister. You will be safe. At midnight I will meet you at the drawbridge."

Elwytha nodded. Her mind screamed down different paths, seeking back up plans and avenues of escape. Tonight she would betray him. What would be the consequence?

⚔ ⚔ ⚔ ⚔ ⚔

The Commander turned away from the half closed door, and the hand that he'd raised to knock long minutes ago fell to his side.

It felt like someone had rammed a sword down his lungs. He felt destroyed, as if his heart had been cut open and left to bleed. Treason! Elwytha plotted to kill him. It had been her plan all along.

He had been a fool. A *fool!* An anguished cry gurgled in his throat, and he shoved a hand at his ear, as if trying to silence the words of treason he'd just heard. Then he realized the Prince's enemies could come out at any minute. He walked away, moving fast, unmindful of his direction. He strode outside, across the court, and found sanctuary in the armory. He leaned against the wall, heaving great breaths, wanting to turn his mind off, and block out the pain, but he could not.

In his weakness, he had dared to hope that she cared for him.

He smashed his fist against the stone wall. His knuckles split and bled.

He didn't care.

The Commander slid down the wall, to the floor.

He squeezed his eyes shut, and lifted his face to the heavens. How had it happened? "*How?*" he roared.

He had dared to hope for something good in his life...but God would not be mocked. He'd sown death and destruction, and so he would reap death and destruction, to his very soul. He could never remember crying, but he wanted to now.

"I *wanted her,* God," his voice broke. "I would do anything for her! I've repented of my past. I'm trying to follow the right path. Whatever else You ask, I would do it."

But it was too late. His bargain with his Maker was useless. Elwytha did not care for him. She had chosen to betray him. He had wanted to tame her, but she had, after all, tamed him, and taken him for a fool.

Anger rose, folding through the hurt inside, but nothing appeased the scorch in his soul. Elwytha had betrayed him, and even now coldly plotted their last night together. He clenched his fists and swallowed back a ragged breath. She meant to lie to him one more time, to use his passion for her to dull his mind to her treachery.

Very well. He would allow it.... He could not lie to himself. He wanted it, God help him. One last time he would satisfy himself with her. And then, when she uncovered the deadly blade of her true intent, he would finish this thing between them. Once and for all.

But for now, he would warn the Prince of Richard's treacherous plot and the danger to them both. Rising on wooden legs, he reentered the sunshine, heading for the castle. But the warmth could not touch him. The cold blackness that had retreated during his two weeks with Elwytha flooded through his soul again. It just might kill him, but he no longer cared.

ᛉ ᛉ ᛉ ᛉ ᛉ

Richard's threat to take care of the Prince worried Elwytha as she headed for her chamber. What did he plot? To kill him? Anxiety twisted through her. She no longer trusted Richard. He frightened her. He had pretty much said he'd kill her if she didn't do as he ordered. And truly, what guarantee had she that he'd spare her, even if she did obey?

Clearly, he felt threatened and suspicious of her. He loved his crown and his life too well to allow a threat such as herself to live within his walls.

Was that why he had ordered her to marry for peace—to push her outside of his walls? Or did he want their enemies to slay her after she killed the Commander? Then he wouldn't need to do it himself.

A shudder shook her.

Richard had killed Thor. She knew this now, but had no proof, outside of his murderous rage this afternoon...and his absolute lust for power, and the treachery that twisted like snakes through their native soil—his heart.

Carefully, Elwytha thought through her plan to trick him this evening. To convince him to leave the palace without bloodshed.

But what if he attacked the Prince?

If so, his treachery would earn its own reward. She could not save him from that fate.

But she could warn Mary. Her husband was the Prince's personal guard. Elwytha need not say she suspected ill of Richard. Her heart still would not let her betray her brother, her kin. Familial loyalty had been bred too deep. But she could tell Mary that when into his cups, Richard could become unruly. Henry could be warned to keep a sharp eye upon Richard, which would help protect the Prince's life.

Yes. Elwytha adjusted her course and headed for the kitchen. The Prince's blood would not be on her hands.

As Elwytha hurried to speak to Mary, she struggled to work out the final details of her plan to trick her brother this evening. Unexpected questions surfaced, as well. How did Richard plan to cross the drawbridge? Or did he plan to kill the Prince's men and then lower it? Disquiet grew within her.

Her plans to outmaneuver Richard's plots twisted inside her, vexing her, sickening her, as she tried to work out all of the finer points. Richard was her brother. She'd loved him all of her life. What if she was wrong about him?

Doubt assailed her.

Elwytha bit her lip, and wished she could flee from this untenable situation. Only one thing remained clear above all. She loved the Commander, and would not let Richard kill him. She would do everything necessary to ensure his safety.

CHAPTER TWENTY-ONE

THE FEAST WAS HARDLY JOVIAL that evening. The Commander never showed up, so Elwytha had to make conversation with Richard and the Prince. An uncomfortable, prickly situation, that. She gladly retired early, eager to escape Richard's cold, meaningful glances, and the Prince's curled lip. Neither ruler had drunk more than one cup of ale. As she knew both loved the beverage, it only boded ill for later.

In her chamber, Elwytha felt nervous as she dressed in the fine white robe the Commander had given her when she'd first arrived. Somehow, it seemed fitting. Their relationship had come full circle. Tonight he could remove it from her with one quick motion. She bit her lip and gazed into the mirror. Worry darkened her blue eyes as she brushed her hair for the last time, but she struggled to ignore it. Even now, her decision to betray her own flesh and blood haunted her. Would he suspect her treachery? Would she live the night?

She turned as the door shut. The Commander stood in the doorway, staring at her.

She forced a trembling smile to her lips. "You're home."

"Yes."

Why was he looking at her like that; as if he'd never seen her before? "Are you all right?"

He moved abruptly into the room. "I'm fine. It was a hard day."

"I wondered why I didn't see you at the evening meal."

He turned to the side and shucked off his jerkin. "I'm sorry I couldn't attend."

An unusual energy radiated from him, making her feel uncertain and cautious. "Perhaps you wish to rest alone," she suggested hesitantly.

"No!" He turned to her, and an unknown emotion glittered in his eyes. "No. I wish to be with you tonight."

She smiled, relieved. "Then I will wait...until you are ready," she said softly. She crawled onto the bed and sat leaning against the headboard, pleating her hands in her lap.

He readied himself for bed, which took longer than seemed necessary. He washed, and put away his clothes, and at last sat on the edge of the bed. His eyes burned like smoke. "You are sure?" he asked.

Elwytha was confused by his strange mood. Surely he could not guess her secret plot tonight? No. Certainly not. "Of course I'm sure. You're my husband."

He reached for her hand. "No words of affection between us, Elwytha?"

Her heart beat hard. "I..."

"Shh." He put his finger to her lips. "Speak nothing you do not mean."

He did not want her to speak, and truly, she felt afraid to share her heart with him. Could he ever accept it? Instead, she kissed his finger, which was still against her lips.

"Come to me, my husband," she whispered, and felt relieved when he did just that. He enfolded her in his great, gentle arms and kissed her with a passion that took wings inside her and soared, thrilling her. She felt his kisses down her neck, and then the slide of his hands, loosening her robe.

She moaned when he took his time with her. She felt his warm breaths, quick and fast against her, and he kissed her mouth again with a quiet intensity. She returned it with a blooming, urgent passion. She touched him, too, aching to show her love for him.

The pace between them slowly quickened. He seemed to savor her lips and her body with a passion edged by desperation.

It matched her own mood.

The fervor between them intensified and suddenly flared hot and urgent. In the darkest recesses of Elwytha's mind, she feared she would never lie with her husband like this again. Never touch him, never love him.

Reason could not silence her tears, and when he came to her, she cried out his name at the same moment he thundered hers. Again he groaned her name, as if in agony of soul.

"Gilead," she whispered on a sob, and gripped him tight. She never wanted to let him go. She never wanted him to leave her. And yet he did. He pulled away and lay on his back.

She felt very alone. Soundless tears ached in her throat and she turned into him and slipped her hand across his great chest. Already, he slept. His gentle breaths stirred her hair. Tears squeezed out of her eyes and she hugged her arm around him, as tightly as she could. She loved him. It was why she could make no other choice tonight.

When she was certain he was deeply asleep, Elwytha slipped from their bed, pulled on her robe, and knelt at the trunk where he kept his knife. She knew he kept the key in his breeches, and now she slipped it into the lock and softly turned it. Silently, it slid open. She pulled out his prized, wicked dagger. Squeezing her eyes tight, she gathered her courage and moved the blade to her arm.

She felt pain, and realized in a disconnected part of her brain that it came from her wrist. The dagger fell with a clatter to the floor, but her husband did not release the pressure on her arm. She stared up at him, alarmed.

"You would love me, then kill me?" Fury shook through his deep voice. And betrayal. But not surprise.

"No!" She shook her head quickly.

"I heard your plan with your brother. Don't deny it." He held both of her hands painfully immobile now.

"No. You misunderstand."

"I misunderstand nothing," he roared, anguished, and fear leaped inside her. "You would whore your body to me, a monster, to accomplish your goal."

"No," she choked out.

"You did. You *did!*"

"No! I love..."

He cringed. "Speak no lies to me. Must you insult my intelligence, as well?" He loomed over her. His anger and displeasure frightened her far more than his physical size. She wanted desperately for him to understand.

"I wanted him to think I would kill you," she whispered.

"Do not take me for a fool."

"I was going to cut my arm and smear blood on the blade. That way he'd think..."

"You lie!" Anger shook through his voice. "No one would do that for me. I forgave you for your treachery last time. I cannot again."

Fear spiraled in her. "Commander..."

"No! You have betrayed me. Do not speak again."

She had to make him see. "I lied to my brother. Truly, I meant to betray *him.*"

He growled, shaking his head, as if trying to shoo off a gnat.

"I meant to protect you," she insisted. "Otherwise, he'd kill you himself."

"Let him try," he roared, and she shook then, with fright. He hauled her to her feet.

"What are you doing with me?"

"What I should have done last time."

"No," she cried out, struggling against him. "You're not the monster everyone says you are."

"I am."

"You are not!" Or was he? Terror galloped through her, but tears burned her eyes. His hatred hurt far more than any punishment he could mete out.

He pushed her into a chair and lashed her hands behind her back. He glowered at her. "I will finish with you later. Now I must stop your brother's plot to kill the Prince."

Her brother's plot to kill the Prince? Horrified, she watched him leave, slamming the door behind him. The Commander suspected... That meant the Prince did, too.

Fear spiraled in her. If only she could stop Richard! If he attacked the Prince he would sentence death upon his head...and hers. Tears ran down her face, and she struggled helplessly against her bonds. She had an awful feeling someone would die tonight. Someone she loved.

And maybe herself, as well.

ϟ ϟ ϟ ϟ ϟ

The Commander rushed into the hall, sword and dagger clenched in his fists. Rage and pain contorted inside him. He'd hoped—foolishly—to find Elwytha innocent. But no, she had taken out the dagger to kill him. To kill him!

He swallowed back an agonized roar as he ran through the halls. Silence. He couldn't warn Richard of his approach—if the Prince hadn't finished him off already. The Commander wanted to be there, should his lifelong friend need help.

He stopped outside the great hall and listened. Nothing. The drinking and socializing had ended for the evening. Then where were the Prince and Richard? He ran next for the throne room. He approached the doors and slowed, listening carefully. One door was ajar. No guards were in sight. Something must be wrong.

Quieting his breathing, he moved closer. That's when he heard it; a faint moan, just beyond the doors.

"Commander."

The Prince! Was he injured? With caution, he looked around the door edge into the blackness. All lights had been extinguished. Unease surged. He felt danger close by. Quickly, he looked left. When he glanced right, he saw a quick, blinding movement and then pain exploded across his face.

With a guttural cry, he staggered. He reached for a wall for stability, and found the wobbly door. He stumbled against it. Out of the corner of his eye, he saw movement again. Through his pain blurred mind, he swung up his sword to defend himself.

His blade sliced into something hard, sticking to it. A wooden beam. His attacker held a wooden beam. Even now, his unseen opponent swung it back for another swing, jerking his sword from his hand.

The Commander was ready this time. Battle precision and long practice had ingrained automatic responses. It was a good thing, because his brain felt fogged with agony. He blocked the blow with his left arm and swung his dagger with his right.

A flash of metal threw off his aim. It was a dagger, flying right toward him. He swiftly blocked it with his forearm, but felt no pain.

The wooden beam fell with a crash.

He saw a shadowy movement, and then another blade shone in the dim light. Another dagger. All of a sudden, he knew the man had three. Elwytha had had three. Three to fling, one after another, at their attackers.

This blade shot toward his leg, but he did not take the bait. He turned quickly, taking it in the back of his thigh, just as another dagger flew toward his neck. Like lightning, he deflected the murderous blade. He recoiled and brought his own blade back, but before he could let it fly, he heard a faint sound behind him. A silver dagger whistled by his ear, straight and true toward the enemy. It sank deep into flesh and bone.

With a strangled cry, the man dropped to his knees. The light from the hall revealed Elwytha's bearded brother. King Richard stared up at him, then beyond him, eyes glazing.

"Reap your treacherous reward, Richard," said the Prince.

And then, with a quickness the Commander would never believe, the dying King flung a fourth dagger straight at the Prince.

Instinct made his own blade flash out, faster still, deflecting the deadly missile. Richard collapsed on the floor, blood pooling on the floor. The Prince's bejeweled dagger was imbedded in him to the hilt.

"Good work, Commander."

He felt light-headed now, and felt stinging in his cut arm and leg. Blood dripped down his face. He swiped at it, and at his nose, which felt the most painful. It was broken yet again, smashed flush with his face this time.

The Prince regarded him. "You look a prize."

Now he noted the blood dripping down his friend's jerkin, and the slash on his arm. "You look no better." He gestured at Richard. "What happened? Where are your guards?"

The Prince looked at the King's fallen form in contempt. "He said he wished to discuss peace, and asked that we speak in my study. I didn't know he'd put a potion in my guards' drinks. When they stumbled and fell on the way to the study, Richard attacked me forthwith." He gestured ruefully at his bloodied wounds. "He caught me by surprise. We battled and he was losing. He ran off. I see now he hid in the throne room."

"He extinguished all the lights." The Commander kicked at the wooden beam, which now lay harmlessly on the floor. "And he hit me with a log."

The Prince laughed. "Good thing you're made of stone, or your face would look less pretty."

"What will we do with him?"

The Prince regarded the Commander. "Tell me first, did your lady love betray you?"

He looked away. The clawing, agonizing pain again seized his heart. During the battle he'd been able to compartmentalize it. Now it felt again like it might kill him. "Yes," he gritted in a low voice. "I caught her with my blade in her hand."

A small silence elapsed. "What will you do?"

He looked at Richard's fallen form. Elwytha had betrayed him. He groaned aloud, and pressed his fist to his face. It increased the agony in his head. He wished only to fall to his knees and weep. "I will take care of Elwytha," he whispered.

The Prince remained uncharacteristically silent for a time. Finally, he said, "I want Elwytha to sign a surrender agreement. Delay your punishment until after that."

"When?"

"Now. I have it ready in my study."

"You never doubted their treachery?"

Another small silence, and then, "Never."

The Commander heaved a breath. "I will bring Elwytha."

"Bring her by here, brother," the Prince said. "Let her see Richard's dead body. Make her understand that her treacherous plot is ended."

The Commander nodded and retrieved his sword, and then, with slow steps, went to summon his traitorous wife to justice.

⚔ ⚔ ⚔ ⚔ ⚔

Elwytha had given up fighting her bonds. They were too tight. She could not escape. As she could not escape the fate Richard would force upon her. If only she could make the Commander see her innocence. But he'd found her with a blade in hand. His blade, stolen from his trunk. What was he to think, especially after overhearing her conversation with Richard this afternoon?

She waited in dread for someone to come.

Long minutes...perhaps an hour later...the door opened, and the Commander entered. She gasped. Blood covered his nose, which was obviously broken, and dripped down his mouth.

"You're hurt," she cried out, unable to help herself.

He did not answer. In silence, he loosed her bonds, then pulled her to her feet, gripping her by the arm with one large hand. He forced her toward the door.

"Where are you taking me?" she gasped. Fear bloomed.

"Walk," he thundered, and she obeyed.

"I didn't intend to betray..."

"Silence!" His grip on her arm hurt now. "Speak no more. I will not hear you."

More tears fell as her terror swelled. What had happened? What was he going to do with her? She knew her fate lay in his hands. The Prince had promised it. So what would the Commander do to her?

What had happened to Richard?

It couldn't be good. More helpless sobs choked out. Richard was still her brother, no matter his plots and treachery. Had he walked into a trap? Wasn't it her fault he was here at all? After all, if she hadn't agreed to marry the Commander, none of this would have happened. Of course, she had followed Richard's orders. His wishes, all along.

Except she hadn't killed the Commander. Had this proven to be Richard's death sentence?

They strode quickly through the halls—toward the throne room, she realized. Did the Prince sit upon his throne, even at night? Would he witness the justice the Commander would mete upon her head, approving it? She gasped, trying to wrench free, but it only resulted in a harder vise around her arm.

Feet flying, unwillingly, over the stone floor, she approached the throne room. The doors were open, and it looked dark inside. So the Prince wasn't in there. ...But a man sprawled on the floor, near the door.

Richard.

She let out a high, keening wail. The Commander allowed her to collapse at her brother's side. He was dead, she knew this. "Richard. Richard!" She wept and pressed her cheek to his lifeless one. All of their days together as children flew through her mind. The good times, and the bad. She sobbed harder, for the boy he had been, and for the man he had become.

"Come." The Commander gripped her wrist, and dragged her to her feet. "Enough." He propelled her down the hallway again, but she looked over her shoulder, wanting one last glimpse of her brother. She knew she would never see him again.

Elwytha did not know where they were going. She couldn't see through her blinding tears. Finally, he shoved her into a small, warm room, and she saw it was the Prince's study. He stood beside the round table, alone. Elwytha saw a parchment upon it. And a quill with ink.

The Commander released her when she reached the table.

Frightened, Elwytha looked from one to the other and brushed the tears from her eyes. What did this mean? Why had they brought her here? To kill her, wouldn't they bring her to the dungeons, or maybe outside?

She waited, barely daring to breathe, for one of them to speak.

The Prince broke the silence. "Your brother is dead, Princess. Now your family's kingdom falls to you."

Elwytha heaved a breath. Surely they did not intend to let her live and rule her kingdom. She waited silently for her sentence to be read.

The Prince's obsidian gaze held hers. "You will sign surrender papers now. You will sign over your kingdom to my throne. Otherwise, we will battle and vanquish your land on the morrow."

Elwytha's hands shook. If she signed it, he would conquer her land with a pen stroke, and the land her family had ruled for centuries would no longer be theirs. The dishonor of it. And the death. The Prince surely would not allow her family to live. He would kill everyone opposed to him.

"No," she said. "I will not allow the murder of my family. Or my people."

"We will kill only those who defy us," the Prince said.

"And I should trust your honor?" she spat. "You, who killed my brother?"

"Your brother," the Prince said through thinned lips, "felled my guards with a potion. He sprang upon me with a stolen sword. And he attacked your Commander with a log and three daggers. He deserved his fate."

Elwytha stared at the bloodied face of her husband. He returned her gaze, his steely eyes cold. Blood congealed on his face and he looked frightful, yet still she loved this man. And Richard had done this to him—had smashed his face somehow. And what of the dagger attack? Swiftly, she scanned him, and for the first time saw the blood on his forearm, and the dark stain dripping down his leg. Horror shuddered through her. Richard could have killed him.

Her brother had attacked him with three daggers, just as she had meant to do. He had lost. And he had earned his fate.

She heaved a breath, and tried to marshal her thoughts, but continued to look at her husband. "If the Commander also swears to their safety, I will believe you."

The Commander frowned at her. He didn't look to the Prince for confirmation. "I swear by my honor."

Hands trembling, she reached for the quill. "As well, promise homes for my family, and no ill treatment for all who cooperate," she demanded.

"Done," he rumbled.

Elwytha stared at the document. A peaceful surrender would benefit her people far more than another bloody battle. A battle they would finally lose, she knew, as they had lost the last battles. And now they had no king, or ruler. Any attempt from one of her distant kinsmen to rise to power and deploy warriors would happen too late.

She dipped the quill in the ink, and with a steady hand, neatly wrote her name. "You have your surrender," she said. "Now what will become of me?"

The Commander stiffened beside her. He did not speak, as if unable to.

The Prince spoke instead, his black eyes fixed on the Commander. Could that be a flicker of compassion in that obsidian gaze? Elwytha found it hard to believe that any kind emotion lived in him. His next words proved it. "Decide soon, Commander. You will ride on her castle at first light."

Elwytha gasped and clenched her fists. "You promised no battle. You promised the safety of my people!"

The Prince's eyes looked as hard as coals. "We will ride under the white flag of truce. The Commander will present the surrender agreement. All those who fight against us will die."

Elwytha went very still. The Commander would enter her castle. He'd be vulnerable, and possibly alone. She turned to him. "Don't do it," she cried. "They'll kill you."

The Prince mocked, "Still, she professes wifely affection."

She glared. "I know my warriors. They will attack him if he enters the castle gates."

The Commander said, "I am not as foolish as your brother. We will meet on the ground of battle, outside your castle."

Although Elwytha felt relieved, she still felt dismayed about the fate of her people, and about her own fate, too. She forced herself to meet the Commander's eyes. He gazed at her with dislike and contempt, and it seemed that he didn't want to look at her at all. Elwytha's heart began to bleed then, as she realized the deep, irrevocable damage done between them. She had come here intending treachery. Richard had tried to kill him. The Commander no longer trusted her. He hated her. He would not believe any words she spoke to him.

"Commander, what will you do to me?" She couldn't stop the small tremor in her voice.

A muscle clenched in his jaw and he glanced at the Prince. Then he looked back at her, his eyes a wintry, bleak gray. Harshly, he said, "I will not decide your fate now. I am too angry to think clearly."

She swallowed. What did this mean? "Will you put me in the dungeon, then?"

She waited, and the Prince remained silent, as if waiting, too.

He thundered, "I will put you where it pleases me!"

She jumped a bit and he seized her arm, which frightened her still more. He told the Prince, "I will return soon." And then he forced her to the door.

Silently, she ran to match his long strides down the halls. Familiar halls. He was returning to his chamber...to her old chamber. He thrust her inside the small room. He seemed barely able to look at her. "I will decide your fate when I return from your castle," he gritted, and slammed the door. The lock clicked.

Elwytha stared at the closed door, barely able to believe her fate. Was this turn of events good or bad? She would live for another few days...or weeks. And then what? Would he kill her when he returned? Was this incarceration meant to intensify her torment and fear?

She couldn't believe this. She did, however, believe he didn't know what to do, and that was why he'd locked her up in here.

Still, her fate remained undecided. Tomorrow he would ride against her castle. Elwytha knew her warriors. Many would rather fight than surrender to the Prince; signed surrender or not. Many men could die. The Commander could die.

Elwytha could not bear the thought of any harm coming to him. She loved him. She loved him so much.

She sank onto her bed and wept for the loss of her marriage, for her brother's death, for her fear of the future...and for her own broken heart.

CHAPTER TWENTY-TWO

ELWYTHA PACED HER SMALL CELL of a chamber, feeling depressed. Gray, early morning light streamed in through the overhead window. It matched her mood. Over a week had passed since the Commander had ridden out to defeat her castle. Was he dead? Had they killed him?

Anguish roiled within her. Though he hated her, she still loved him with all of her heart. Even if she was to die, she wanted him to live a long, good life. It was what he deserved.

As she had received what she deserved. She had plotted treachery and had lied. No one would believe that she had changed her mind. The Commander hadn't. He didn't believe she had married him because she wanted to. She loved him— but hadn't told him so. He would believe nothing she said now, anyway. He didn't believe that she had wanted peace. Or that she'd tried to stop Richard's murderous plot. More tears trickled down her cheeks. She had cried bucketfuls in the last eight days. It seemed like they would never end.

The Commander hated her, as did everyone else in this palace. Her two friends, Hagma and Mary, hated her, too. It was unbearable. Every day Hagma brought her food, and Elwytha couldn't look at her anymore. She couldn't stand the disappointment and anger in her friend's eyes.

She heard a sound at the door, and knew Hagma had arrived with breakfast. She sat quietly on the bed and watched the maid enter.

"I've bread and eggs this morning," Hagma said, and then attended the necessary chores in the chamber. She moved quickly, as if anxious to leave.

All of a sudden, Elwytha couldn't stand it anymore. "I know you hate me," she said softly. "I know you all do."

Hagma turned on her, her eyes hard. "You betrayed us all. How else should we feel?"

Elwytha swallowed. She had to try, at least, to explain herself. Over and over again, she'd rehearsed her speeches of innocence...and remembered her sins. She was about to go crazy in this tiny room, cut off from people, and from the outdoors she loved so well.

And feeling the hatred of others shriveled up her soul. She couldn't stand it anymore. She had to speak, and try to make someone understand. And struggle—perhaps hopelessly—for someone to believe her.

Quietly, she said, "I committed no treachery against the Commander. It's true I intended to when I first arrived, but..."

"Because you hate us so much?" Hurt and further anger sounded in Hagma's voice.

"No. Because of Thor." Elwytha drew an anguished breath. "I thought the Commander murdered him. His sword was found deep in his back. Richard wanted vengeance, and so did I. So he sent me here under a false peace agreement." Elwytha felt even more depressed, as she confessed her guilt, and further shame. She did not feel better, as she had hoped.

"The Commander would kill no one in such a manner," Hagma stated, her tone sharp and condemning.

"Of course not." Elwytha bit her lip. "I learned that quickly. So I decided to abandon Richard's plot. But when Richard came, he told me he'd kill the Commander if I wouldn't; so I told him I'd do it. But really, I meant to smear my own blood on the blade so Richard would think he was dead. Then we'd both escape from the palace and go home. But it didn't turn out that way." That horrible night again blasted through Elwytha's mind.

Hagma said coldly, "Richard plotted to kill the Prince."

"I didn't know," Elwytha cried out. "I didn't even think to suspect it—not until he actually came. And then I told Mary to warn Henry that Richard would need watching. I hoped I was wrong. I didn't know, for sure. Since I first got here, I wondered if Richard might be plotting something else, but I never dreamed then... I thought he might try to attack the palace, but I never guessed he'd try to assassinate the Prince."

"Really?"

Elwytha looked away. "I know you don't believe me. I know you hate me, and everyone hates me. The Commander hates me...." Unable to help herself, she burst into tears. "I never wished for any of this to happen."

Hagma looked sad, and wary. "Truly, miss?"

"Yes." Elwytha felt hopeless. Helpless. The man she loved hated her. She was incarcerated in the enemy palace, and every friend she'd made here distrusted and hated her. It made her feel sick to her stomach. In fact, she felt like she might vomit right now.

With difficulty, Elwytha took a deep breath, trying to calm herself. But her relentless thoughts beat on. Her honor had been irrevocably sullied to these people. Forever, they would be her enemies. She wiped her face with her sleeve and surveyed the unappetizing eggs before her. The sick feeling intensified and she pushed the tray aside.

"What is to become of me?" she appealed to Hagma. "I've been locked up here for over a week. Has the Commander vanquished my land? Am I to die?"

Hagma bit her lip and backed toward the door. "The Commander has not returned, and I do not know, miss."

Of course not. She was only a servant.

"I will speak to Mary," Hagma said. "I'll be back later."

Hopelessly, Elwytha watched her go. Another mindless day lay before her, to be spent in her prison. If only she had a parchment to write upon, or needlework to occupy her mind. She feared she might go crazy soon.

The food looked revolting now, and Elwytha flopped back on her bed and stared at the ceiling. Light streamed through her tiny window. Oh, if only she could go outside. But condemned prisoners could not partake in such joys. And when the Commander returned, not only would her joy be ended, but perhaps her life, as well.

Was he all right? As always, Elwytha's mind returned to her husband. All week, she had prayed fervently for his safety as he rode on her castle; as he battled to vanquish her land.

She missed him so much, and she loved him so much. And she longed for the hopeless—for things to return to the way they were on their wedding day. Before Richard came.

It would never be. Wretchedly, Elwytha wept into her pillow until she had no strength to cry anymore.

※ ※ ※ ※ ※

Later that day, Elwytha heard a noise at her door and slowly sat up. She felt exhausted, and still had not touched the foul eggs.

It was too early for Hagma to return.

The door opened and the Prince entered. With a startled gasp, Elwytha leaped to her feet. The enemy ruler wore no crown upon his black hair, and a dagger sparkled at his belt.

Her eyes narrowed in confusion. "Why are you here? I didn't know your royal feet tread these pedestrian hallways."

His teeth gleamed, but it could not be called a smile. "Your pleas of innocence have reached my ears."

Surprised, Elwytha said, "Hagma spoke to you?"

"Henry, my guard."

Quickly, she remembered that Hagma had said she'd speak to Mary. Perhaps Mary had spoken to her husband, Henry. She swiftly marshaled her wits, knowing the Prince paid her no social visit.

"Do you believe in my innocence? Have you decided to set me free?" Elwytha didn't believe this for a moment.

His eyes looked like coals, and his aquiline nose looked as sharp as the blade tucked into his belt. "No." Venom bit through the word.

Fear slid through her. "Then why are you here?"

"To interrogate you."

Elwytha crossed her arms. Though what defense this might prove against his blade, should he decide to wield it upon her, she did not know. "Ply your questions then, and I will answer."

"With more of the lies you're spreading around my palace?"

She opened her mouth, but he raised a finger for silence. "I will put an end to your lies. Answer me now. You plotted with Richard to kill the Commander. You swore to a false peace. You say now you changed your mind and forsook your plot to betray us. But you still knew of Richard's treachery, and did not speak of it." The Prince watched her with condemnation in his black eyes.

The breath caught in Elwytha's throat. And guilt. "Tell me, could I betray my own brother?"

"The Commander deals with you too kindly," he flashed.

"Yes, you would adorn your flagpole, I know. But I did not betray the Commander, Prince. I did not put a blade to his throat. I would *never* do that." Anguish sparked her temper.

"Your silence was treachery enough."

"How could I serve honor to Richard and honor to the Commander? Pray, what would you have done, if you are so wise?"

The Prince took a menacing step toward her. "I would *kill* the bastard who killed my brother!" His black eyes cut into her like knives, shocking her.

It took her a moment to understand what he meant. "I didn't know that Richard killed Thor. I still have no proof. You would have me kill an innocent man?"

"You purposed to kill the Commander," he said silkily. "An innocent man."

"I didn't know," she cried out. "Not at first. And then...finally, I believed him. I never would have married him, otherwise."

"You love him so tenderly, then?" the Prince mocked. "Spare me a woman who would serve a lie and pretend it the truth."

"Truly, Prince, you have all the answers, don't you? I did not want Richard to die, or the Commander, or even you. That is the truth. If I failed," she spurted, "it is because I have not your infinite wisdom. You are faultless in all your ways, are you not? No, Prince," she said with scorn, "You are as blackened as the rest of us. You knew Richard planned treachery. You suspected me...and him...all along. Yet still you sported with us. We are the only ones who suffered."

"As you deserved," he returned in a cutting tone.

"Pretend no innocence, Prince," she lashed. "True, I plotted treachery at first. But you plotted it to the last—Richard's last breath. Did you lure him here and taunt him to attack you? Did you commit the cold blooded murder of my last brother?"

Anger flared, giving the Prince's features a dangerous edge, but Elwytha no longer cared.

She hissed, "You hate my words? Perhaps now you understand how it feels to be accused when you can provide no proof of your innocence."

As the Commander had felt when she'd repeatedly disbelieved his innocence. Tears burned her eyes.

"Judge me then, Prince. I have admitted my crime. But torture me no further with your presence or your false piety. Leave me to the hell the Commander has subscribed me to!" She burst into tears and turned away.

He was right. Perhaps she should have warned the Commander and Prince directly. Maybe they would have thrown Richard into the moat instead of killing him.

But now her fate was sealed. The Prince despised her. The Commander hated her. Her tears came faster. Clearly, that would never change. When would they take her life? Or would she spend the rest of her days locked in this tiny chamber, tortured by her thoughts and memories? She gulped, choking on uncontrollable sobs.

Behind her, she heard slow, deliberate hand claps. "Well done, Princess," the Prince said softly.

Elwytha shuddered, unable to bear his mocking taunt. "I am not playing a game," she screamed out. "This is real life. *Mine*. But how could you possibly know the difference?" Further fury flared, and she whirled in a rage, but he was gone. The door softly clicked closed behind him.

※ ※ ※ ※ ※

The next morning, Hagma came with a guard.

Elwytha sat up, glad she had dressed this morn. Since the interrogation by the condemning Prince, she had felt little desire to do anything. Even food did not appeal.

"This is Mary's husband, Henry." Hagma indicated the helmeted warrior. Elwytha had seen that mustached face before. "The Prince has agreed you may go outside for an hour each day. Henry must accompany you."

Joy soared in her. With wonder, she looked from Hagma to the guard. "But...the Prince doesn't believe in my innocence. Why would he allow this?"

"Mary and I believe you. And she asked Henry to speak again to the Prince for you. It's a small comfort, but it's the least we can do."

"You believe me?" Tears filled Elwytha's eyes. "Truly, you do?"

Hagma nodded. "And Mary is worried. Why are you not eating your food?"

Elwytha could not even look at the glistening scrambled eggs. "It makes me want to vomit. I do not know why."

Hagma scooped up the tray and offered Elwytha a small smile. "What would you like?"

Elwytha burst into tears at the unmerited kindnesses. "Perhaps toast and fruit, if it's not too much trouble."

Hagma nodded, but before she could leave, Elwytha leaped to her feet and hugged her friend. "Thank you, Hagma," she whispered brokenly.

Hagma pulled away, seemingly embarrassed, but pleased as well. "Do not carry on, miss. These are only small things."

"But they mean everything to me."

"After breakfast, Henry will return to take you outside."

Elwytha smiled at the helmeted man. "Thank you, Henry."

The gray mustached man said, "Hmmph."

"And please thank Mary, too," Elwytha told them as the door closed.

Relief and joy brightened her spirits as Elwytha waited for their return. To go outside! To smell the breeze and see something besides these boring four walls. But she didn't delude herself. Her fate may still end up at the edge of a sword, but for now, the life remaining her would be more bearable.

CHAPTER TWENTY-THREE

TWO WEEKS TO THE DAY after Richard's death, Hagma entered Elwytha's chamber, bearing her usual breakfast of toast and fruit. She set it down on the dresser.

"The Commander returned last night."

Elwytha's heart leaped. He lived! "Is he all right?" she asked anxiously. "Has he been injured?"

"Nay, miss, not that I could see." Hagma bit her lip. "I'm sorry, miss, but..."

Dread sank to her toes. "He wishes to sentence me for my crime."

"He wants you to dress and pack. You will leave in an hour." Hagma blinked quickly.

Elwytha felt a bolt of surprise. "But where am I going?" Would he have her pack if he meant to kill her? Surely not. A blade of hope sprouted in her heart.

"I know not." After a hesitation, she said, "Goodbye, miss."

Elwytha hugged her friend and watched her go. Tears prickled in her own eyes. But she also felt hopeful. She would be delivered from this tiny chamber—perhaps to another tiny chamber? The dungeon, perhaps? Some small part of her did not believe this.

Quickly, she dressed and packed, unable to deny her eagerness to see her husband. She only nibbled at the toast. Her stomach roiled, sickening her. Nerves? Or did she have the flu? She spent a few minutes struggling not to throw up.

But she was so hungry. When her stomach calmed, she ate a little more toast and felt better.

Elwytha was easily ready within the hour. Two guards came and collected her trunk. Later, another came for her.

Where was the Commander? Evidently, he had no wish to see her.

Further pain withered her heart. She followed the guard to the stables. Sir Duke was saddled, and nuzzled her hand eagerly. Closing her eyes, she pressed her cheek to her old friend's face. At least someone loved her.

"Mount," the guard told her. She obeyed, and then followed a small envoy of horses, including one that pulled her trunk in a cart, over the drawbridge to the field below. There she saw her husband upon his black stallion, and her heart leaped. He looked well and strong. Just as she had hoped and prayed he would be.

As soon as they cleared the castle he rode ahead, clearly leading the small troupe. Equally clear, he intended to shun her.

No chamber imprisoned her now. No shackles tied her legs or hands. Therefore nothing, she determined, would stop her from speaking to him. She could not stand being apart from him for one more moment. And she longed for him to hear her, and to believe in her innocence. As well, she wished to know where they were going. What future did he intend for her?

Elwytha patted Sir Duke, and he broke into a glad gallop. When they neared the Commander, she pulled back on the reins. With reluctance, Sir Duke slowed. Her heart beat fast as they drew alongside the black stallion. "Commander."

He glanced at her and frowned. A white bandage covered his nose. Evidently the break had been terrible if it still needed healing. Did it pain him?

With him glowering at her, all questions fled from her head except one. "What is to become of me?" It was the same question she had asked two weeks ago. Would he answer now?

He gritted his teeth and looked away, as if it were painful to look at her. "You will return to your castle and ready it for the new king."

Elwytha digested this. She would not be put to death. Relief soared, and hope, too. She could go home, even if it was only to ready her palace for another. "What new king?"

He looked back at her, and the wintry gaze forbade further questions. Elwytha ignored the warning. Now was her chance to speak. "Commander, please," she begged, "listen to me."

He turned his head away and rumbled harshly, "I spared your life. Speak no more to me." As though he couldn't stand the sight of her, he kicked the stallion into a gallop and left her behind.

His rejection stabbed like a dagger through her heart. He refused to hear her. He hated her! Tears wet her cheeks. How many had fallen since she'd first arrived at the Prince's palace? A month's worth. And still they did not end. Nor would they end anytime soon. Not as long as she loved him. Not as long as her heart beat.

Depressed, Elwytha rode on, and as noon approached her stomach rumbled. As well, the nausea from this morning returned. Remembering how toast had settled her stomach, she nibbled on bread from her bag. It did not help. Sir Duke's steady rising and dipping gait seemed to worsen it, for the queasiness increased as they continued.

Elwytha gulped, feeling her throat convulse. Suddenly, she couldn't hold it back. Clinging to Sir Duke's neck, she leaned forward and retched to the ground.

She hoped it would make her feel better. It didn't. She retched again. Weak and trembling, she pressed her face into Sir Duke's neck. Elwytha wanted to cry, but did not.

When she opened her eyes, she saw a black horse beside her. Eyes watery, her gaze flickered to the Commander. His mouth looked grim, and he looked at her as if she were an unwanted annoyance. "You are ill?"

"I have the flu." Elwytha sat up in an attempt to regain her dignity.

"Is it why you don't eat?" he asked harshly.

"How did you know?"

"Hagma pained my ears with reports on your health."

"Did she also say she believes me innocent of treachery?" Again, desperately, she appealed to him.

The wintry eyes turned to flint, and Elwytha quailed inside. He said, "I spared your life. Test me no further."

"Commander, I have not lied to you," she cried out, unable to keep silent for another moment. "Please, I did not betray..."

"No," he roared. "Speak to me no further!" He snapped the reins and the black charged ahead.

He would not hear her words. It was time for her to accept this. No peace would exist between them, ever again.

She watched him gallop ahead, and her heart bled out hope. Without him, home held no cheer. Her life would be as drab and gray as imprisonment in a dungeon.

❧ ❧ ❧ ❧ ❧

Castle Iolaire, two weeks later

The Commander lifted a blade and ran it down his cheek. The Prince had asked how long he would delay the inevitable. He had no answer. Not yet.

Warm water dripped down his smoothly shaven neck. He barely recognized the man staring at him in the metal mirror. He lowered the blade and wiped his face with the rough cloth.

It was his hair. He still wasn't used to it. He fingered the black strands. It was longer than two inches now. Part of him itched to shave it off, too.

But it pleased her. So he would continue to let it grow...to torture himself still further.

He had hoped the pain would abate as time went by. It hadn't. So far, it had only intensified, eating at his heart, his mind, his soul. He loved her. Her betrayal had slain him, and he felt like half a man. When would the pain end?

He wished for her, even now, God help him.

Escorting her to the palace had almost unmanned him. Her sickness made him wish to gather her in his arms and forgive her, protect her, and care for her. And he'd wanted to believe her pleas of entreaty. To believe her innocent of treachery.

He was a *fool*. He clenched his fist. A weak fool. His weakness for her could only be his undoing.

Yet again, the Commander wished for a battle to fight. Taking over her castle had been far too easy. He could find no release for the anguish tormenting his soul—only vicious sword fights with his best swordsmen, who were all too easily defeated.

He ran his hand through his hair again and turned away from the foggy mirror. If only this mantle would fall from him.

He could not see her. Not yet. But the inevitable would not be denied forever.

$$ \text{\Large Y\ \ Y\ \ Y\ \ Y\ \ Y} $$

Castle Cor na Gaeth

Elwytha had been home for three weeks now. Today she would clear Richard's personal items from the King's chamber. She had no idea when the new ruler would arrive, but no doubt the new king would wish to claim the room for his own.

Pain still simmered, deep in her soul, like a wound that would not heal. She missed the Commander desperately. But at least now—in her mind—she accepted her fate. Her heart still resisted this unpalatable truth.

He had allowed her to live. For this, she would be grateful. But she would spend the rest of her days alone. She knew this, too. No other man could ever take his place in her heart. She would love him forever.

Reluctantly, she entered the King's chamber. Already Richard's clothes had been removed, and the linens changed. She only needed to go through his desk. She carried a large bag to put all the papers in.

Richard had written prolifically. He'd written missives to other rulers and kept all of their correspondence, and he'd written piles of other things, too...lists, battle plans, and more. Elwytha swept them all into her bag. She opened the drawer of his desk and discovered a bound book. A rare commodity. For what purpose had her brother used it? She fingered the leather cover.

It felt strange to be in his room, going through his private items. Richard had been an intensely private man. But now he was dead. His wrath could no longer hurt her. She opened the bound book.

A quick flip through proved that each page was dated. She read the first entry, and was shocked. The page detailed Richard's thoughts, and what he'd done that day. The bound volume was half full.

Overcome by a guilty fascination, Elwytha read the next page, and the next. Nausea told her it was time for the next meal, but she nibbled the cracker she always carried with her now, and read on. Soon she would need to speak to a doctor about her illness. But not yet. It wasn't as bad as it had been in the beginning. Perhaps she was healing, even now.

The sun lowered in the sky, darkening the chamber. She lit the fire and sat beside it, reading on. She had already learned much about Richard that she'd never known before. His paranoia, for one. He'd wondered, even before Thor died, if Elwytha would kill him if he ever gained the throne. Next, his fears turned to Thor. Would Thor kill him to protect his throne?

She also learned of his desperate lust for power, and his secret dreams of becoming king. He wrote detailed plans of what he would accomplish as monarch; primarily to tax more and obtain more luxury items. She checked the dates. It neared the date of Thor's death.

She turned the page and read,

Lance will kill Thor with the sword I found in battle. The Commander's sword. How perfect. Now he will be blamed for

Thor's death. What a pretty find, that day on the battlefield. The fates must be looking upon me. They must wish for me to be ruler.

Horrified, Elwytha felt a surge of nausea. She gulped it back. Richard had plotted Thor's death and framed the Commander, even from that early day. She skimmed on, reading of Thor's death, and Richard's elation. Not a scrap of remorse for the horrific deed he had ordered could be found.

She drew a shuddering breath. What a waste. Thor's life had ended for no reason. He had been murdered only to satisfy Richard's greed for power and wealth. And Richard's twisted reasoning throughout the journal entries justified his actions by stating, again and again, how he suspected Thor meant to kill him.

Of course he had not. Had Richard begun to lose his mind?

Elwytha flipped ahead to read about when Richard had sent her to the Prince's palace with the fake peace plan. Yes, here it was. Her nausea intensified as she read it.

The perfect plan. The Commander is framed for Thor's murder. Elwytha will happily avenge her favorite brother. And when he is dead, the Prince will win no more victories. With that monster dead, his forces will fall to my hands...and Elwytha will pay for the Commander's murder.

Elwytha. My only remaining sibling. For pure sentiment's sake, I feel saddened. I hope they kill her, for I have not the heart to do it. A true warrior. And the last threat to my throne.

Sickened betrayal twisted through Elwytha, although Richard's words came as no surprise. She had suspected the truth long weeks ago. But to have them confirmed in ink on parchment... From Richard's own pen!

Pain billowed through her.

Richard had meant for her to kill the Commander, and then be slain herself, so Richard wouldn't have to do it. That's why he had come late to the palace. He had thought she would murder the Commander before her wedding. He'd counted on his belief that she would be too repelled to wed the 'monster.' And yet she hadn't. Richard had been incensed, she remembered. If she hadn't promised to kill the Commander that night, he would have killed her in his guest quarters.

Treachery. Betrayal. Murder. A path of blood from her castle to the Prince's. Only the Commander's mercy had spared her life.

Could healing ever be possible between their two lands? Or for her heart?

꙳ ꙳ ꙳ ꙳ ꙳

Castle Iolaire, six weeks later

"Why do you continue to delay your departure?" the Prince inquired, relaxed on his chair in his study.

The Commander restlessly paced the room. No matter what he did, however, he could not escape the pain that still ate at his soul. He chose not to answer.

The Prince said, "You did not allow Elwytha to play her hand fully."

He frowned in surprise. "You are speaking in her defense?"

The monarch sat silently for a moment. "I spoke to her while you fought Castle Cor na Gaeth. I can discern a lie. I looked, but saw none in her testimonies."

The Commander felt even more surprised, but growled, "I cannot trust her. She held my blade in her hand. I heard her swear to her brother that she'd kill me."

"True." The Prince nodded, and said after a moment, "I will speak no more. Except it pains me to see you wretched, as you are."

The Commander turned away. Cravenly, he wished to believe his friend's words. He wanted to believe in Elwytha's innocence. But at the cost of all reason? He knew well enough that he could not think clearly where she was concerned. He turned back and said, "Do you have proof of her innocence?"

"No. But she did warn Henry to watch Richard that night." The Prince watched the effect of his words on the Commander, who felt a twinge of hope. "Have you spoken to her about that night?"

"No," he admitted. He was afraid to. Afraid his foolish heart would too readily believe whatever she told him. He wanted to find hope in his discerning friend's words. Seldom, he knew, did the Prince ever affirm a hint of faith in another. "You trust her, then?"

The Prince gave a cynical smile. "I trust no woman. And she is not completely innocent. She admits as much. However, a little truth may lie in her story. It is up to you to discover how much."

He would see Elwytha soon. This he knew. He dreaded it and he longed for it, but he could avoid it no longer. Soon, he would find the answers his heart feared...and demanded.

Perhaps hope was possible. Perhaps not. He would tread carefully.

The Commander drew a fortifying breath and turned for the door. "Thank you, old friend."

"Godspeed, brother."

CHAPTER TWENTY-FOUR

Castle Cor na Gaeth
January 716 A.D.

THE DAY SHE HAD LONG DREADED had arrived. Elwytha rested her palms upon the rough stone parapets of the tower. The wind sang through her hair, mixing with the thunder of horses' hooves galloping across the grassy hills.

It wasn't the only change in the air. King Osred of Northumbria was dead. Rumors whispered that he'd been murdered by Coenred, the new King. What would happen to Cor na Gaeth now? Would the brutal new ruler be satisfied with token tributes? Perhaps it would take months to sort out. And right now she must face a new King of her own.

The new ruler now approached. The castle and its lands would no longer belong to Elwytha or her clan. She had had three long months while preparing the castle for the enemy king to accept this unpalatable truth. She could swallow it no easier now than before.

Who had the Prince sent to rule over her people, Elwytha wondered for the millionth time. She knew he had no brothers or sisters. Perhaps a cousin or an uncle.

Which of the riders was he?

Her eyes strained as the horses galloped nearer, and then one large warrior vaulted off his horse and strode toward the castle drawbridge. Instinctively, she knew this was he. He held himself with confidence. He also wore a King's full warrior armor, and even from this distance she could see that he was huge and fearsome, with flowing black hair...

Elwytha gasped. He looked exactly like the image in the portrait the Prince had shown her. Of his father, the King.

She strained for more details of the man. From his profile, all she could make out were a straight dark brow and a straight, strong nose. All were a mirror image of the dead king. In fact, if Elwytha wasn't certain he was dead, she would think this was he—only he would be much older than this man. This powerful, intimidating visage possessed the full strength and vigor of prime manhood. He was the new king of *her* palace. He must be a cousin, or a close relation of the Prince.

Elwytha looked for the Commander, but did not see him. Disappointment sickened her, foolish as that was. She had longed to be the one to tell him.... Soon she would not be able to hide the babe growing in her womb. He would learn of it soon. Would he come then? Or would he leave her to raise the child alone? At least the babe would not be a bastard. The Commander remained her husband. For now. She twisted the ring on her finger. Though she knew her marriage was dead, she could not bear to take it off.

Despair again bit through her heart, and tears threatened to flow. They came much too easily these days. She could not just blame it on her pregnancy. She missed her husband. She longed for him, foolish and hopeless as that was. It cut like a sword through her heart to know he would hate her forever. That he wanted nothing to do with her, ever again.

But no time to think on that now. The drawbridge lowered. She had to welcome and pledge servitude to the new king. Would he throw her out of the palace? Or would he allow her a small corner to live out her days, alone? Perhaps she would be expected to become a maid.

Elwytha adjusted the ample, flowing lines of her royal blue dress and slowly descended the steps. By now the King would be stepping onto the drawbridge.

She reached the bottom step. *Now he would reach the front gate.*

With slow, measured steps, she crossed the great hall to the front door. *Now he would be striding across the grassy courtyard, ready to vanquish her palace and claim her throne.*

The guards beside the doors cast her a look of sadness and pity. It had been a long day coming, and it pained them all to see it arrive. She nodded, and they opened the doors wide, letting in a spill of sunshine. How could one of the darkest days of her life be so bright?

Elwytha stepped out into the sun. It came from the east, directly before her, and momentarily blinded her.

She saw the great figure of the new king striding closer— only ten paces away now. She closed her eyes, readying to curtsey before him. To pledge subservience. Everything within her rebelled at the idea, but she had no choice. Opening her eyes, she fixed them upon his black boots, which now stopped three paces away.

Swallowing her pride, she curtseyed deep, and after lingering for an obsequious moment with a bowed head, she rose to her feet. Slowly, she raised her eyes from his feet up his powerful legs and torso to his thick, flowing black hair, to his straight brow...but instead of the King's black eyes she had expected to see, she saw silver.

The Commander!

The hair had thrown her off. In shock, she scanned his face. Still the scar remained over his right eye. But his nose...his nose was straight, with a slight hook in the middle. She remembered it, bloody and broken when she had signed the treaty. The bandage had still covered it when he had escorted her to her palace. And now...

He was King?

Mouth agape, she stared into cold gray eyes. "But you look like..."

"My father."

She had almost forgotten his deep rumble. It shivered along her nerve endings, as did his declaration.

Her husband, the King, the son of the enemy King, stood before her. At last, all of the pieces fell into place—the Prince treating him like an equal, and the hints that they saw each other as brothers. Now she realized the Prince had shown her his father's portrait in order to see if she recognized the resemblance between the Commander and the King. Yet another of the mind games he loved to play.

But as Elwytha's gaze rested upon her husband's face, all of these truths faded to nothingness as her heart wrenched yet again inside her. Pain erupted, like a scab ripping off a fresh wound. Misery flowed like blood from her heart. How she loved him! But clearly, he hated her still.

Elwytha searched for her well-rehearsed words. "Please come in," she said quietly. "We have prepared a feast for you."

She led the way into the palace, glad to turn away from the Commander's...the *King's*...cold gaze. She walked past the silent guards into the dining hall. With a hand, she indicated that he should sit at the head of the table, and his men beside him.

Elwytha wasn't certain if he wished for her presence or not. But for the sake of the delicate transfer of power, she placed a tentative hand on the chair at his right hand, and looked at him questioningly. He nodded curtly, and she slid into her seat.

For a great feast, it was quiet. His soldiers jested a little with one another, but the Commander...King...sat silently, cutting his meat with swift slices of his sharp blade.

Elwytha felt it her duty to submit pleasantries. "The Prince? How is he?" she asked, chewing on a bit of bread. It tasted like ash in her mouth, and she put the hunk down, glad that her nausea had at last abated. No need to tempt it, however.

He cast her an unfriendly glance. "The King sends his best wishes."

Elwytha digested this. She could well imagine that comment delivered in a mocking tone from the Prince. And then the title caught her attention. "King? He's declaring himself King now? After all these years as Prince... Why?"

He chewed the meat, jaw movements harsh, as if he took no pleasure in what he ate. "The Prince always considered me to be the true King. Foolish of him."

Because the Commander was the King's bastard son, she realized. He had no true claim to the throne. However, he was clearly his son—his eldest son. The resemblance was uncanny. Only his bent nose, vicious scar, and shorn head had concealed his true identity before.

"When did you guess?" she asked.

"That the King was my sire?" His well cut mouth twisted down, and Elwytha remembered the feel of it, kissing her, loving her, and pain scorched her, so she barely heard his next words. "The Prince noticed our similarities first. I didn't believe it. Then he tricked my mother into admitting it to us."

Elwytha could well imagine that. The Prince, sporting with his tricks and games from an early age.

The Commander continued, cutting more meat. The blade flashed in abrupt, precise motions. "The Prince was glad to have a brother. He flaunted it to the King. It was why I was allowed to learn to read. And train with the best warriors. But the King refused to acknowledge me as his son. And I understood."

Elwytha nodded, overcome with empathy for this man she loved; for all the pain he had suffered as a child...taunted, rejected, face broken, and then mutilated. But he had matured into a fine man. The best, most honorable man she had ever met. "The Prince...King...has been a true friend and brother to you all these years."

His steely eyes impaled her. "I know no one with more loyalty."

Quick tears flooded her eyes, and she looked down at her food to conceal them.

In silence, she finished a few more bites of her meal. After he'd finished, she said, "Do you wish for a tour of the castle, or of the grounds?"

He looked at her unsmilingly. "I wish to see my chambers. And I want you to take me there. Alone."

Alarm sparked. She tried, but failed, to read his expression. "Very well," she agreed, and rose.

He spoke to one of the men at his side and then strode beside her up the stairs leading to the King's chambers. She'd had them scrubbed and readied. Elwytha had never resided there, knowing she would never be queen.

She pushed open the door to the great chamber and allowed him to enter first. Sunshine spilled in on lavish rugs, tapestries, and the massive bed was covered in blue silk and soft pillows.

Elwytha laced her hands. "Does it please you?" She felt a little uneasy, being alone in his presence like this. It was the first time since that terrible night over three months ago.

By way of an answer, he closed the door. Now they were completely alone. Cut off from the world.

She stared up at him, at the face she loved—a little different now, but still the Commander. The harshness of his expression stabbed into her heart like daggers. "Can I do something else for you?" she whispered, and moved a step across the room. "Perhaps show you the other chambers..."

His large hand caught her wrist, stopping her, and she looked up at him, startled, and apprehensive.

He heaved a great breath and said harshly, "Yes. You can do one more thing for me." She trembled at the burning smoke of his eyes. "You can please me, my wife, if you would lie with me."

Elwytha stared at him in shock, her mouth open. "But you hate me. Why would you wish to...to touch me?"

"I can wish for nothing else," he roared. His fist clenched. "At night I dream of you...during the day I want you. You are a fever in my blood I cannot purge."

Passion. Need. But no words of love.

Elwytha's heart beat very fast. She longed for him, too, but not like this. "Commander...King...Gile..."

"Commander," he demanded roughly.

She took a breath. "You are my husband, and I will not deny you what you wish. But first, please, I would like to speak to you."

"Words mean nothing between us," he growled.

"I must speak. Pray, listen!" It was her first spark of temper in months.

His eyes narrowed, and a little of the old Commander flashed through. "Speak," he gritted.

Elwytha searched for the words she'd practiced so often. They failed her now. She blurted, "I was not going to betray you that night."

He turned his head away, and a great scowl contorted his features.

"Listen, drat you," Elwytha exclaimed. "Please, listen to me. You told me over and over again that you were innocent of my brother's murder. You had no proof. But I believed you."

"Because I spoke the truth," he snarled back. "You spoke nothing but lies."

"It's true I came intending treachery," she admitted, feeling shame for it, but she continued to meet his eyes. "Please forgive me for that. In truth, it sickened me from the first. I wanted vengeance for Thor's death, true. But the lies and murder I'd agreed to commit haunted me more every day. That first time at the chapel, I realized plotting to kill you was wrong. That I would be no better than Thor's killer. So I decided to battle you face to face for Thor's honor. The next time we went to the chapel, I realized even that was wrong. I could not kill you.

"Richard wanted me to kill you before our wedding. He promised to come with his forces to rescue me. He didn't come. And I had assembled no knives to kill you.

"By our wedding day I believed you. I knew you were innocent. I gladly married you...because I *loved* you." Her voice broke. "And that night when Richard expected me to kill you, truly I had planned to trick him. I was going to tell him I'd killed you, and convince him to leave...." her voice trailed off. "I had no true plan beyond that. But I did warn Mary to tell

Henry to protect the Prince. I wanted only to protect you...and him."

The Commander stared at her. "You expect me to believe you after all of your lies?"

"They ate at my soul," she cried out. "Why do you think I cried at the chapel? I knew I was sinning before God, and I couldn't stand myself anymore. Remember when you held me and kissed me?"

He gave a curt nod.

"That's when I decided to abandon my brother's treacherous plan. It was wrong and deceitful and I couldn't bear it any longer. And I was falling in love with you, even though I didn't realize it yet."

Elwytha looked at him, awaiting a response. Anything.

For the first time, the hostility in his gaze wavered. "You didn't love me."

"I *do* love you!" Her voice shook. "With my whole heart."

The Commander took a deep breath. He shook his head once, as if to clear it. "You love me? Verily?" The words scraped, low and rough.

"Yes." Elwytha could no longer keep still about her surprise. She took his great hand and placed it on her abdomen. "And I carry your babe, Commander. I want you to be his father...and my husband, forever." She couldn't stop her tears now. "I know you don't love me, and you don't trust me. I know I can never prove my innocence. I understand that, but I will accept whatever part of your life you'll give me." Tears ran down her cheeks.

A cautious wonder overtook his features. His large hand spread gently over her stomach. "My baby?" Awe sounded in his deep voice. "You carry my babe?"

"Yes." Elwytha sniffed. "The midwife says I have just over five months until delivery. Already I feel little pops inside. Mayhap a strong warrior, beginning his first kicks."

His fingers stroked her stomach, and then slid around her waist. His other hand brushed the tears from her eyes.

Here was her husband again. The gentle man she loved.

"You love me?" he asked, searching deep into her eyes.

"*Yes,*" she whispered. "And I've missed you terribly. I've been so miserable without you."

Both of his hands cupped her waist now, pulling her closer to him. "You believe I didn't kill Thor?"

"I *know* you didn't. I knew it in my heart all along, and then I found Richard's diary. He ordered Thor's murder. He wanted to gain the throne." Pain again stabbed her, remembering the awful day she'd made that discovery.

The Commander nodded, his gaze still locked with hers. "And I believe you now."

Joy took wing in her heart. "You do?" She flung her arms around his neck and hugged him tight.

He said, low and rough in her ear, "I wanted you to love me. But I never thought it could happen for one such as me."

"You mean an honorable man? A brave and gentle and kind man?" She looked up at him with a wobbly, teasing smile. "What woman in her right mind wouldn't want you?"

"Ones who saw only my ugly scars and low birth. No woman has ever seen beyond those things."

"Then that's their loss. And I'm glad," Elwytha said fiercely. "I want you all to myself, forever."

He smiled at last, and it was like sunshine lit his silver eyes. "I'll confess the truth."

"What?"

"I fell in love with you the first time I saw you. I wanted you for my own. I was glad the Prince gave you to me."

"Because he thought you were the true king, and deserved first choice?"

"Yes. And because he didn't want to stop his philandering lifestyle."

Elwytha giggled. "That sounds like him."

He smiled. "I pursued you from the first minute you promised yourself to me. I set about it as a battle plan, to break down every one of your walls."

"To gentle me, like a horse," she reminded him.

"It worked."

She grinned, and tightened her arms around his neck. "Are you sure I'm not the one who gentled you?"

"That you did." At last, he kissed her and Elwytha melted into him, hungry for his touch, his kiss...for her husband.

He pressed more kisses onto her skin, raining them down her chin to her neck. She arched back, eager for his touch.

"Elwytha," he growled against her throat.

"Hmm?" she sighed.

"I love you."

She stilled, her fingers in his black hair, and gazed into his eyes. She smiled so big she thought her heart might burst. "I love you too, my wonderful, battle-plan minded husband." Fear flared when a memory surfaced. "But promise me no more wars. I was scared to death you'd die when you left to conquer my land."

He gave her a slow smile. "No more fighting. Except for our wars of words. I enjoy those battles, for the prize is so great."

Elwytha smiled and kissed him, with love giving him the prize he sought. More kisses sealed their peace covenant, and promised an eternity of loving each other.

The End

ABOUT THE AUTHOR

JENNETTE GREEN HAS ALWAYS had a passion for writing. She wrote her first story over thirty years ago, and her first romance novel, *The Commander's Desire*, was published in 2008. This new, revised version, was published in 2013. This book has been given the accolades of "Top Pick" novel and "Reader's Favorite Hero for 2009." In addition, *The Commander's Desire* was optioned to be translated into Thai and published in Thailand.

Her second romance novel, *Her Reluctant Bodyguard*, is also a reader favorite, and has received a number of top pick reviews. *Ice Baron*, a science fiction romance, has been well-received as well, and won third place in the Global Ebook Awards in the Science Fiction category, as well as a "Reviewers' Choice Award" from Two Lips Reviews.

Jennette loves to travel with her husband and children, and particularly likes long walks along the ocean, dreaming up new stories.

Jennette loves to hear from readers. You can find her on the web at Facebook, Twitter and at www.jennettegreen.com.

Sign up for Jennette's newsletter by contacting her at:
jennettegreen@jennettegreen.com

Connect on Facebook:
www.facebook.com/JennetteGreenRomanceAuthor

Twitter:
twitter.com/Jennette_Green

CPSIA information can be obtained
at www.ICGtesting.com
Printed in the USA
BVHW070005110419
545236BV00001B/83/P

9 781629 640044